Dr. Anwar Hamdan Sajwani is an award winning Emirati Consultant Ophthalmologist.

He worked at hospitals under Dubai Health Authority for more than 25 years and was also a senior lecturer and examiner at Dubai Medical College.

Anwar quest for medical knowledge and expertise took him to multiple countries including Pakistan, Lebanon, Egypt, Ireland, UK and France. Whilst his passion to treat patients drove him to volunteer at different medical camps.

Love in the Season of Hate is his first book, first published in 2020.

I dedicate this book to my late parents who encouraged me, to achieve knowledge, even though they never attended school.

To my family, my wife and 3 children, who have supported me throughout all stages of my challenging life. A special appreciation to my youngest daughter, Fatma, who helped me with the technical (computer) work, and advised on different aspects of my story.

Last, but not least, to all my teachers and trainers who taught me at school, medical colleges and various hospitals (Egypt, Ireland, France, Pakistan, the United Kingdom and the UAE), where I was trained.

Dr. Anwar Hamdan Sajwani

LOVE IN THE SEASON OF HATE

STRUGGLE OF A YOUNG DOCTOR TO
SEEK HUMANITY AND LOVE

AUSTIN MACAULEY PUBLISHERS™
LONDON * CAMBRIDGE * NEW YORK * SHARJAH

Copyright © Dr. Anwar Hamdan Sajwani 2023

The right of Dr. Anwar Hamdan Sajwani to be identified as author of this work has been asserted by the author in accordance with Federal Law No. (7) of UAE, Year 2002, Concerning Copyrights and Neighboring Rights.

All rights reserved. No part of this publication may be reproduced, stored in a retrieval system, or transmitted in any form or by any means, electronic, mechanical, photocopying, recording, or otherwise, without the prior permission of the publishers.

Any person who commits any unauthorized act in relation to this publication may be liable to legal prosecution and civil claims for damages.

This is a work of fiction. Names, characters, businesses, places, events, locales, and incidents are either the products of the author's imagination or used in a fictitious manner. Any resemblance to actual persons, living or dead, or actual events is purely coincidental.

The age group that matches the content of the books has been classified according to the age classification system issued by the Ministry of Culture and Youth.

ISBN – 9789948785491 – (Paperback)
ISBN – 9789948785507 – (E-Book)

Application Number: MC-10-01-6991043
Age Classification: E

Printer Name: iPrint Global Ltd
Printer Address: Witchford, England

First Published 2023
AUSTIN MACAULEY PUBLISHERS FZE
Sharjah Publishing City
P.O Box [519201]
Sharjah, UAE
www.austinmacauley.ae
+971 655 95 202

Table of Contents

Chapter One: Daraa, Syria; Winter 2016	12
Chapter Two: University of Sharjah, Summer 2009	17
Chapter Three: College of Medicine, Year One	26
Chapter Four: Global Day and Elections	37
Chapter Five: Training in Ireland	44
Chapter Six: The Massacre, Winter 2016	51
Chapter Seven: College of Medicine Years Three, and Four	62
Chapter Eight: Graduation Ceremony	67
Chapter Nine: Internship Year in Egypt, 2014	72
Chapter Ten: 'A Marriage and a Death', Summer 2015	83
Chapter Eleven: Islamic Group in Syria , Winter 2016	91
Chapter Twelve: Sudan Medical Camp,Summer 2015	103
Chapter Thirteen: Amman Trip	110
Chapter Fourteen: Jordan Refugee Camp	119
Chapter Fifteen: Back to Jordan, Winter 2016	129
Chapter Sixteen: Escaping the Jihadists	134
Chapter Seventeen: In Safe Hands	144
Chapter Eighteen: Explosion in Damascus	151
Chapter Nineteen: Lebanon and the American University	158
Chapter Twenty: Psychiatric Therapy	166
Chapter Twenty-One: Language School in Munich, 2017	174
Chapter Twenty-Two: Back to Egypt and Sudan	180
Chapter Twenty-Three: A New Friendship	188

Chapter Twenty-Four: Back to Lebanon 195
Chapter Twenty-Five: Only Love 203

From the Author's Desk
Dr. Anwar Hamdan Sajwani

When I was asked to write the biography for my book, I hesitated for some time.

Since, I am a medical consultant (*Ophthalmologist*) by profession, my readers might expect a story related to medicine or my professional life. However, my book is not about (boring) medicine. It's about difficult college years. It's about charity work. It's about the suffering of refugees and, most importantly, it's a deep love story of a young doctor.

However, there are some light and enjoyable passages that will make you smile, laugh and feel satisfied and relieved. My only request to readers is to be patient in the first few chapters of the story and try to imagine the pain and difficulties faced by medical students in their academic years.

After the first few chapters, the story will change to include moments of excitement, suspense and even some unexpected events.

As I am a national of UAE, you might expect a story related to the area, but this is a story of the recent events in the Middle East that will touch the hearts of every human being living anywhere in this world.

It's also my life story. After secondary school, my quest for medical education took me to Pakistan, Lebanon, Egypt, Ireland, the United Kingdom and France.

I also worked in free eye-camps in many places as a volunteer. I am reminded of a time in my life when I came down with a serious case of malaria in one of the camps. I became very sick with a high grade fever and shivering; I thought for sure I was going to die. Fortunately, one Pakistani doctor diagnosed me, treated me and saved my life. Thus, I have interjected some of my own life experience in this story as well.

For most of my life, I worked at Dubai Hospital and Rashid Hospital in the UAE. I was a senior lecturer and examiner at Dubai Medical College for over eight years. I was also elected President of the Emirates Ophthalmology Society for three terms (i.e., six consecutive years). My last official appointment was Consultant and Head of Department at Dubai Hospital.

This is my first book. I have always wanted to write it; but due to the commitments of my job, I could not complete it.

During the Corona virus (COVID 19) Pandemic, I used my free time to write this novel.

Finally, I must thank my editors, Hajer Al Mosleh and Diana Tattarakis, without whose support this novel was not possible.

I hope you will enjoy reading it.

Dr. Anwar Hamdan Sajwani

The special awards that I have gratefully accepted:

1 – Sheikh Rashid Award for Doctorate in Ophthalmology.

2 – Sheikh Mohammed bin Rashid award for Best Medical Project in the private sector.
(LASER MEDICAL CENTER)

3 – Award for Most Distinguished Ophthalmologist in UAE by Emirates Ophthalmologist society.

4 – Most Distinguished Ophthalmologist in Dubai Healthcare city Year 2020.

5 – Best medical Project in DHCC 'Laser Eye-Care and Research Centre' Year 2020.

Chapter One
Daraa, Syria; Winter 2016

Dr. Humaid woke up at six in the morning. He peeled off his smelly, blood covered shirt and trousers and jumped in the hot shower. As he scrubbed his body, he tried to remember his dream. The details escaped him. All he could recall was the feeling of sand between his toes, the scent of sunset on the shore and an overwhelming feeling of being swept away into the Gulf.

Abu Jaber had already prepared their breakfast. They were extremely hungry. They ate all they could, devouring the food on their plates. They washed their hands before leaving the apartment in the two-storey building in Deraa.

Abu Jaber's black pickup truck was waiting in front of the gate. They proceeded to the opposition's Army hospital. Once they reached the hospital, Dr. Humaid stopped for a casual discussion with the staff, and the medical director, before he proceeded to check in on his patients. The patient with the chest injury was awake in the ICU, and was being fully monitored.

Nurse Rima was at his bedside checking his vital signs. She accompanied Humaid while checking on the rest of the patients in the other wards. She updated him on the medicine and doses given to the patients as well as their current status.

The patient with an abdominal injury was not fully conscious and his blood pressure was very low. Dr. Humaid examined his abdomen and found it abnormally swollen. He was quite concerned, and wasn't sure if the patient's low blood pressure was caused by internal bleeding, or some other injury the patient might have sustained during the explosion. However, he decided to take the patient back to the operation room to explore his abdomen.

'Prepare him for surgery,' Dr. Humaid told Rima. 'I will be down in thirty minutes.'

'May I please assist you with this case, please?' Rima asked. Dr. Humaid nodded in agreement.

The operating theatre was located in the basement. There, the anesthesiologist was waiting for the patient, who was wheeled in and put under anesthesia. Humaid washed his hands and changed into a clean pair of scrubs. Rima had already sterilized, and cleaned the incision area in preparation for the procedure.

Humaid began by cutting the stitches and opening the previous incision, which was not yet healed. He started exploring the patient's abdomen, and found it full of blood. After removing the blood with a tube connected to a vacuum pump, Humaid noticed that the blood vessel, which he had sutured the day before, had opened again. Humaid then realized that because he was in a hurry the day before, he used the wrong stitches for the blood vessel. In order to rectify his mistake, he now removed the previous sutures, and replaced them with proper ones. The bleeding stopped immediately. Following that, Humaid closed the stomach with watertight sutures, and asked Rima to apply the bandages.

Together, Dr. Humaid and Nurse Rima checked on the rest of the patients, looking for any complications that might have arisen due to his hurried work the previous day.

Everyone at the hospital respected Humaid. They knew how much he had helped them in the last two days, especially Rima. In the short time they were together, she shared with Humaid her life story, including the loss of her husband and how her two children were living with her mother in another town, as well as the difficulties she faced to feed her family.

In the staff meeting room, Humaid told everyone that this was his last day at the hospital. The next day, he would be heading to Jordan, and from there he would return to the UAE. Everyone hugged Humaid goodbye and kissed him on the cheeks, even Rima.

'You're like my younger brother,' she said, tears brimming in her eyes. 'Please don't forget us. Come back and help us again.' Humaid promised he would come back soon.

Before he left, Humaid gave Rima five hundred dollars. She refused to take the money at first, but Humaid insisted.

'It's for your children,' he said. 'If you want to call me your brother, then you must let me help you.'

Outside, Abu Jaber was in the car waiting for Humaid. On the way to their apartment, he told Humaid to get plenty of rest, as they would be driving back to Jordan early the next morning. Humaid was happy that his contribution to the hospital had helped several Syrians, who had fallen victim to the war atrocities, and were in serious need of medical help. He was also glad that soon he would be back with his family, in the safety of the Emirate of Sharjah. Little did he know that his mission was not over. God had a different plan for him. Back in the apartment, unaware of what was to come and thinking of his journey to Jordan, Humaid fell into a deep sleep.

Around four in the morning, right before dawn, Humaid was jolted awake by the sound of a deafening blast. The walls in the room shook, as if an earthquake had hit. All the windows shattered, and there was broken glass strewn everywhere. The blast had catapulted Humaid out of his bed, and thrown him violently onto the floor. He was unconscious for some time, not knowing what struck him. As soon as he came to, he pulled himself up. He noticed that the door of the room had blown off. Humaid found his backpack under the broken bed. He pulled out his jeans and shirt and slipped into them as quickly as he could. He retrieved his jacket and torch from under the scattered furniture and ran for the door, almost forgetting his backpack. He grabbed it and ran outside.

Humaid couldn't believe what he saw. The entire building in which he and Abu Jaber lived had been reduced to rubble. His room was the only structure left intact. As he searched through the debris, he found Abu Jaber buried up to his waist under the rubble, his torso bent over, his forehead touching the ground as if he was deeply immersed in silent prayer. Humaid tried to pull him out but could not muster enough strength to do so. He noticed that Abu Jaber's body was ice cold and there was no pulse in his neck. With his torch, Humaid checked Abu Jaber's eyes, only to find no pupillary response. To his horror, he realized that his dear friend and guide, who was supposed to take him back to the refugee camp in Jordan, was dead.

Humaid found the black pickup overturned on the ground, covered by debris. He soon heard another explosion, much louder and closer than the first one. Flames rose in the distance from the spot where the opposition stored their ammunition. Bombs began exploding all around Humaid; coming from planes flying above him. Humaid ran faster than he had ever run in his life. He had to run away from the town, as the entire town was under fire.

He ran and ran until the sound of the explosions was reduced to a distant muffle and, completely exhausted, he started walking. Realizing that his face and body were covered with blood, from the wounds he sustained during the explosion, Humaid took the first aid kit out of his backpack, cleaned and sterilized the cuts, and applied bandages to them. He continued walking in the darkness until he saw some lights in the distance and then quickened his pace as he walked towards them. Suddenly, he heard gunfire and the sharp crack of bullets over his head. He crouched down in a trench and remained in that position for some time.

Suddenly, a high-pitched voice demanded, 'Who are you?'

At the same time, someone pulled Humaid up. Humaid saw two heavily-bearded men wearing long shirts and trousers that reached their ankles. Their guns were pointed at his chest. Humaid was sure they were going to shoot him; his heart was pounding and he was breathing heavily. He raised his hand and said, 'I'm not armed. I am a doctor.'

'Where are you from?' one of the men asked him, aware now that he spoke Arabic with a different accent.

'From the United Arab Emirates,' Humaid replied.

The armed strangers thought a little and asked, 'Do you have your passport or ID with you?'

'Yes,' Humaid said, as he slowly slipped his hand into his pocket, found his passport and handed it to them. They looked at the passport and seemed satisfied. They searched his backpack and jacket and tied his hands behind his back. Holding him by his shoulder, like a prisoner, they walked him to a nearby old house.

The two men opened the front door to a small room and pushed Humaid inside. 'Please tell me who you are. Why are you taking me as prisoner?' Humaid implored.

'We're from the Islamic Army,' one of the two men replied. 'Tomorrow morning, we will take you to meet our Chief. He will decide what to do with you.' Having said that, the two men left Humaid alone in the room and locked the door.

Humaid lay down on the bare floor. He was totally exhausted. Every part of his body ached. He tried to sleep but couldn't. He started crying and admonishing himself. 'Why did I leave the comfort and safety of my home to come here?' he said to himself over and over again, remembering his family in Sharjah, his mother, father, sister, Afra, and best friend, Saleh, all pleading with him not to go to the refugee camps. But he was stubborn and didn't listen to their advice.

His college days at Sharjah University flashed in front of his eyes. Beautiful memories of the five years he spent there, especially that first day at university when he registered at the College of Medicine, came rushing by like a surreal dream from a long time ago.

Chapter Two
University of Sharjah, Summer 2009

The first day at the university was one of the happiest days in Humaid's life. After all his hard work in high school, staying up until the wee hours of the morning, studying, memorizing, researching and barely lifting his head from his books and notebooks, he graduated with flying colors, achieving the highest rank among his fellow Emirati students. Suddenly, all doors were wide open for him and the opportunities were limitless. He won open scholarships from the Ministry of Health to either study abroad, enroll at Sharjah University, or any other higher education institution of his choice.

After lengthy discussions with his parents, Humaid chose to apply to the School of Medicine at Sharjah University. He made the decision after taking into consideration the political situation in Europe and the US. Humaid was spoilt for choice. There were many excellent schools of medicine in the UAE, but Sharjah was home. In addition, Humaid lived in close proximity to the school.

The day before, he trimmed his beard at the local barber, made sure his *kondora* and *ghotra* were starched and wrinkle-free. His new sports car, a gift from his father and mother, was in the driveway ready for the morning ride. Humaid got dressed early in the morning. The scent of *bukhoor* wafting from every seam in his *kondora* and *ghotra*, filling his lungs with the heady exuberance of peace and purpose. He wore his new watch, a gift from his sisters.

On his way to university, Humaid drove carefully as he didn't want to scratch his new car or jeopardize his chances of getting into an accident. It was the first day for all schools and colleges to resume after such long summer holidays, so he wasn't the only one on the road. The cars of other eager students were causing heavy traffic on University Road.

After forty-five minutes, Humaid finally reached the gates of his new university. The security guard checked Humaid's enrolment documents and pointed at the parking area where Humaid was to park his car. As he entered the car park, he noticed almost all the parking spaces were occupied. He circled around for a bit until he managed to find a narrow empty spot. Relieved, Humaid pressed his foot on the accelerator ready to swerve in and claim the spot before anyone else could beat him to it. However, as soon as he signaled his intention, a limited-edition red Porsche, with dark tinted windows slipped in the space.

Humaid was furious. The door of the Porsche opened and a young, tall, stunning beauty stepped out, adjusting the strap of her Chanel black shoulder bag, her eyes hidden behind a pair of oversized Gucci sunglasses. Her silky smooth brown hair reflected the sun with its daring streaks of reddish highlights, cascading down her back and reaching her waist like a flame.

Nevertheless, Humaid was in no mood to even admit to himself that he noticed her beauty, her fair skin, her mischievous smile or her red lipstick.

He waved at her indicating his disapproval, but she just walked by, neither noticing him, nor even aware that she did anything wrong. Humaid had no choice but to keep on searching for another parking space. He hoped he wouldn't have to wind up parking in the far, sandy overflow parking bays surrounding the university, but that's exactly where he ended up parking. Determined not to let this incident affect his day or ruin his happy mood, Humaid walked in the blazing sun, towards the large registration building designated for all colleges. He climbed up the steep steps and walked through the sliding doors, letting the cool air-conditioned air tickle his face and calm his nerves.

The Islamic architecture of the building was similar to the other buildings in University City. Sharjah University campus was huge. It was home to over twenty buildings, each housing a different college. Some buildings accommodated universities from the other Emirates and some even from other countries.

On the first day of class, the registration hall was booked for four Sharjah Colleges – The School of Medicine, Business School, Engineering, and Law. The indoor area was divided into the four areas accordingly.

While Humaid was looking around for the medical students' waiting area, someone touched his shoulder and called his name. It was Saleh, his childhood friend. They had attended the same high school and were both determined to become doctors. Saleh was from a small town on the outskirts of Ras Al Khaimah. To go to the School of Medicine in Sharjah, he rented a studio in a building near the university to avoid driving a distance of three hours every day, back and forth to college.

Humaid and Saleh were seeing each other after eight weeks of summer vacation. They hugged and sat next to each other, on two chairs in front of the College of Medicine registration desk. Other students were already gathering, each one taking the next available seat proudly, holding their admission papers.

By 10 a.m., the University staff behind the desk started to call the names of the students alphabetically. The number of students registering for the school of medicine was the smallest, about ninety students in total. Other colleges had a much higher number of new registering students, the highest being Business and Arts. It was a running joke among medical students that the Arts College naturally had the easiest curriculum and the least number of years to graduate. After just three and a half or four years, Arts students could walk away with a B.A., whereas medical students would have to spend six long, excruciating years at school before they could graduate and start their careers as attendants.

As Humaid waited for his name to be called, he turned and noticed the girl who stole his parking space earlier in the day, waiting in the Business and Arts College registration area. When Humaid's name was called, the lady behind the desk congratulated him and handed him his ID, first-year curriculum class papers and schedule. Finally, after three hours had passed, registration was over. Students were given the opportunity to meet each other. They gathered in clusters, talking. Old friends were happy to see each other again. Saleh introduced four foreign students to Humaid, all four of them residing in the same building as Saleh.

'This is Gibran,' Saleh said. 'He's from Lebanon. And this is Rajan, he's from India, while Jamshed here is from Iran and John come all the way from Nigeria.' Humaid greeted them politely and welcomed them warmly.

'Since all of you are guests in my city, I will invite you all to coffee today, but don't make it a habit.' Everyone laughed and walked towards the students' coffee shop. Inside the coffee shop was very crowded, so Humaid and the others found a table outside.

As everyone started to sit down, Humaid asked them what kind of coffee they liked. There was a long line. The three baristas and two cashiers could barely keep up with the orders. As he waited in line, Humaid noticed the same girl from the parking lot standing directly behind him. Although he was generally a shy person and not very sociable, especially with girls, Humaid was itching to say something to her. He placed his order and paid for it, but just before leaving, he turned around and looked directly into her honey-colored eyes. Her face turned red in an instant, as if she had recognized him. He said in English, 'I'm glad you didn't steal my turn this time.' She didn't reply, but shot him a look of utter disinterest and indifference right before she turned her attention to her latest model iPhone, swiping the screen nonstop as she waited for her order.

She has speckles of jade in her eyes, Humaid mused. *Like sparks of impish elves dancing in a forest of green*, Humaid thought. She couldn't have been Emirati. Something about her spoke of faraway lands and histories beyond his grasp.

Humaid carried the tray of drinks, and delicious slices of chocolate and carrot cake to his table outside.

Humaid found his friends talking excitedly about their future plans. As everyone thanked him for his kind hospitality, Humaid glanced across the room and noticed that the same girl, which he now had named *Daloa, spoiled girl*, was sitting nearby with a group of girlfriends. They were speaking loudly and excitedly in a mixture of English, Arabic and French. The girls were all wearing full makeup and bright lipstick. As if they were on a fashion runway, each one of them was wearing the latest haute couture fashion, from their sunglasses to their watches and slim leather purses down to their shoes. Like *Daloa*, almost all of them had streaks of red and purple in their hair and in-your-face highlights.

The girls seemed to come from rich families. Two of them appeared to be local. They were wearing expensive, embroidered, colorful abayas and their hair was not covered. The entire group acted as if they owned the world.

Humaid never liked girls who showed off, especially those who would sabotage and disrespect the Arabic language by mixing it with other foreign languages. He overheard the *Daloa* saying, 'I honestly don't like local boys. They're too bossy and close-minded.'

'If some local boy asked you for your hand in marriage, what would you do?' one of her girlfriends asked.

'I would refuse straight away,' She replied, tossing her hair to the side, exposing a graceful fair neck as if in that subtle move she was bestowing a divine gift to a world undeserving of all that beauty.

'Mai, if you don't like him, please pass him over to me.'

So her name is Mai. A small dear. A beautiful young girl. Humaid thought. As if the essence of beauty was condensed in those three letters.

The girls laughed so loudly that almost all heads turned in their direction, although they didn't bother to lower their voices. They were young and beautiful, and it was their first day in college.

Humaid's family lived in the quiet outskirts of Sharjah. Since he was the only boy, Humaid was the apple of their eyes. His two older sisters, Afra and Asma, were students at the Higher Colleges of Technology in Sharjah, while his younger sisters, Sara and Maitha, aged seven and eight, were the loves of his life. He would not spare a chance to play with them and read them bedtime stories. They were his buddies and they loved to kick the ball with him in the yard. Sara and Maitha hated to play with dolls like other girls of their age. Whenever Humaid came home, they'd both jump on him and make him carry them piggyback around the house. And that's exactly what they did as soon as Humaid walked into the house after his first day at college.

'Mama,' Humaid giggled. 'What are you feeding these two devils? They're getting too heavy to carry.' Humaid's mother came out of her bedroom as soon as she heard his voice.

'How did it go, Dr. Humaid?' she asked, hugging him and smiling, feeling immensely proud of her grown-up son. 'Did everything go smoothly with your registration today?'

'Couldn't have been better,' he replied. 'Where's Dad?'

'He went to the mosque,' Sara said, covering his eyes with one hand as she tried to take off his *ghotra* with the other.

'He'll be back soon. Where's your stethoscope?' Maitha said as she jumped on the couch and tinkered with Humaid's backpack. 'And your syringes? Did you cure any people today?'

Humaid burst out laughing. 'I didn't even get to see the inside of the lab today, let alone cure people, sweetheart.'

Afra and Asma raced out of their room. 'Dr. Humaid!' They said in unison, hugging and kissing their brother and congratulating him on becoming a college student.

Humaid loved his family, but he felt closest to his dad who succeeded in creating a delicate balance between loving his children beyond measure and relentlessly providing for them and taking care of them, while making sure Humaid and his sisters did not end up spoiled or feeling entitled. Their dad had a great impact on all of them. He was truly Humaid's idol. He always urged Humaid to work hard to achieve something great.

'Never settle for less than you're worth, son,' he'd say. 'Always aim for the sky. There are so many shining stars in the sky, but only one is the brightest. Always aim to be the best.'

Humaid's mother, Maryam and father, Abdullah were both university graduates, from Cairo University. That's where they met and fell in love. They got married a few years after their graduation.

Maryam, as was usual for women in those days, chose to become a teacher. Abdullah, chose to join the Ministry of Foreign Affairs. He loved to travel and explore the world. His job took him to every country in the world. He travelled often, either by himself or with his family. But regardless of how beautiful and rewarding their travel was, they loved the UAE more than any other place, and missed it when they were gone for long periods of time. Abdullah was a highly refined and well-read individual. He spoke five languages. However, his reading, research and inquisitive mind led him to study most of the religions and he was well versed in Hinduism, Buddhism, Christianity, and Judaism, and of course Islam.

When Humaid was a child, his father would quiz him. 'Do you remember what Caliph Ali bin Abi Talib said?'

'Human beings are two types,' Humaid would answer excitedly. 'Either brothers in religion or brothers in Humanity.'

When Abdullah came home, he too greeted Humaid with, 'Dr. Humaid!' He was full of anticipation and kindness, inquiring about Humaid's day. Humaid told him everything, leaving out nothing, except his encounter with Mai. The two continued their chat at the dinner table. After dinner, Humaid asked his parents to advise him and give him pointers about how to succeed in his new academic endeavors.

'You're at a stage where you can make your own decisions,' his father said. 'Don't try to be like me or anyone else. Carve your own path. Your mom and I always taught you to be honest, at whatever cost. Being honest is not easy and you'll soon find that there are a lot of people who don't like straight talk. Always help the poor and the weak. Don't tolerate injustice, wherever it may come from. But most importantly, don't cross red lines. Be respectful, and abide by the law. Also, don't make decisions when you're angry, upset or sick. There, that's my two-penny worth of advice, the culmination of my age-old wisdom. How about you, Maryam?' his father turned to his mother with a contented smile. 'What would you say to Humaid, Maryam?'

'I want to add one more thing. Never ever miss your prayers. These are the things that will give you strength in everything you do.'

His older sister Afra shouted jokingly, 'Enough! Enough advice for the day! It's the poor guy's first day at college!' Everyone laughed.

As usual, Humaid and his family continued talking until late in the night. When his parents went to sleep, Humaid's older sisters started asking him more about college, the students and if he made new friends. They all chatted for a few more hours, until Humaid yawned and implored, 'I can hardly keep my eyes open. I have a lot of work to do tomorrow. Please, let's call it a night.'

***

Saleh phoned just as Humaid was about to fall asleep.

'God! It's almost one in the morning, man,' Humaid said as he answered the call.

'I know, I know,' Saleh said. 'I'm so tired, man, but I can't go to sleep. It's either some sort of adrenalin rush from all the excitement, or maybe it's the extra shot of espresso I had in my coffee at college. Or maybe both. Yeah. I guess it's a combination of both. I'm so excited about tomorrow. Did I say that already? Where should we meet tomorrow? What time?'

'Take a deep breath and slow down, Saleh. You're talking a mile a minute.' Humaid was as excited as Saleh, but he knew better than to let that show; otherwise, Saleh wouldn't hang up at all. 'Let's go to sleep now, or else we'll be too tired to enjoy our full day at school tomorrow.'

Humaid and Saleh had many beautiful memories growing up. They spent their afternoons either playing football or fighting with each other or other kids, but never ending the day without making up.

In those days, Saleh visited Humaid at his house regularly and Humaid's parents were very fond of him.

Saleh was three years older than Humaid. Growing up, Saleh's town did not have a school. By the time his parents became aware of the benefits of education and decided to enroll him in school, he was already the oldest student in his class. Humaid and Saleh were in the same class in sixth grade, and they had been inseparable since that time.

One incident that Humaid would never forget happened at the end of that year. Humaid drew a cartoon of one of his teachers, who was hated by almost all his students. When he was done, Humaid passed the drawing to Saleh under the desk. Saleh looked at it, and when he decided to make a tiny change, the teacher caught him. Fuming with anger, he sent Saleh to see the principal, who threatened to have him expelled from school. Nevertheless, Saleh kept silent and didn't reveal to the principal that the cartoon was actually drawn by Humaid. That day, Humaid returned home from school very upset and deeply saddened.

When Humaid informed his father about what had happened, his father advised him to do the right thing, tell the truth and be brave enough to live with the consequences of his actions. The next day, Humaid timidly approached the teacher and confessed to him, exonerating Saleh from all wrong-doing. Despite being extremely upset with both Humaid and Saleh, the teacher was impressed by Humaid's courage and honesty. He didn't want to seem too lenient and let them think they could get away with this kind of behavior, so he told Humaid that he needed time to think about it. Before the end of the school day, he called them into his office and told them that he decided to pardon them both.

As they grew older, Humaid and Saleh started meeting at coffee shops or shisha lounges after school and on weekends. Sometimes, Humaid would visit Saleh's family farm and spend the day with them there. During high school, Saleh stayed with his uncle who lived in Sharjah. In the beginning, Saleh didn't want to study medicine but Humaid convinced him. 'Our country needs doctors,' he'd say proudly. 'And you'll make a great doctor.'

Ever since he was a child, Humaid dreamed of becoming a doctor. He used to get sick quite often and, in those days, most of the doctors in Sharjah were expats from the sub-continent. Humaid's father used to visit a family doctor named Dr. Mushtaq, in his small clinic. Dr. Mushtaq was originally from Pakistan. He was good natured and a gentle soul, treating poor laborers free of charge. Abdullah used to arrange for Dr. Mushtaq to pay them a house visit to treat his parents, who were quite old. Abdullah's family liked him so much that they would feel instantly better when he visited their house, especially Humaid's grandmother, who had refused to see any doctor other than him.

Humaid's grandparents used to live in Miraijah, an old and historical area of Sharjah where Abdullah was born. As a child, Humaid used to visit his grandparents there and would sometimes stay with them overnight. He would tell his grandmother, 'Grandma, when I grow up, I will become a doctor just like Dr. Mushtaq.'

She would stroke his hair and say, 'But Humaid, you're very frail and can hardly tolerate washing your hands so many times a day. You better choose another specialty.'

'But that's what I want and that's what I will become,' Humaid would stomp his feet, upset that his grandmother whom he loved dearly, couldn't see how much he wanted to become a doctor so he would take care of her one day.

Humaid's grandparents had a special bond with Humaid and loved him unconditionally, as he was their first grandson. When Abdullah built their new house on the outskirts of Sharjah, he asked them to move in with him, but they refused to leave their old house and wound up living in it for the rest of their lives.

Chapter Three
College of Medicine, Year One

The next day, the students toured the university and visited the different lecture halls. They mingled with each other and got to meet the faculty. There were about ninety first-year medical students that year, half of whom were Emiratis, others from neighboring Gulf countries and even some international students; with parents working in the UAE. As for the faculty members, they were mostly foreigners, with only one Emirati professor. In general, it was a multinational environment where everyone felt comfortable and at home.

Humaid, Saleh and the rest of their cohort walked around the college, appreciating everything they saw, from the lecture halls, laboratories and dissection rooms to the massive medical library. Finally, their advisor asked the assembled students to get into groups of ten students each. Each student was given the choice of selecting which group he/she wanted to be a part of.

'But if you don't form your groups within five minutes, I'll have to do that for you. And trust me, you don't want me to do that. It's your last chance if you want to be in the same group as your friends.'

By the time he was finished, nine neat clusters of ten students each were already gathered.

'Excellent!' exclaimed the advisor. Each group was given a number.

Humaid and Saleh were in group 5, along with Gibran, Rajan, John, Farah, Mona and Manal, as well as Hanan from Bahrain and Hilal from Oman. Because of the colorful and varied multinational and multilingual atmosphere, they quickly learned about each other's countries, beliefs and cultures. Each celebrated and embraced the others' differences without passing judgment.

Respect was a key word. Rajan, a Hindu from India, was an only child. His parents worked at Abu Dhabi Petroleum Company. In marked contrast to his friends, Rajan was terrified of his mother. He was possibly the most hardworking, studious and promising student among them all.

'If I don't get straight A's, my mother will kill me,' Rajan would say, causing the others to laugh at him and his exaggerated consternation. As a joke, they'd tease him and tell him that his mom was waiting outside with a stick.

John's father, on the other hand, was a civil engineer working in Bahrain. After thorough research, which included comparing the academic rankings of various colleges, the international acclaim they received and the living standards of the respective countries where the universities were located, John chose to study at Sharjah University. Both Rajan and John had plans to move to the USA after graduating.

Out of the five girls in the group, Humaid liked Mona the most. She was an Emirati girl from Dubai. Mona was attractive, polite and had a strong personality.

She had fair skin, long black eyelashes, deep dimples and a small beauty mark, on the crest of her left cheek. She wore hijab and no makeup. Her modest style was in sharp contrast to the flashy clothes some of the other girls, like Farah and Manal wore to college. She didn't pay attention to boys but preferred keeping a low profile and concentrating on her studies. Farah was from Abu Dhabi, while Manal came from the Eastern Region of the UAE. They had enrolled in the College of Medicine because they loved the look of doctors in their white coats, without seriously considering the difficult, long years being a medical student entailed.

Hilal and Hanan were two very different people. From the way they looked to the way they acted, the two were polar opposites. Hanan dressed up in the latest western fashion trends, while Hilal was never seen wearing anything but traditional Omani *dish-dashas,* either white, brown or black and an embroidered *kuma*. He never worried about his looks.

Their differences didn't stop at the way they looked and dressed. Hanan liked to do most of the talking, while Hilal was a man of few words. Yet, the two were probably the most competitive students when it came to their studies. From day one, they showed that nothing was going to stop them from excelling in college. Despite their differences, Hanan and Hilal liked each other from the day they met, and an innocent and mind-boggling relationship bloomed between them.

Overall, the atmosphere in the college was very relaxed and laid back, except for a group of six students with long beards and narrow-sighted views regarding co-education. They had fundamentalist beliefs and looked with dissatisfaction, if not pure unmitigated anger, at what they referred to as *the end of time and the lax morals allowing for mingling between the sexes.*

Humaid had no problem whatsoever with their appearance, but he did not like the way they treated other people at the university. They despised students who were non-Muslims. They even antagonized Muslim students who showed any kind of moderation. Additionally, they shunned other students and didn't socialize with them, especially with girls. When they met Humaid at the mosque, they tried to corner him and ask him, 'Why are you sitting with non-believers? And why do you have uncovered girls in your group?' Humaid put his foot down, looked them squarely in the eye and replied firmly, 'This is none of your business.' Finally, they gave up questioning him and stayed away from him. He found out a couple of years later that some of them quit school to join Jihadist groups in Afghanistan and Syria.

During the first year of the College of Medicine, otherwise known as the foundation or pre-medical year, the students had four subjects: English language, Biology, Chemistry and Physics. All subjects were taught in English. Humaid, Saleh and the local girls had some difficulty in adapting to the language, especially as the language they used, in the School of Medicine, was rooted in Latin and was predominately related to medical terms.

Conversely, that wasn't the case with the native English-speaking students. Most of them were already familiar with the terminology. However, Humaid's group helped each other. Each day after classes, they gathered to study and clarify any ambiguous points. Rajan was always helpful and ready to stay at school for however many hours it would take until he was sure his friends were caught up on all assignments. Soon, everyone found their footing and managed to maneuver around the Latin words and medical terms and sail smoothly through the intricate scientific jargon of biology and thick chemistry books. Whereas Humaid loved Biology and hated Physics, Saleh loved Physics but had a problem with Biology, especially when they had to dissect frogs and rabbits in the lab. It wasn't a strange sight the first few weeks of school to see Saleh rushing out of the lab and heading to the bathroom to vomit. Some girls even fainted. However, soon everyone grew accustomed to the sight of a rabbit's abdominal cavity and a frog's small intestines scattered on tables.

What Humaid liked most in his group was how they supported and encouraged each other. When Saleh was asked to dissect a rabbit in class once, he collapsed on the floor. Now, Saleh was not a small guy. He was quite tall and rather chubby. It took four guys to hold him upright. They understood how serious it was for Saleh to overcome his fear, so they supported him and helped him with his dissection challenge. Soon, he became as comfortable dissecting a rabbit as he was cutting a slab of medium-rare steak. However, that didn't save him from becoming the butt of his friends' jokes. They made sure he never forgot that fainting episode by giving him the nickname 'Bunny'.

Saleh was an easy-going guy. He didn't mind their jokes. In fact, he outsmarted them. Sometimes, during Biology, as the others were busy dissecting an animal or putting it under chloroform, he would stick a post-it note on the back of one of them, usually Rajan, with *Dracula* written on it.

Since each college was in a different building, students from the various colleges hardly intermingled, except during annual events like Global Day.

The university held Global Day in the outdoor area directly in front of the main registration building. All the colleges participated in the event. Students from various countries would reserve a space for a stand to best present their different cultures and heritage; for example, wearing their national dress and gowns as well as showcasing their handicrafts and paintings. Most of the organizers were students from senior years who were familiar with the event from previous years. Towards the end of the fair, student elections were held, with two students from each college voted as President and Vice President, representing the rest of the student body for the next year.

Humaid, Saleh and their friends strolled around the fair, stopping at the various stands and chatting with their organizers. The UAE stand was by far the largest and most rewarding. The students who oversaw it were dressed in stunning traditional Emirati clothes and jewelry, some of them busy cooking local dishes and offering them to the visitors with dates and coffee. Nearby were stands from Lebanon, Syria and Jordan. Slightly in the distance were stands representing India, Pakistan and various African countries.

It was interesting to see most of the other students arriving to the event with parents wearing their traditional clothes. Humaid too came to the event with his parents and sisters. This was something new and interesting for them. On the last day of the three-day event, the elections were held. The students erupted into cheers and applauded each time a name was called out. Amidst the laughter and shouts of almost 1,000 students, Humaid picked up the euphonious chocolaty tenor of Mai's voice. His eyes scanned the rows of students. Her flaming red hair waved at him like a pennant in the breeze, although he didn't try to approach her and she in turn pretended she had other more important things that demanded her attention. Mai's group was undoubtedly the noisiest. They cheered and clapped for each and every elected student.

Finally, Ahmed, a fifth-year medical student, was elected student president. Ahmed was a popular and charismatic student from Egypt, born and raised in Dubai. His parents had left Egypt and settled in Dubai during the 1960s, when his father started a successful real estate business with a local partner. His company was now amongst the top-tier real estate companies in the Middle East, with offices in the UAE and MENA region.

The two-week winter vacation started during the first week of December, right before UAE National Day.

Humaid's group utilized their time off to study and prepare for finals. There was a lot of studying as everyone tried to review all the information they learned during the semester. The group was in constant touch with each other to understand and clarify various points in their books.

Their short holiday was over in the blink of an eye. They hardly had any time to take a break from their studies, let alone visit other family and friends. Once again, everyone returned to college. Lectures and labs resumed their daily schedules; books were checked out of libraries; coffee shops were teaming with excited eager students. However, this time it was much easier than the previous semester.

Easier for everyone, that is, except for Mona whose mother was diagnosed with breast cancer right before the holidays. Poor Mona barely had any time to study. As soon as her friends found out about her mother, they offered to help her, especially Rajan, who had spent the two-week break at his desk, cramming in every single essay and lesson they covered throughout the previous months. His mother kept her sharp eyes on him, her metaphorical stick ready to strike any time she sensed him dilly-dallying or shifting in his seat.

'You can relax and take a break after the end of the year, Rajan,' she'd say, bringing him a glass of sweet tea with milk. 'Better yet, you can relax once you graduate,' she'd add changing her mind and shaking her head and adjusting the flap of her sari.

'Man! It was a nightmare for me!' Rajan said to his friends as soon as he saw them after the holidays. 'Now I can sleep.' For the first days after they came back, he'd fall asleep in class. Sometimes when Saleh caught him sleeping, he would shake him and whisper in his ear, 'Your mom is here!' Rajan would either jump up and rub his eyes, or scream, causing everyone to laugh, including the instructor.

Mona's tenacity amazed everyone. She worked diligently to catch up with all classes, committing the new ones to memory as she navigated previous lectures, reviewing them and making sure she was on par with her group, if not ahead of them. She stayed late in the library, sometimes all alone, sometimes with Hanan, both of them no-nonsense hard-working students with a passion to succeed.

Before they knew it, the spring semester was about to wrap up, catapulting everyone into panic mode. Finals were creeping up on everyone faster than they could prepare for them.

Everyone in the class was busy studying. In the evenings, after college, Humaid and Saleh would study together, sometimes in Saleh's apartment and sometimes at Humaid's house, where Saleh was often invited and encouraged to stay for dinner. He joined Humaid's family for dinner a few times but was determined not to overstay his welcome or make a habit of it, especially to avoid inconveniencing anyone. Any time he stayed for dinner, Humaid's mother and sisters would wear head covers in front of him and he felt he was imposing on them, regardless of how warm and welcoming they were. Consequently, Saleh preferred asking Humaid to come to his apartment. There, they would order takeout or Saleh would cook. He loved to cook, especially local dishes. His favorite dish was *Majboos*, not an easy dish to make, but he excelled at it, producing a mouthwatering fiesta of flavors and aromas, every single grain of rice a celebration for the taste buds. He made it with chicken when he was in the mood for chicken, with fish when he managed to get some fresh *hamour* at the fish market and with lamb when a baby lamb leg caught his eye at the local butcher a few blocks from where he lived.

'Don't tell my mom I said that, but man!' Humaid said one evening, licking his fingers after eating one of Saleh's creations and wiping his plate clean. 'This is better than her cooking. You've taken *Majboos* to another level. This is art man. I'm beginning to have some doubt about the advice I gave you. Maybe you should have become a chef.'

'I got it figured out. I'll become a Chefysician. Get it? Chef and physician merged into one. By the time we graduate, there will be a huge market for *Chefysicians*, and I'll be the only one applying for the job.'

'And I'll be your attendant, Bunny!' Humaid chortled. They laughed so hard they had tears in their eyes.

The exams were scheduled during the last week of June 2009. The students needed to pass with an A+ or A-. They could even move up to the next level if they got a B or a B-, but a C in any subject meant the student had to repeat it during the summer. Everyone agreed that the multiple-choice part of the exams, although tricky and requiring quick analytical thinking and a strong ability to isolate the distracting answers from the correct ones, felt much easier than the essay-writing part. On top of that, each subject had a lab exam. Humaid feared that Saleh would have weak knees when it was time to dissect an animal, especially because his final grade depended on his performance in the lab. However, Saleh surprised everyone by performing an award-winning dissection of a common lab rabbit and was the first to finish.

'And the Bunny crosses the finish line first,' Rajan clapped him on the back, amazed at the transformation in his friend.

'You fooled us all,' Gibran said. 'We were so worried about you throwing up or fainting and flunking the class. How on earth were you so poised and focused?'

'I had to,' Saleh said with a serious note. 'I'm going to be the first doctor in my town. I thought of this in the morning as I was heading to the mosque for the Fajr prayers. I couldn't let my parents, my town and my country down. I had to recall every single detail of every single lecture. I felt the weight of the responsibility and I had to live up to it. Also, I have a photographic memory. All I had to do was trust in myself and reach into my memory and bring up everything I learned to the dissection table.'

'I say we celebrate by having rabbit Majboos,' Humaid said out of nowhere. 'What do you say, Chefysician?'

'No way!' Saleh laughed.

'What are you two talking about?' the others asked.

'A long yummy story,' Humaid said, as they walked towards the coffee shop.

One week after the exams, the results were announced. Everyone in Humaid's group got either an A+ or an A-. Not surprisingly, Rajan came out on top of the entire first year medical students, head to head with an Egyptian girl from another group. Another unexpected result was Mona's. She got an A-. Nobody expected her to achieve better than a B-, considering how her mother's sickness had greatly affected her concentration and freedom to dedicate more time to studying. During the spring semester, she hardly laughed or participated in group extracurricular activities. She even became more reticent than she was before. Humaid and Saleh were thrilled to pass their overall classes with A+ and A-. There were ten failures in all.

Those students would have to either repeat the classes over the summer or transfer from the college. They had no other choice.

The semester was finally over. The eight weeks of summer holidays were a very welcome respite from months of studying. Almost everyone had plans to travel, except for a few students, including Mona. Humaid felt sorry for her. When he related Mona's unfortunate circumstances to his mother, she and his two older sisters insisted on visiting Mona and her family in Dubai.

After informing Mona, Humaid drove his mom and sisters to her house, bringing with them a beautiful bouquet of flowers and a box of fancy chocolates.

Mona lived in the relatively newer area of Jumeirah. Her father was a businessman and her mother a homemaker, who dedicated her time and energy to taking care of their four children. Mona and her mother were delighted by the visit. As soon as the door was opened, the first thing Humaid's mother noticed was how pale and tired Mona's mother looked. Cancer was taking its toll on her. Mona was the oldest child in the family.

In addition to caring for her mother, she also took care of her two brothers and two sisters. Over sweet tea, *balaleet* and *basboosa*, Mona and her mother chatted with Humaid's mother and sisters. It wasn't long before Maryam found out how kind, generous and down to earth Mona's family was. She liked Mona a lot and wished deep in her heart that she would become her son's wife.

After their visit, Humaid drove his family to Dubai Mall, where his mother and sisters loved to shop. Humaid bought a few new outfits for their summer vacation. After a delicious meal at their favorite restaurant in the mall, they returned home to Sharjah.

They arrived home fairly late but found Abdullah, Sara and Maitha still awake. They too had finished school for the summer and were waiting anxiously for the rest of the family to return.

Once everyone was settled down, Abdullah said, 'I have a surprise for you.'

'What is it, Dad?' Sara asked, settling in her father's lap.

'Tell us quickly, Dad,' Maitha urged, her expectant eyes wide open.

'I have four weeks off from work and free tickets to the destination of our choice,' replied Abdullah. 'Tell me where you want to go, but please don't select a warm destination. I want to go where it's cool and breezy.'

'You're the best, Dad!' Sara couldn't contain her happiness, circling her dad's neck with her arms and kissing him.

'Where do you suggest we go?' Humaid's mother asked.

'I have a destination in mind, but I'm going to let Humaid tell us where he wants to go as it was a very difficult year for him.'

'Not fair,' Afra poked Humaid in the waist. 'I want to choose.'

'No way! You *always* choose London,' Asma rolled her eyes at her sister.

'I *always* choose England,' Afra said. 'London happens to be my favorite city in England.'

'Smarty pants,' Asma said, resisting an urge to stick her tongue out at her sister.

'Fine. I'll let it slide this time,' Afra said. 'But just because he shared his cheesecake with me earlier.' Afra winked at Humaid, knowing for sure which country he was going to choose. She knew all the global destinations on his bucket list.

Humaid had heard from his college friends that Australia was a very beautiful place to visit in the summer as it was winter there during that time of year.

'Australia?' Humaid said, testing the waters. Abdullah had already been to Australia a few years ago on an official visit with his boss.

Abdullah jumped at his son's suggestion. 'Yes! I like your idea, but let's let the others also give their opinions,' he added, seeing how thrilled they all seemed at the idea of going to Australia.

'That settles it then,' Humaid's mother said. 'We've been to Europe and the US plenty of times. I'm actually quite eager to visit the southern hemisphere.'

The only problem was the long flight time. Since there were no direct flights from the UAE to Australia, Abdullah said, 'There is a two-hour layover in Singapore and then we proceed from there to Sydney. That gives us a break to walk a little bit at the airport after sitting on the flight for a few hours. By the time we walk from one terminal to the other, it will be time for our flight to take off to Sydney.'

In a week, their suitcases were packed. They didn't forget to pack warm winter clothes, which took up a lot of space in the suitcases, leaving hardly any room for souvenirs from the places they were going to visit.

Australia was a very different experience for Humaid and his family. It was a country unlike other countries they had visited before. It had a great deal of nature, resplendent city life and a plethora of amusement parks, so there was something for everyone. The kids enjoyed the parks. The adults liked nature, while Asma and Afra enjoyed their favorite hobby of shopping.

One of the major highlights of their vacation was the full day trip to the Blue Mountains near Sydney. The mesmerizing beauty of the green mountains with their blue tops, the soothing majestic waterfalls, and the wildlife with its spectacular array of colorful bird species made everyone fall in love with the scenery and the trip and wish it would never come to an end.

Humaid always wanted to see the Great Barrier Reef, the largest natural reef in the world, a natural wonder. From the city of Cairns, the family rode on a catamaran to the reef. The catamaran was anchored in the middle of the barrier reef, it was the perfect place to see the underwater wonder all around. They took a submarine for a closer look of the colorful reef and rare fish species—a glorious sight they had never seen before.

Abdullah and Humaid went on a snorkeling tour with a certified guide to have an even closer view. That proved to be an unforgettable experience for the two of them. After visiting Cairns, the family headed to the Gold Coast via Brisbane. There, they came across many Emiratis and other tourists from the Gulf. Abdullah and Maryam were not surprised to see many of their old friends there. Some of them had been in Brisbane for over a month. They even hired cars and learned how to drive on the left side of the road.

Abdullah and his family also wanted to explore the beaches and mountains around the Gold Coast. Abdullah knew how to drive on the left side of the road, so he taught Humaid, who was a quick learner.

After a few lessons, Humaid was able to drive their rental car smoothly and without any issues so he took over the steering wheel.

The entire family got in the habit of rising at eight in the morning, have their breakfast and then head out to explore the area until five in the evening, or until it became dark. The Gold Coast was inexhaustible. Its exquisite nature was unequaled, from the mountains and waterfalls, to the sprawling jungles. Although Humaid's family stayed there for ten days, with so much to see and do they could hardly scratch the surface. All too soon, it was time to return to the UAE. After a short layover in Singapore, they boarded their final flight and landed in Dubai. It was already August, with just a few days before the end of the summer vacation.

Chapter Four
Global Day and Elections

As soon as he returned to Sharjah, Humaid started calling his friends. The first one he called was Saleh, who was just back from a two-week trip to London. He went there with a group of friends, as his parents were not interested in travelling to Europe. The other students had returned to the UAE, except for Rajan whose cellphone was continuously busy.

Year two of the College of Medicine was considered year one of the medical curriculum. The cohort was to start studying the human body from every aspect. The main subjects that year were Human Anatomy, Human Physiology, Histology and Pathology, incredibly difficult subjects, but the logistic problems were much less than those of the first year.

By the start of the year, everyone knew everyone. The faculty, staff and students recognized each other by name. The language difficulties that intimidated the students the year before were much less now.

The registration requirements for the second year were limited to paying tuition, signing a form and obtaining a new student ID. Everyone from year one was there, except for five students who dropped out—and for Rajan.

'John, have you seen Rajan?' Humaid asked. Fear started creeping up on everyone when they realized that Rajan's parents lost their jobs at Abu Dhabi Petroleum Company.

'Oh God! Do you mean to tell me that they have no savings to pay for Rajan's tuition?' Saleh asked.

'Unfortunately, they put all of their savings in one bank,' John replied. 'The bank went bankrupt and all of their savings are blocked now until the Central Bank is done with its investigation.'

'We can't just sit here idly and do nothing,' Humaid said. 'There has to be something we can do to help.'

'What do you suggest we do?' Farah asked. 'It's a lot of money.'

'How much can each of you contribute?' Humaid turned to his group and asked as he started checking his bank statement on his cellphone. 'Rajan helped us all last year in every way he could. He's a brilliant student and an asset to any university. I don't know how this could happen. He was the top student in our class.'

Finally, after checking their own bank accounts and squeezing out every penny they could, the group collected around 20,000 dirhams between them. Unfortunately, this amount was barely enough to scratch the surface, as they would need 45,000 dirhams to cover Rajan's tuition and fees for the current semester plus another 45,000 dirhams for the next semester.

An idea came to Humaid. 'Let's go and meet the student president,' he said.

Ahmed, the current student president, was very helpful.

'I have some funds for the next Global Day,' he said in perfect Emirati dialect which came naturally to him since he was born and raised in the UAE.

'I can spare 20,000 dirhams, but I must seek permission from the college administration.'

Ahmed immediately called the office of the College Dean, Mr. David Maloney.

'Two of you can come with me,' Ahmed said after hanging up. Humaid and John volunteered to go.

Mr. Maloney was Irish. He was well known in academic circles as a strict, yet just person. He had the university's best interests and the students' support services on top of his priorities, believing that those two factors were essential to a reputable university and successful students.

Mr. Maloney was always available to help any student in need. He himself came from a poor Irish family before acquiring a scholarship to study at the Dublin School of Medicine.

'How can I be of help?' Mr. Maloney said after Ahmed, Humaid and John introduced themselves and shook his hand.

'This is about Rajan, sir,' Ahmed said, as Mr. Maloney motioned for the three of them to sit down.

'Oh yes,' Mr. Maloney said, nodding. 'I know Rajan very well indeed. He is a brilliant student. He was the highest achieving student in pre-medical last year.'

'Yes, sir,' Humaid agreed. 'But, unfortunately, it doesn't seem he will be joining us this year.'

'Why wouldn't he?' asked Mr. Maloney, taken aback by the revelation.

'Sir, his parents are in a tough financial predicament,' Humaid said. 'That's why we're here. We're asking for your help.'

'How can I help?' Mr. Maloney asked, genuinely touched by the magnanimous spirit of the three young men in front of him.

'We managed to scrape up around 20,000 dirhams between our group of friends,' John said, leaning forward and trying to stop his voice from shaking. Mr. Maloney was one of his role models, and to be in his presence was naturally both rewarding and intimidating. 'Ahmed wants to contribute 20,000 dirhams from the college fund, but he needs your permission for that.' Then, out of nowhere, unprompted as if illuminated by some invisible power, John added, 'We're also wondering if it would be possible to award him a scholarship to cover the remaining amount, so that he doesn't miss school this year?'

'How can I do this in such a short time?' Mr. Maloney asked, knitting his eyebrows with a confused look on his face. 'Well, let me think. We do have some emergency funds set aside. Let me see what I can do. I'll have to call the office of the university chancellor and see if we can dig into the funds for this noble cause.'

Mr. Maloney picked up the phone and dialed the chancellor's office. The chancellor's educational secretary replied immediately. Mr. Maloney first apologized for calling at such a time. He explained the situation to him. There was a pause for a couple of minutes. Humaid and the others sat quietly, their eyes locked on Mr. Maloney. After a few seconds which seemed like an eternity, Mr. Maloney said on the phone, 'Yes, I'm still here.'

'You have the chancellor's approval. Go ahead, Mr. Maloney. We don't want to lose our best student.'

'A million thanks,' Mr. Maloney replied, beaming. 'Please thank the chancellor from all of us here at the School of Medicine.'

Mr. Maloney put the phone down and looked at the smiling faces of the three young men who could hardly contain themselves from springing to their feet and high-fiving each other. 'Problem solved,' he said.

'Thank you so much, Mr. Maloney,' Humaid, John and Ahmed said in unison.

'Please save your money,' Mr. Maloney added, shaking their hands as he walked with them out of his office towards his secretary's desk. 'We can support Rajan fully for this year at least.'

'Nancy, please call Rajan's parents and ask them to come immediately to sign a few papers and register Rajan today,' Mr. Maloney told his secretary.

Humaid and his friends shook Mr. Maloney's hand again and thanked him profusely.

'Not at all, gentlemen. It is you I must thank for spearheading such a noble initiative. I must admit though, this is the first time I ever received such a quick reply and immediate help for a foreign student. All the best, everyone. Keep up this good spirit and positive attitude and you will achieve a lot in life.'

Once Humaid and the others informed the group, everyone breathed a sigh of relief, delighted that Rajan would be back. They also agreed among themselves not to tell anyone else outside their group about what happened, so as not to embarrass Rajan.

'We have a charity organization,' Ahmed confided to Humaid later that day. 'I need someone like you to manage it. Would you be interested?'

After considering Ahmed's offer and after giving the matter some thought, Humaid agreed. 'As long as it doesn't affect my studies,' he said to Ahmed.

'It won't,' Ahmed replied, and they shook hands to seal the agreement.

As expected, the second year of the School of Medicine was not complicated. However, the curriculum was very long. The students had to study Human Anatomy. The eleven major organ systems in the human organism had their own heavy study requirements. Luckily for Humaid and Saleh, one of the required subjects for year two was Embryology, their favorite subject.

In addition to that, they were required to study Human Physiology, Histology and Biochemistry. They were also required to attend lab for these subjects. It was very difficult to remember the names and functions of the human body in the beginning, but with repetition and group study, everything started to become much easier.

After being informed that they would be expected to travel to Ireland to work on real human cadavers once that year's final exams were over, each group was given a full human body made of silicone to work with. Each group was assigned one instructor. Most of the instructors were either Egyptian or Asian, with at least five years' experience teaching human anatomy.

The students started with the lower limbs, from skin removal to severing superficial nerves and blood vessels, to diving deep into each and every muscle. That was immediately followed by intricate dissection which called for tearing tendons and ligaments until they reached the bones.

As usual, the names of most of the medical phrases used were in Greek.

Humaid's group was assigned an Indian instructor named Arjun. He had taught at Delhi College of Medicine for more than ten years and was extremely knowledgeable and hands-on.

Outside the classroom, Saleh enjoyed teasing Rajan. 'Today we are going to see your brother,' Saleh would say.

'Is that so, Bunny?' Rajan would quip, his quick wit the perfect match for Saleh's good-natured humor.

Time was of the essence for Humaid and his group. They were busy studying the whole day and would sometimes wind up returning home very late in the evening. They had to review everything they learned numerous times to make sure they didn't miss anything. Students with a good ability to retain information had a greater advantage. Mona and Farah were extremely lucky. Their ability to retain information and analyze it critically proved essential. The two of them never hesitated to help their friends, especially when they studied for monthly quizzes and exams.

By December, they had covered half of the year's curriculum requirements and were now gearing up for the mid-year exams. Humaid and the others barely had time to scratch their heads. Humaid would go home late in the evening, totally exhausted. His mother and sisters would try to cheer him up. He would chat with his family for a short while after dinner, before heading straight to his room to study some more. He hardly went out with his family or friends anymore, even on weekends.

Again, the exams were made up of multiple-choice questions. Each exam took at least three hours to complete. The results were to be announced after the two-week holiday; nevertheless, everyone in the group was happy with their performance.

As had been the case the previous year, Global Day was held in early December to coincide with UAE National Day and the winter holiday. This time, Humaid and Saleh participated as organizers. Humaid was beginning to seriously entertain the idea of running for student president and was planning to enter his name for the elections.

After their daily studies, Humaid and Saleh would stay at the university to work on their election campaign. Ahmed was very happy Humaid had decided to run that year and was sure that he would be elected. He advised Humaid and helped him prepare his agenda and took it upon himself to email it to all the students. He also asked Humaid to open an online portal where other students could chat with him.

Humaid's parents were not very happy that he was so busy after exams. They were afraid he might burn out. Maitha and Sara missed playing with him, and his parents and older sisters wanted him to join them for holidays and picnics.

On 2nd December, which was the UAE National Day and first day of Global Day, Humaid, Saleh, Mona and Farah were sitting in the UAE stand chatting with visitors while serving them local coffee and dates. They were all wearing national dress. Suddenly, Humaid heard somebody calling him from a distance.

Humaid couldn't believe his ears. It was Mai.

'Humaid!' Mai called his name again, waving at him as she approached the stand. As usual, she was full of life and wearing the latest fashion from head to toe. With her impeccable makeup, she gave the impression that she just stepped out of a fashion magazine.

'How are you?' she smiled as she asked Humaid and entered the UAE stand.

This was the first time Mai had ever spoken to Humaid directly.

'Hello, Mai,' Humaid replied awkwardly. Even after a year in college, he was still feeling socially awkward when in close proximity of girls. 'I'm fine. How about you?'

'Good, good,' she said, her smile widening, her dimples deepening, revealing a shapely set of perfect white teeth. 'I've been hearing lots of impressive stories about your success. My friends and I will vote for you this year.'

'Thank you, Mai,' Humaid said, feeling flattered.

'I'd like to introduce you to my parents,' Mai said, as a middle-aged man from the Levant and a European lady walked into the stand and stood next to Mai. 'This is my father, Ashraf, and my mother, Alice.'

Mai's father shook Humaid's hand.

'Bonjour,' Alice said, shaking Humaid's hand and kissing him on both cheeks.

Humaid blushed a deep crimson as he was not used to strange women kissing him. Mona and Farah noticed this and smiled but didn't say anything. However, Saleh would not let this opportunity pass without a witty remark.

'Seriously,' he whispered to Mona and Farah. 'If I knew I would get a kiss from a beautiful lady, I would have registered my name for student president.' The girls almost fell backwards laughing.

Ashraf, Mai's father, was from Syria. He came from a well-known family who had businesses all over Syria. His father had sent him to France to study. There, he met Alice and fell in love with her. His family did not approve of the relationship and were against the marriage, but Ashraf went against their wishes. Soon after graduating, he and Alice tied the knot in Paris. Ashraf decided to stay in Paris because it was what Alice wanted. He found a job at a large, well reputed bank. There, Mai and her two brothers were born. When Ashraf's bank opened a branch in Dubai, he was selected to manage it.

Alice, however, didn't want to move to Dubai but she really had no choice. When they finally moved to Dubai, Alice liked the multinational, multicultural environment. The six-figure salary Ashraf received in Dubai and the luxurious quality of life and financial security it brought with it were too tempting for her to refuse.

To keep herself occupied, Alice taught at a French school in Dubai. She didn't like to socialize with non-French, Arabs or Asians as she considered them third-world people. Every summer, she would go back to Europe and stay for at least two months in France with or without her family. Her plan was to eventually go back and settle there.

Ashraf, on the other hand, preferred to stay in Dubai during the summer. He planned to go back to his native country Syria and settle there after his retirement. Ashraf and Alice used to argue a lot about that, confusing their kids and creating unnecessary tension in their household.

Later that day, Humaid's family came to visit the Global Day. Humaid introduced them to Mai's family, as well as to the families of Farah and Mona. The fair was a great opportunity for the families and students to meet each other and learn about the different cultures.

At the end of the second day of the fair, which was Global Appreciation Day, the elections were held for student representatives and student president. As expected, Humaid was elected student president for the year.

Chapter Five
Training in Ireland

The 2011 university global event was the most successful of all the years, thanks to Ahmed's hard work and the active participation of Humaid and his group. It was also Ahmed's last year at the College of Medicine. He had plans to go to Egypt for his internship, spend two or three years there before proceeding to the United Kingdom for further post-graduate studies.

Humaid and the other students struggled throughout the rest of the year with their studies. Everything was getting more difficult. Studying required and demanded more hours in the day than there were.

Manal couldn't tolerate the pressure and seriousness of the prolonged medical studies and lost interest in medicine. She decided to change majors that year before it was too late. Mona did well as usual. Although her mother was still under treatment, Mona managed a delicate and hard balance between her college studies and her home responsibilities with calm and confidence.

Since becoming student president, Humaid started dedicating every free minute he had to the responsibilities that the position demanded. He was well regarded and admired for promptly addressing and managing student affairs. He was very popular and respected among the school students as well as by the college administration. The only complaint he received was from his parents and sisters because of the little amount of time he spent at home.

Humaid missed the family gatherings and the time he used to spend playing with his younger sisters. On a Friday evening, if he was free, he would go with them for dinner or perhaps watch a movie. His parents were mainly interested in Arabic movies, while Humaid loved Hollywood movies, his favorite movies being *Killing Fields* and *Deer Hunter.*

He was especially impressed by doctors in the movies, who worked as volunteers in war zones. In retrospect, that year seemed to pass very fast. The finals were approaching. All college students started putting more effort into their studies as they prepared for their respective exams, studying in groups, reviewing and sharing lecture notes while preparing to ace their finals.

It was like a Eureka moment for all of them that took about two years to happen. Anatomy, Physiology, Histology and Biochemistry were like four pieces of a puzzle that finally fit perfectly together.

Anatomy explained the shapes, sizes and the full structure of the heart and liver, Physiology explained how those parts worked, Histology explained the microstructures, whereas Biochemistry explained the enzymes and metabolisms that made them work. Similarly, Anatomy taught them where muscles were attached. Physiology explained how muscles contracted, while Biochemistry identified how muscles produced heat and kept the human body at a fixed temperature. Once the students understood that, everything became crystal clear.

From that moment on, there was nothing more enjoyable and rewarding for them than opening their books and learning more about the natural phenomenon called the human body.

The eighty students who now remain enrolled at the College of Medicine got to know each other better throughout the year. Some of them often complained of having no time to study at home. Some, like Rajan, would study at home and at school and still manage to help others without ever complaining. Saleh kept everyone entertained with his funny jokes. The others still called him Bunny, but Saleh was the master of nicknames. He called Rajan *Bookworm* or *Dracula*, depending on his mood and the occasion.

'Is your brother, Arjun, Dracula too?' he'd look at Rajan and ask out of nowhere, making everyone laugh.

'Hey, you never told us,' Saleh turned to Humaid once in the middle of a serious discussion on the functions of the various muscle tissue types. 'How was the kiss from Cinderella's mom? Was it worth it?' Everyone in the group laughed, except for Humaid, who felt upset and annoyed by Saleh's persistent joking about that isolated incident. However, since Humaid was naturally used to Saleh's banter, he learned to ignore him and not let the jokes affect him.

The final exams were quite different from the mid-year exams. They included written and multiple-choice questions plus lab and an entire section focused on the human body. In addition, there were oral exams conducted by teachers from overseas or other universities, grilling the students for fifteen minutes with intensive, laser-focused questions about random parts of the curriculum.

The exams were thorough. They covered almost everything the students studied throughout the year. Most of the students were well prepared and passed their exams with good grades. Surprising everyone, the student who had the highest grades among the entire cohort was Mona. After seeing the results, Saleh exclaimed, 'Mona, were you studying in secret behind our backs?' Everyone laughed and congratulated her on her well-deserved success and achievement.

Now that the exams were over, the students had a two-week reprieve which they planned to spend with their families.

'I'm going home to see my parents for two weeks,' Saleh said. 'Don't call me or show your faces within a ten kilometer radius of my house. I'm sick of seeing you all every day, even in my dreams.'

Humaid now had some time for his family. He played with Maitha and Sara and tried his best to make up for the time he spent away from them, preoccupied with his studies.

The Arab Spring, which erupted in Tunisia in the spring of 2011, soon spread to Algeria, Egypt and Syria. Arab masses were demanding changes of government. They wanted freedom of speech and free elections. In countries like Syria, it was most intense and extremely bloody. Abdullah and Maryam discussed this subject most of time. Now that Humaid had free time, he would join in the conversation, eager to hear his parents' views and learn from them.

They were aware of the situation in those Arab countries before the Arab Spring took different Middle Eastern countries by storm, and so it was interesting for them to know what was happening there now. Their dream was for Arabs to unite and fight against the occupation of Palestine.

Through their discussions, Humaid and his two older sisters learnt a lot and discovered what was happening in the world around them. Their interest was piqued. It was young people like them filling the streets of cities they either visited in the past or read about in books. They had friends from those countries. They wondered if they were safe, if the demands of the masses would ever be met, if peace and justice would prevail one day.

The two weeks passed. It was the time the students from year two anticipated eagerly. They were to travel to Dublin, Ireland's capital, for a six-week intensive summer course at the Royal College of Surgeons where they would study and work on human cadavers.

The air tickets were to be paid for by the students themselves, but all costs of studies and accommodation in Dublin were covered by the College of Medicine in Sharjah. The students were given a choice of either staying at the Royal College of Surgeons' student hostel in Dublin, or with Irish families. The students travelled separately but were to arrive in Dublin on the same day.

Humaid travelled with Saleh, Farah and Mona on the same flight. On arrival at Dublin airport, they were met by a beautiful Irish lady, who introduced herself as Caira. They were expecting her and appreciated the extra mile the school had gone to ensure their comfort by signing them up with the best tourist agency in town. Caira asked the students their names, pointed at a limousine waiting at the arrivals gate and asked them to put their luggage in the trunk. They did that and got in the car. Caira sat next to the driver, Humaid and Saleh took the seat behind them, and Mona and Farah had the whole back seat to themselves.

Caira turned her face to them, 'Welcome to Dublin,' she said, in typical Irish accent. She efficiently explained their schedule. She also gave them a brief history of Ireland, most of which they did not understand, due to her accent.

Humaid and Saleh were going to be dropped off first at the student hostel of the Royal College of Surgeons where they would share the same room.

After arriving there while they were getting their bags from the limo, Saleh asked Humaid in Arabic, 'What was she saying, man? Was it even English?'

Mona told him to be quiet and not to embarrass Caira.

'Well, I hope you understand the accent, otherwise, you'll die of hunger,' Saleh said to Mona and Farah, who had chosen to stay with an Irish family.

'Don't worry about us, Bunny,' Farah said. 'We know how to take care of ourselves.'

Before resuming their journey, Caira explained to Humaid and Saleh where to check in and how to get their room keys. She was back in the car in no time to drop Mona and Farah off at the house of the Irish family the university had arranged for them.

It was a typical Irish household. Besides the mother and father, the family had two daughters. The accommodation they prepared for the girls consisted of a nice cozy room and an adjoining bathroom on the first floor. Everyone was very kind and treated Mona and Farah as a part of their family.

The hostel room, on the other hand, was basic with two single beds, writing desks, two chairs, two small cupboards for clothes and a small TV. It was comfortable. After all, they were going to spend most of the time at the college, or out exploring and discovering the beautiful city of Dublin.

The room had no air conditioning, but Irish summers are pretty cold, so there was really no need for it. The room had a small toilet with a shower. They later found out that it was one of the better rooms in the hostel. Not many rooms had a private toilet. The students from Sharjah University had similar rooms. It was summer vacation for Irish students, so most of the rooms were empty.

The Royal College of Surgeons was just a short walk from the hostel. After breakfast in the hostel cafeteria, the students proceeded to the college. Built over ninety years ago, the Royal College of Surgeons was one of the oldest colleges in Ireland. It was situated right in the center of Dublin, in front of a large park, called Stephen's Green, and a mere five-minute walk from Grafton Street, a major shopping street in Dublin.

The students got together in the main hall of the college. Caira was there on their first day at the college. She introduced them to their Irish teacher, Mr. Connor. The Anatomy instructor from Sharjah University, as well as Dr. Arjun, were also there to assist them. Some of the instructors from Sharjah University had themselves studied at the Royal College of Surgeons, so were familiar with the system.

'Your brother is also here,' Saleh told Rajan. 'At least one of us won't be missing his family.' They laughed. The groups were with the same instructors. Each group was given a human cadaver to dissect and to study its different parts.

The students soon discovered that a human cadaver was completely different than a silicone model made to resemble a human body. So far, that was all they worked with back in Sharjah. The cadavers they were presented with at the Royal College of Surgeons were stored in formalin which gave off a very strong, pungent smell. In the beginning, everyone was hesitant, if not reluctant to proceed, but their instructors were there to help and encourage them and show them how to handle the cadavers.

At first, some of the students looked scared, but soon enough, everyone grew accustomed to touching the cadavers and studying them in detail.

After removing the skin, they separated the muscles, blood vessels and nerves until they reached the bones. Their previous work on silicon models of the human body helped them work on real human cadavers.

Soon enough, the students required less and less help from the instructors, who would stand by and sip coffee in one corner of the room as they chatted with Mr. Connor and observed the students from afar.

The students took advantage of the weekends to visit nearby shopping districts or go to the movies. During these trips, all the students got a chance to know a lot more about each other as they had plenty of spare time.

Humaid and Mona also grew very close to each other during these trips. They used their spare time to sit together and chat about their families, their college and their future plans. Sometimes, late in the evening, they would find an excuse to call each other on their cellphones and would wind up chatting for hours. Although they developed very special feelings towards one another, neither opened their heart, probably because they were not completely confident about their love for each other.

A funny incident happened to Humaid, one evening while he was alone in his hostel room. Someone banged on his door. When he opened it, he found a young Irish woman standing there.

Her cheeks were flushed and she looked extremely uncomfortable. She said something with a heavy Irish accent, which Humaid did not understand. She slurred her words as she pointed at the room, indicating that she wanted to enter.

'No! No!' Humaid refused her entry. 'You can't come in.'

The woman looked very upset and started shouting at him. One of the instructors heard her and came out of his nearby room. He explained to Humaid that she wanted to use his toilet urgently as hers was blocked. Humaid apologized to her and let her in to use the toilet. He never relayed this incident to Saleh, knowing that Saleh would relentlessly tease him about it for rest of the year, if not for the rest of his life.

During their stay, the students also visited Irish museums, Trinity College and the Irish Parliament. They made Irish friends, and sometimes, on the weekends, they went out to play football with them in Phoenix Park, Dublin's largest park. They also visited other nearby cities like Kerry, Waterford and Shannon.

After their six-week stay in Dublin came to an end, it was time to return to the UAE. The night before their scheduled trip back to home, Mr. Conner invited them for evening coffee and snacks.

Another funny incident occurred during the party. The students were offered Irish coffee. Thinking that it would be nice to experience authentic local treats and flavors before leaving Ireland, all of them tried it. The taste of the coffee was very strong, so Farah wondered out loud what they put in it.

'Nothing much, really,' Mr. Connor said, emptying his tumbler. 'It's just coffee with Irish whisky.'

'What?' Humaid exclaimed, shocked and in disbelief. 'Whisky?'

All the Muslims present stopped drinking immediately, but they had already consumed enough to feel the effects of the whisky. Since it was the first time any of them had ever tasted alcohol, regardless of the small amount they had ingested, it went straight to their heads.

'If my father finds out that I drank alcohol,' Saleh said, slurring his words and swaying slightly, 'he will kill me.' As he said that, he ran his forefinger across his neck, to drive his point across.

The next day, still groggy and slightly hung-over, they finished packing their luggage and headed to the airport.

'Guys, what happens in Dublin stays in Dublin,' Saleh told the others as they were waiting at their gate to board the flight.

'I need an aspirin,' Humaid winced, rubbing his temples and closing his eyes.

'I need coffee,' Mona said, adjusting her sunglasses to hide the black circles under her eyes. She couldn't sleep the night before. She was excited to be heading back to the UAE. At the same time, she was becoming increasingly worried about her mother. On top of that, the alcohol in the Irish coffee upset her stomach and gave her double vision.

'But not Irish coffee,' Farah added, resting her head on her neck pillow and dreaming about the moment she will reach her room back home and crawl into her own bed. Boarding started and soon they took off. On the plane, the students fell asleep even before takeoff and dreamt of Dublin and all the pleasant memories they had there.

Chapter Six
The Massacre, Winter 2016

After dinner at the Emirati Refugee Camp hospital in Jordan, Dr. Humaid rested for a few minutes in his room before Abu Jaber came to pick him up around 9pm. Humaid stuffed a few articles of clothing in his backpack, some basic medical equipment and emergency medications. He made sure he took his ID card, driving license and Emirati passport with him. He had a few hundred dollars and some Jordanian dinars which he put in his wallet.

'Are you ready?' Abu Jaber asked.

'Yes,' Humaid replied. He wore a pair of jeans, a warm pullover and a heavy winter jacket he bought from a shop near Petra. Under all of that, he was wearing woolen thermals to keep him warm on the long journey.

It was only November, but the weather was already harsh. It felt like the middle of winter.

'Let's go, Abu Jaber,' Humaid said after surveying the room, making sure he didn't forget anything.

Humaid had arranged for his transportation personally, engaging the services of Abu Jaber, since he was not permitted to use a camp car for personal trips. The two men walked between the refugee caravans, crowded next to each other on the campgrounds. It was very quiet there, as almost everyone was sleeping. Except for a few dim streetlights providing Humaid and Abu Jaber with just enough light to see their immediate surroundings, there was no other light to guide them as they walked.

Abu Jaber guided Humaid through a small rear gate in the wall separating the camp from the outside world. They stepped outside without being seen by any of the sleepy security guards. Abu Jaber's black pickup truck was waiting for them. The cargo bed of the car was full of wooden boxes and other items

Humaid couldn't identify. The two men took their seats in the front and Abu Jaber quietly pressed on the gas pedal.

Humaid removed his backpack and made himself comfortable. He noticed that Abu Jaber had a walkie-talkie which he used to speak with someone in Syria, asking him for the safest route to cross the borders.

Abu Jaber drove on the paved road for about thirty kilometers before swerving into a muddy road and driving for another ten kilometers, ending up at a long stretch of barbed wire fencing separating Jordan and Syria. The car was quite comfortable with a strong engine and big tires good for off-road driving, and Abu Jaber seemed to know his way very well. He drove on a bumpy road along the border wall for about thirty minutes until he found a gap in the wall. He drove through it.

'We are now in Syria,' Abu Jaber announced.

Humaid felt the adrenalin rush through his body. The excitement of entering a new country, of entering Syria out of all countries in that specific time of history, was enough to make him hear his own heart thudding loudly in his chest. This was something he would want to remember and talk about forever.

Abu Jaber drove on through Daraa, one of Syria's fourteen provinces. The name of that small southern province Daraa became a synonym for unrest. It made it into history books and appeared on screens all over the world as the spark that ignited the Syrian revolution. From there, it spread like wildfire all over the country.

'We're not going to the city of Daraa itself because of the heavy fighting going on there,' Abu Jaber said. 'Instead, we'll go to a small town about fifty kilometers away from there.'

Humaid nodded.

Throughout the journey, Abu Jaber maintained contact with various people over his walkie talkie, enquiring about the road situation to his destination. He would sometimes change direction, depending on the instructions he received. At one point, he switched off all of the car lights. It was pitch dark outside without even a glimmer of moonlight. However, Abu Jaber seemed to know his way, even under these difficult circumstances.

At about 11.30 p.m., Humaid saw some lights in the distance.

'This must be our destination,' he said excitedly. Before entering the town, they were stopped by armed men.

'Abu Shadi, it's me!' Abu Jaber said to one of them.

'Welcome, Abu Jaber,' a voice responded.

Humaid could now see outside. There were around twenty men standing on either side of the car with assault rifles and submachine guns hanging from their shoulders.

'These are the brave fighters of the Opposition Army,' Abu Jaber said to Humaid. All the fighters seemed to know him.

'I brought Dr. Humaid with me to help us in our hospital,' Abu Jaber said to the others. When they heard that, the men approached the car and, one by one, shook Humaid's hand and thanked him for joining them. Humaid felt welcome and appreciated, which put him at ease, since the sight of the guns at such a close proximity had left him with an uneasy feeling in the pit of his stomach.

Humaid and Abu Jaber stayed inside the car the entire time. The armed men pointed them in the direction of the nearby town. Abu Jaber went straight on, expertly maneuvering the car between the damaged houses surrounding them. He stopped the car near a small two-storey building and got out. Humaid followed him. The two walked through the unlocked main door and headed to an apartment on the ground floor. Abu Jaber opened the door.

'This is the safest place in this building,' he said. 'The top floors are risky.'

It was a two-bedroom apartment, nicely maintained and clean. There were some fresh fruits and food on a table in the foyer. They ate some of it and then headed straight to their bedrooms. Abu Jaber wished Humaid good night.

'I'll take you to the hospital first thing in the morning,' he said and closed the door of his room behind him.

Humaid could not fall asleep for some time. He opened a book given to him by Dr. Jihad about the treatment of war injuries, like from explosions and burns. Soon, he drifted off into deep sleep.

At 6am, Abu Jaber knocked on his door and told him that breakfast would be ready in ten minutes.

Humaid got up and went to the toilet. He washed up and got dressed quickly and prayed Fajr. Abu Jaber had prepared a typical Syrian breakfast of fresh eggs, white cheese, honey, hummus, fresh olives and bread. It was more than delicious, and the two men, knowing that lunch would not be an option, ate heartily. On their way out, Humaid grabbed his backpack and jacket. Abu Jaber reminded him to make sure he always had his passport and cash with him.

The pickup truck was outside the building, right where they left it the night before. Humaid was curious about the bulky packages filling up the truck bed.

'What are these?' he asked Abu Jaber, pointing at them.

'They're medical supplies and ammunition for the fighters,' Abu Jaber replied matter-of-factly. 'Courtesy of some friendly governments and fundraisers. I must unload all this first before we go to the hospital today.' Humaid nodded in approval.

Abu Jaber drove around the house and headed towards a stretch of olive and fruit orchards. Adjacent to them, were a few small vegetable farms. The sun was already up, throwing its golden rays on the horizon. It was beautiful and peaceful in the morning. *'I would love to buy a farm here once the war is over'*, Humaid thought to himself.

The car stopped suddenly at what looked like a secret tunnel hidden by trees and leaves. It was guarded by five soldiers carrying heavy guns. The soldiers waved to Abu Jaber, cleared the entrance of the tunnel and let him pass through.

As they drove through the tunnel, Humaid had the feeling they were slowly sliding down, deeper and deeper into the earth. The end of the tunnel opened into a huge hall full of arms, ammunition, different types of guns, rocket launchers, and military trucks and other sealed crates and boxes.

There was no one inside. Abu Jaber asked Humaid to help him unload the boxes from the pickup. Both men got out of the car and started looking around. Some of the boxes showed their origin. Humaid noticed that some of the boxes had *'Made in USA'* printed on them, while others indicated they came from Eastern Europe and Turkey. Humaid was astounded. He couldn't believe the opposition had possession of so many arms.

After unloading the items from the pickup truck, Abu Jaber and Humaid proceeded to the hospital.

'Can I ask you a question, Abu Jaber?' Humaid asked as they approached the hospital.

'By all means,' Abu Jaber replied.

'It might be a sensitive subject. Please don't get me wrong, but is the opposition army getting arms from foreign countries?'

'Absolutely,' Abu Jaber replied without taking his eyes off the road. 'Those countries are helping us in this war. We need arms from anywhere we can get them.'

Humaid didn't like the idea at all, but felt it was best to stay silent.

As they drove past what seemed like a football field, Humaid saw a large formation of around three hundred fighters training there, carrying guns similar to the ones he just helped to offload in the secret storage place at the end of the tunnel.

Abu Jaber stopped the car so Humaid could have a better look.

'Those are my cousins you see there,' he said, pointing towards the men sitting on nearby chairs. He got out of the car, shook hands with the men and they chatted for some time.

'This is Dr. Humaid,' Abu Jaber said, motioning to Humaid to get out of the car and join them. 'He's a surgeon and has come to help us at the hospital.'

Humaid overheard the army trainers shouting in English with a foreign accent.

'What are those foreigners doing here?' he asked, confused.

Alarmed by the question, Abu Jaber took Humaid to the side and advised him.

'Don't ask these questions here, please,' he said, almost in a whisper. 'Otherwise they might think you're spying on them.'

Humaid understood the gravity of the situation and knew he had to heed Abu Jaber's advice. Nevertheless, he was very disappointed to see that the opposition was being trained by foreigners as he was always under the belief that they were fighting alone and nobody was there to help them.

Abu Jaber and Humaid finally arrived at the hospital. The white three-storey building had both the Red Cross and the Red Crescent signs painted on it. It was actually a villa originally owned by Daraa's previous mayor. Abu Jaber introduced Humaid to Abu Rami, the Hospital Director, who promptly took Humaid on a tour of the hospital.

The ground floor housed the administration offices and was also used as an outpatient clinic. The second floor was converted into two separate wards for men and women, each ward with ten beds. The ICU units were on the third floor. They were fully equipped with oxygen, cardiac monitors, respirators and most of the usual life-saving equipment found in other hospitals. There was an elevator that led to the basement. The Hospital Director and Humaid rode the elevator down revealing a basement converted into two modern operating theatres, sterilizing rooms and recovery rooms. Every room was furnished with equipment Humaid recognized to be made in Europe.

Humaid was introduced to the rest of the hospital staff, two physicians, two anesthesiologists, two surgeons and ten nurses.

'Just two surgeons?' Humaid asked, shocked.

'Yes,' one of the surgeons replied. 'We were four, but two surgeons disappeared last week. That's why we asked Abu Jaber to get us help right away.'

The two surgeons were young Syrians, fresh out of medical school.

'We have three ambulances to transport injured patients from war zones to the hospital,' the Hospital Director said to everyone, but seemed to address Humaid in particular. 'Our outpatient emergency department is working full-time. A lot of patients are waiting in the outpatient clinic right now. Try not to admit any more patients unless it's absolutely necessary. We now have fifteen patients and two soldiers in ICU on ventilators. The wounds of five patients are severely infected and they need surgery immediately. Chances are we will still receive new injured throughout the day. Remember that we're covering the Daraa and Sweda areas around us. Fighting has started there again, so let's go everyone.'

Humaid was assigned a Syrian nurse, Nurse Rima. She was about thirty years old and had two children. After losing her husband in the war, Rima decided to volunteer at the hospital. She took Humaid to the Accident and Emergency clinic and showed him where all the medical equipment he would need was kept.

Right away, Humaid started checking on the ICU patients. Some of them were front-line fighters who were injured. Their wounds were not sutured properly.

'I want to see the very serious trauma cases only,' Humaid told Rima. 'The other doctors will be able to handle the less traumatic cases.'

One of the ICU patients was a militia member. He was lying on his bed unconscious, both legs clearly damaged by rockets and shrapnel. By the time the ambulance brought him to the hospital, he had lost a lot of blood. Humaid asked Rima to give the patient a dose of plasma and saline without delay. After checking the patient's blood type and making sure the hospital had an adequate supply of it, Humaid asked Rima to prepare the operating theatre immediately.

Once the patient was under general anesthesia in the operation room, Humaid discovered that the right leg was damaged very badly. At first glance, he realized there was no hope of saving the leg, so he decided to amputate it at the end of the surgery. The other leg also had multiple wounds. The main artery had ruptured, causing no blood to flow to the lower part of the leg, which had turned a deathly shade of white. Humaid decided to use a technique he learned in the Sudanese and Jordanian refugee camps. The technique called for taking a vein from one thigh and transplanting it into the place of the damaged artery in the other leg. This vein would then supply blood to the injured leg and save it.

The junior doctors had not seen this technique employed before, so they came to watch Humaid operate and learn from him. After stitching the vessels and suturing the wound, Humaid felt the lower limb with his hand and it felt warm, an indication that the graft was working and blood was flowing in the leg again. He was relieved that he could save at least one of the patient's legs. Everyone knew how important that was. Managing life with one leg was much easier than with no legs at all.

The hospital surgeons, doctors and nurses were immensely impressed by Humaid's technique and poise.

Hours passed before Humaid heard the call for Isha prayers. He went to the bathroom and washed up. Abu Jaber was waiting for him outside the hospital. They walked to the nearby mosque. Inside the mosque, the medical staff, fighters and civilians came together. Abu Jaber's cousins were there as well. They had already heard about Humaid's phenomenal performance in the operating room and thanked him wholeheartedly.

When the Isha prayers were concluded, the Imam raised his hands and prayed to God to protect the fighters, destroy the wicked forces of the army and give victory to the mujahedeen. When he was done, everyone got up and headed to a large room connected to the mosque to have dinner.

Humaid and Abu Jaber drove back to their apartment, chatted a little bit about the hospital and the patients Humaid saw and treated that day. Humaid did not discuss the topic of the foreigners that were there or the ammunition that was in the storage. He was extremely exhausted anyway, so he retired to his room and skimmed through the war injuries book given to him by Dr. Jihad. While reading the chapter on bomb blast injuries, he fell into a deep sleep.

At about 5 a.m., the sound of an explosion in the distance woke him up, but he didn't worry too much and went back to sleep. Soon, he heard a loud knock on his door.

'Dr. Humaid! Dr. Humaid!' Abu Jaber called out to him urgently.

Humaid got up and opened the door.

'They hit the nearby village with barrels. We need to go to the hospital as soon as possible. Get ready please. I'm preparing us a quick bite to eat,' Abu Jaber said, already turning to head to the kitchen.

At first, Humaid didn't fully comprehend what Abu Jaber meant. He would later find out over breakfast that barrel bombs were dropped on a nearby village. Humaid knew that a barrel bomb was made from a metallic container filled with highly charged explosives, sharp objects and chemicals. He had learned that they were typically dropped from helicopters and, if they missed the target and fell in civilian areas, would cause severe casualties.

Humaid changed his clothes quickly. He and Abu Jaber had only a couple of bites and wrapped up a couple of sandwiches and drinks so they could finish their breakfast on the way to the hospital. Humaid was filled with a sense of impending doom.

When they arrived at the hospital, Humaid saw something he knew he would never be able to forget. The image was going to haunt him for the rest of his life. In the garden outside the hospital, bodies covered with blood were laid out. The dead and the dying covered the ground. Over one hundred and fifty of them. Men and women of all ages, bleeding, moaning, screaming with pain, calling for loved ones or severely shell-shocked. Children as young as a few months old were covered with blood and debris. The sound of sirens wailing as the ambulance sped by to the village to bring more bodies shrouded the cold dawn with the pallor of death.

Some of the injured were brought in on foot, carried on stretchers and on the backs of those who were not hurt. About fifty workers from the local civil defense, doctors, nurses and anesthesiologists were on the spot, trying to deal with the situation.

The Hospital Director, Abu Rami, was moving around giving instructions to them. When he saw Humaid, he waved for him to come quickly.

'The injuries are classified alphabetically,' he said, showing Humaid metallic plates with A, B, C and D written on them. 'A is for patients needing emergency surgery. They will be taken to the operating theatre directly. B is for the emergency room on the first floor. These require suturing and other procedures to stop the bleeding. C is for patients with less serious injuries. These are to be taken care of by the civil defense or their relatives. All they need to do is clean the cuts and bandage them.'

'And D?' Humaid asked.

'These are the dead. They're to be transferred to the morgue behind the hospital.'

'Noted,' Humaid said. Once he understood the system, all he had to do was start taking care of the injured.

Nurse Rima hurried towards Humaid and handed him a stethoscope. She brought surgical clamps to help staunch the bleeding wherever required.

Some of the injured had lost their legs and were bleeding profusely. Some had lost an entire arm or had the forearm barely hanging from the elbow. Others had worse injuries. Their heads cut open, brain matter spilling out of their gaping skulls. Humaid noticed a young injured man. His chest cut open by shrapnel from a barrel bomb, showing his heart still beating.

'This one, Rima!' he shouted. 'Let's take him to the operating room. I will operate on him first.'

There were others who had their abdomens opened, with their intestines an entangled mess outside their bodies. They needed bandages and morphine immediately. Humaid placed signs on the patients accordingly and instructed Rima what she had to do. She stayed with him the entire time and followed his instructions. Everyone onsite seemed to know their jobs and they performed them quickly and efficiently, as if they were already used to working with this scale of injuries. Once all of the injured were seen, the surgeons went down to the operating theatre in the basement, while the physicians and nurses headed to the emergency room on the first floor. The civil defense and the volunteers started moving patients to the designated areas based on the signs Humaid and the other doctors had placed on them.

The information Humaid read in the book, given to him by Dr. Jihad, certainly came in handy. He remembered reading about injuries caused by bomb explosions. When a bomb or a barrel bomb was dropped, it created a shock wave that traveled to a distance, depending on the strength of the bomb. The shock wave could cause extensive damage and heavily injure everyone in the vicinity. There was very little or almost no chance of survival from it. The second type of injury from a falling bomb was caused by shrapnel and sharp metallic parts bursting out from inside the exploding bomb.

The third type of injury was by 'blast winds' caused by the vacuum blasts created in the air. The strength of such blasts could lift a person up from the ground and smash him forcefully against walls or rocks or concrete, sometimes creating traumatic amputation.

The last type of injury was caused by a falling roof or a wall or by burns. Most of the patients admitted to the hospital that day had one or more of those injuries.

Humaid and the other two surgeons were racing against time to save those who could be saved in the operating theatres.

Humaid washed his hands thoroughly and dried them. Rima assisted him with his sterile mask, gloves and scrubs. He started first on the patient with the chest injury. First, he cleaned the blood from the patient's chest and sterilized the whole chest area as well as the abdomen. Humaid then widened the chest wall. The heart was still beating, but there was a lot of debris and shrapnel on it and it was covered with blood. Gingerly, Humaid started removing the foreign bodies inside the patient's open chest.

Then he opened the pericardium to drain the blood surrounding the heart muscles. As the pressure was released, the heart started beating strongly and pumping blood to the body. There were still some bleeding points which Humaid repaired with special sutures. He pressed down on the gauze until the bleeding stopped. He had to do the repair while the patient's heart was beating as there was no heart-lung machine available. Satisfied with the results of the procedure so far, Humaid started suturing the patient's severely damaged muscles and ribs. Assisted by one of the young surgeons and a nurse, the three-hour operation went efficiently and without complication.

As the scrub nurse was dressing the stitches, Humaid headed straight to the second operating room. There, he found one of the surgeons struggling with the patient who was brought with an open stomach. He seemed a little confused.

'I don't know which part of the intestine this one is,' he said to Humaid. 'It's is very badly damaged.'

Humaid, who had worked on a silicone human body in college and on a human cadaver in Ireland, remembered his anatomy lessons very well.

'Let me have a look,' he said to the surgeon. The young Syrian surgeon moved to the side. Humaid started with clamping a large bleeding vessel. Once the bleeding had stopped, they were able to identify the different intestine parts. The very badly damaged parts were excised, and the two ends of the intestines were sutured, end to end. Once that was accomplished, Humaid asked the surgeon and the nurse to close the wound and to dress the stitches.

The next patient had a head injury. Humaid did not have too much experience with head injuries, so he asked the other surgeon to take over and offered to assist him. While they were busy in the operation room, the other doctors and nurses were working on the first floor to treat other less severe injuries. If they ran into any complications, they would change the sign and send the patient to the basement for the surgeons to determine if an operation was required.

Later came the patients who needed amputations. The two surgeons and their nurses had a lot of experience in amputations and they operated independently. When they came across a patient whose limbs could be saved, they immediately called Dr. Humaid to do a graft and save that leg or arm.

They worked nonstop until midnight, little to no opportunity to grab a quick bite to eat or have a sip of coffee or juice. Almost all the bodies that were on the ground outside were removed. Some of the patients were admitted into the wards on the second floor, some were already in ICU. Those with minor injuries were treated, discharged and sent home. Almost all the patients were given antibiotics because there was a very high risk of sustaining infection from war injuries.

When his work at the hospital was done for the day, Humaid headed out into the open night. He realized he hadn't seen the light of day all day long. He had gone inside the hospital before the sun was out and it was now nearing midnight. Abu Jaber had the car ready directly outside the hospital door. The two went straight to their apartment. Abu Jaber headed to the kitchen and started to prepare dinner right away.

Without changing his blood and sweat-covered clothes, Humaid dropped on his bed and fell asleep instantly.

Abu Jaber tried to wake him up to eat, but he couldn't, so he covered him with a warm blanket, switched the light off, and closed the door on him.

Chapter Seven
College of Medicine Years Three, and Four

Years three and four at the College of Medicine were similar to each other as they were the years the students' learning branched out into different subspecialties. Year three concentrated on Pathology, Forensic Medicine, Pharmacology and Parasitology, while year four focused primarily on Gynecology, Obstetrics, Ophthalmology and ENT. These two years were not exactly easy, but they were quite interesting and engaging. The students enjoyed learning about diseases and the different functions of the human body.

There was no longer time for the students to participate in social activities like the Annual Marathon and Global Day.

Humaid didn't run again for student president. He wanted to focus on his studies as well as yield the way to other driven students to run and assume that responsibility. At the end of the fourth year, students from the other colleges completed their curricula and were getting ready to graduate. In the summer of 2013, they received their diplomas during a large graduation ceremony officiated by the university chancellor and vice chancellor. All university staff from the six different colleges attended the ceremony, along with the families of graduating students.

Humaid and Saleh were keen to be there during the ceremony. They had a few friends who were graduating and wanted to congratulate them. The graduation ceremony was held in the main hall, which was big enough to accommodate about three thousand people. After the guests and staff were seated, the nine hundred graduates, wearing their black graduation robes and caps, proudly entered from the side door to the right of the hall. Everyone clapped and cheered for them.

Some whistled while others shouted the names of their friends, brothers or sisters as they entered and took their seats on the stage facing the audience. The chancellor, the dean and the teachers entered last.

As soon as the University Chancellor was seated, the UAE National Anthem rang throughout the hall. Later, there was a brief Quran recitation highlighting the importance of knowledge. Following that, the chancellor climbed up to the stage and gave a heartfelt speech, thanking all the students, faculty and university staff, stressing to the graduates the importance of their future and how best to be prepared to go about life.

A class valedictorian was selected every year based on his or her overall academic achievements. The student would be tasked with giving a speech on behalf of all students. In 2013, the valedictorian was Ahmed from the College of Medicine.

Almost everyone knew Ahmed and cheered for him. He thanked all parents, especially his parents, for giving him their full support, which made it possible for him to call himself a doctor. He thanked the School of Medicine faculty who taught and supported the students from their first day at the university until that day.

Finally, it was time to confer the diplomas, which involved the chancellor and the vice chancellor shaking the students' hands, congratulating them and handing them their diplomas. When it was the Business School graduates' turn to receive their diplomas, Humaid heard the name Mai Ashraf, followed by clapping and cheering from her friends who were either graduating with her or there to support her and cheer for her.

Humaid was curious to find out Mai's GPA, not expecting her to achieve a high one. He was surprised to find out that she graduated *magna cum laude*. As was her habit, Mai was wearing the latest fashion under her graduation robe, her makeup spotless, her green eyes shining with excitement, the red highlights in her hair brighter and her six-inch heels amplifying the echo of every step she took up to the stage to receive her diploma. She was a sight to behold. Her beauty, intelligence and energetic personality took everyone's breath away.

Once the ceremony was over, Humaid approached Mai and congratulated her. Mai's father, Ashraf, was there alone without her mother. Humaid was both surprised that she had missed her daughter's graduation and relieved because he was saved the embarrassment of being kissed by her. However, Saleh couldn't keep quiet about it.

'Oh! Are you disappointed, Humaid?' he poked his friend as they walked out of the hall. 'No kiss for you today from Cinderella's mom?'

After the graduation ceremony, Ahmed and his classmates arranged a farewell party at a restaurant in Dubai for their graduating friends. Even though Humaid and Saleh were not among the graduates that year, Ahmed still invited them to the party. The excitement was palpable among the graduates at the party. Everyone happily called each other doctor. They ate and talked about their future plans, where they would go for their internship and training and how much they would miss college. Ahmed informed his friends of his plan to go to Cairo and finish his internship there. Ahmed saw it as a win-win situation. With Cairo's dense population, he would get a chance to see more patients with varied diseases and ailments and therefore enrich his medical knowledge. He advised his friends to try to go there if they could.

Time flew by during the fourth year of college. It was a strange feeling for Humaid and his friends. They were full of excitement and trepidation. That was it. One more year and they would become real doctors. College might have been tough and demanding at times, exhausting and exhilarating at others, but it was still fun. Where would their careers take them? What did the future hold in store for them? Where would Rajan be in a few years with his sunny attitude and constant teasing of the group, never missing a chance to bring up the memory of the Irish coffee they unwittingly sipped in Dublin? Where would Saleh be with his relentless jokes? Who would poke Humaid in the waist, blow him a kiss from across the road and say, 'Just in case you miss your Cinderella kiss?'

During that year's finals, Mona's mother passed away after a long struggle with cancer. Mona was not able to finish her finals. When the finals were over, all the students went to visit her and her family to offer their condolences. Mona was grief-stricken but did not show any kind of weakness. She didn't even cry. She was the glue that held her family together during that difficult time. Her father and brothers would have fallen to pieces if it weren't for her.

'It's God's will,' she said, holding her mother's memory in her heart, believing that she was in a better place now where no pain would ever come near her. That memory of her mother and the pain she endured would remain with Mona as long as she lived.

That summer, Mona made up for the finals she missed by taking extensive summer classes and passing them all with very high marks. In contrast to Mona's loss that summer, Rajan shared a piece of good news with his friends. His father had found a very good job as the CEO of another gas company. The job came with amazing benefits, including a better salary, housing, vacation pay and full coverage of Rajan's college tuition and fees. That came as a huge relief to everyone, since Rajan's scholarship was approved for two years only.

Until now, Rajan did not know for sure what Humaid had done to get him the scholarship. He did have a hunch, though, but waited for Humaid to tell him. He had become very close to Humaid and felt comfortable enough around him and Saleh to tell them his family situation.

They in turn were kind enough to share their books with him when he couldn't afford to buy his own, which happened every now and then.

Before the summer holidays, their college instructors warned them that the fifth year would be the toughest year and they should be prepared. They must review all the material they learned in the previous years, go through their books and refresh their memories. And that's exactly what they did. They also went ahead and bought next year's books from the university bookstore to familiarize themselves with the subjects as much as they could.

Since most of the medical students stayed in the UAE during the summer of 2013, they thought of having some fun before the start of their final year. So, on the last weekend of the summer holidays, they organized a two-day trip to Sir Baniyas Island, about 180 kilometers from Abu Dhabi.

In the 1980s, the UAE President and Ruler of Abu Dhabi, Sheikh Zayed Bin Sultan Al Nahyan, issued an order to establish the island as a wildlife sanctuary and to round up endangered animals who were at the risk of extinction and bring them to the island. Those animals included the Arabian Oryx and gazelles, sea turtles, cheetahs, peacocks and various bird species.

Forty male and twenty female students, including Humaid, Farah, and Saleh, signed up for the trip. Saleh oversaw the trip logistics. He had visited the island in the past and was fascinated by its lush nature and diverse variety of animals he encountered there. He arranged for a tour bus with a driver and a guide. The students were picked up from the university hall at 8 a.m. the morning of the trip. Everyone packed light-weight clothes and swimming gear. As soon as the students board the bus, Saleh did a quick head count and the bus began the journey towards Abu Dhabi. At one in the afternoon, they hopped off the bus at Jebel Dhanna and boarded a yacht that took them to Sir Baniyas Island. When they arrived, they transferred to another bus that took them to Anantara Resort. The resort was right on the beach. Saleh had booked enough chalets to accommodate them all, with six students per chalet. The girls had their own chalets. The weather on the island was five degrees cooler than it was on the mainland.

As soon as they settled in their rooms, some students changed into their swimming costumes and jumped into the sea. The water was very pleasant and warm. There were facilities for boating, kayaking and diving. The area was surrounded by underwater corals and colorful sea creatures.

Exhausted after such a long active day, the group ate dinner at a nearby restaurant, afterwards, they headed straight to their beds and slept right away.

At 5 a.m. the next morning, the students were up and ready for the most exciting safari tour on the island. Led by an experienced guide, they boarded special safari jeeps. The guide pointed out the wild animals in their natural habitat. The three-hour safari was very much like an African safari but covered a much smaller area. The students loved every minute of it.

After a short rest and lunch, the group resumed their adventures. This time, they were heading to the oldest Christian Monastery in the Gulf built around 1,400 years ago. The students were amazed to learn that Christians lived there, and monks prayed in those very ruins long before the federation of the UAE was formed in 1971.

The last day of the trip was a free day. The students spent it on the beach, taking part in their favorite water sports or simply relaxing in the many gardens and parks surrounding the villas, as gazelles sauntered close to them and birds chirped on tree branches. Late in the afternoon, they checked out and boarded a yacht to head back to the mainland. Their tour bus was waiting for them in the designated area. On the way back, everyone reflected on the two peaceful days they spent on the island and made plans to return soon with their families.

Chapter Eight
Graduation Ceremony

The final year was as demanding as their instructors had warned, but it was by far the most rewarding of all the years. The students visited the university hospital and gained first-hand experience seeing patients face to face and taking their medical history.

A typical day started with accompanying the attendants on their rounds. Each department had a doctor in charge. He would give a brief summary of the diagnosis and go over the prescribed treatment with the department consultant. The consultant would then examine the patient to see if he or she should continue with the treatment, change to an alternative treatment, or, if the patient had recovered, stop treatment altogether and recommend his or her discharge.

The students spent three hours at the hospital every day. They were there at seven in the morning and left at ten. They would take a short coffee break after that and head back to college to resume their classes.

Year five had three main subjects: General Medicine, General Surgery and Pediatrics. Each subject was divided into various specialties. General Medicine, for example, was divided into Neurology, Pulmonology, Urology, Gastroenterology and Cardiology. Each specialty had its own group of instructors and required its own set of books. Students were also required to study Pediatrics, which had similar divisions as General Medicine but for children. The future doctors learned the different types of surgeries, be it brain, chest, stomach, or surgeries for the upper and lower limbs. They were also required to learn emergency surgeries, examine the patients and learn how to deal with them.

In addition, they were taught the different types of anesthesia used for different surgeries. In some surgeries, only local anesthesia was required; whereas in others, it was essential to administer general anesthesia.

The future doctors and surgeons were also allowed to visit operating theatres and observe surgeries in progress. Humaid and his group did well in general. But in the beginning, everyone, especially Saleh, Mona and Farah, felt overwhelmed when they saw fresh blood pouring out of wounds, and felt unsteady and nauseated. They ended up leaving and waiting for the others in the hospital lobby; however, as time passed, they got used to it.

Year five was not only for studying diseases and their treatment, but also for practicing everything the students had studied in the previous years. Humaid's group would meet at the end of every day to go over what they learned that day. As it was getting close to finals, they started meeting weekly as well to review what they had learned throughout the week. They would get together on Fridays and Saturdays outside the college library. Some of them, especially the girls, brought food and drinks or they'd order coffee or tea from the college coffee shop. Mona and Farah would usually cook local food and bring it with them to share with the others.

In November that year, the students had their mid-year exams. Theory exams were carried out at the college and practical exams at the hospital where the students examined patients and gave their diagnoses. Most of the students did well and passed.

The students had a two-week vacation after exams. Humaid and Saleh decided to attend and enjoy Global Day that year. There, they met new first-year medical students. It was like déjà vu for Humaid and Saleh. They felt nostalgic for the early days of their college, but proud and relieved to be almost done. They moved from one stand to another, talking to the new students, listening to their fears and hopes and sharing their experiences with them.

The new students were as excited as Humaid and Saleh were when they started college. When the new students found that Humaid and Saleh were previous organizers and that Humaid was once elected student president, they surrounded them and started asking them about their experiences. Some asked whether it was quite difficult to get to where they were. Some were still not sure whether they would be able to persevere and stay in their major until the end. Humaid and Saleh addressed their many questions and spoke to them honestly.

'Success as medical students requires hard work,' Humaid said.

'But more than anything else, it requires patience,' Saleh added.

'And not being scared of dissecting rabbits,' Humaid said, tongue in cheek. The new students laughed, but they probably did not understand exactly what he meant.

As they moved on to the Syrian and Lebanese stands, Humaid could not find Mai. Even after graduation, some of the alumni were still invited to take part in different events. When he asked about Mai, he was told she moved back to France with her family. He could tell Mai's absence was strongly felt that year by her friends.

After the two weeks were over, the students went back to college. It was their last semester before graduating. They studied harder than they ever did.

On a good day, Humaid would get home after six in the evening. His parents and sisters felt for him and worried that he wasn't getting enough rest, but he always laughed and joked with them and said it was nothing. He rarely found time to play with Maitha and Sara, but when he found the time after a long day of stress and concentration, he felt a sense of exhilaration and relief. His parents and older sisters pampered him and brought him sweets and tea and were delighted whenever he had time to join them for dinner.

Humaid was conscious of becoming overweight. Before he started college, he was in the habit of going to a nearby club for swimming or he would hit the gym four times a week. Now, he could not remember the last time he visited the gym. He also noticed that his older sisters, especially Asma had also gained weight. They loved to cook and try out new dishes. Humaid would tease them saying, 'Please have pity on the bathroom scale. I can hear it moaning under your weight every morning.'

'Yeah? I heard it cry and beg for mercy when you went on it the other day,' Asma retorted.

'Take it easy,' Afra, always calm and good natured, got between the two. 'Humaid was only joking.'

'Well, I wasn't,' Asma said, as she clicked her feet and left the room.

'You know she's sensitive about her weight,' Afra admonished Humaid when she thought Asma wasn't within earshot of them.

'So am I,' he said. 'But I was really joking. I never heard the scale moan in the morning. I think Asma weighs herself at night. I guess that explains the cry the scale sends out in the middle of the night.'

Afra threw an accent pillow at him playfully as she raised her forefinger to her lips motioning for him to keep quiet.

'I can hear you!' Asma called out from her room.

Asma was a bit hot tempered and quick to respond, sometimes without considering the consequences, unlike Afra. She had her own opinions on life and believed in enjoying it to the fullest with her friends. She surrounded herself with a circle of friends who were like her. Their main interests were focused on visiting shopping malls together or spending time chatting in cafés. She didn't like to wear the *abaya* and preferred to dress according to the latest Western fashion.

Abdullah and Maryam didn't mind as long as her behavior remained within the accepted norms and culture of Emirati society.

Finally, the year was over. Most of the eighty students remaining in the 2014 class at the College of Medicine passed their finals and clinical with flying colors. Mona had really aimed for an A but was not disgruntled or sad when she got a B. After all, she had dedicated so much of the time taking care of her family.

As usual, the graduation ceremony was held in July. Eight hundred and fifty students were graduating that year from the different colleges at the University of Sharjah. The parents of almost every student were there at the graduation. Mona looked especially sad that day as she missed her mother very much.

Humaid was voted class valedictorian that year. In his speech, he thanked his parents for everything they had done for him, and swiftly extended his thanks to the university and the entire faculty at the College of Medicine for supporting the students and believing in them.

'On behalf of the class of 2014 College of Medicine graduates,' Humaid said, his voice strong, clear, and resounding, 'I would like to thank you for preparing us for the future, for making us feel proud and worthy today to stand in your presence to take the Hippocratic Oath with confidence to call ourselves doctors.'

The entire audience stood on their feet and clapped for him when he was done. His mother and sisters could not hide their tears and his father beamed with pride and raised his eyes to the sky, thanking God for blessing him with the best son a father could wish for.

The year's conciliatory award was given to Mona. The dean of the College of Medicine introduced her as a brave and hard-working student who faced all manner of difficulty, including the death of her mother during finals, with bravery and strength, never complaining or slacking in her studies. He said Mona was a shining example for all students, to persevere and not give up in the face of calamities.

When Mona went on the stage to collect her award, everyone clapped and cheered for her. She was smiling, but her eyes were full of tears. Her father too, who was sitting near Abdullah, was also happy, but tears flowed down his cheeks. He didn't know if they were tears of happiness for his daughter's graduation or tears of sadness because her mother wasn't there to feel the pride he was feeling at that moment.

The next day, the graduating students organized a graduation and goody party for themselves. It was held at a spacious hall at a five-star hotel in Sharjah. It was an emotional time as they knew that once they left the party and started their new lives, they might never meet again.

Many had plans to travel to another city or country for their internship, although some of them chose to stay in the UAE and do their internship there. Most of the female graduates did that. Hanan and Hilal decided to go back to their countries as well. Everyone assumed that the two would get married soon after they were done with their training, but strangely enough, no one heard from them again after that day. Some, like Rajan and John, decided to go back to their countries for the time being, after weighing the pros and cons of finishing their internship in their home countries. Some were still undecided.

Humaid and Saleh had already decided to follow Ahmed's advice and go to Cairo, Egypt, for their internship. They were already in touch with Ahmed who promised to help with everything they needed, from determining which hospital to train at to deciding where they would live.

As he hugged Rajan goodbye after the party, Saleh, who could not stop joking for a minute, said, 'I will never forget you, Dracula. Will you still haunt my dreams and wake me up in the middle of the night?'

'You bet, Bunny,' Rajan replied. 'I'll never ever forget either one of you as long as I live.' By that time, Rajan was fully aware of the role Humaid and Saleh had played in securing his scholarship during his second year of college.

Chapter Nine
Internship Year in Egypt, 2014

Even after studying for five years and graduating from the College of Medicine, the young doctors were still not allowed to practice anywhere until they finished no less than twelve months of an internship program at a recognized hospital. Humaid and Saleh, being the top Emirati graduates from the College of Medicine, were both invited to do their internship and training at any of the various world-renowned hospitals in the UAE. They were torn between their desire to work in Cairo for a year and the tempting offers they received. So, they decided to do both. They accepted the invitation to continue their residency training in the UAE after finishing a year of internship in Cairo.

Humaid's parents were glad that he was going to be training in Cairo, where they themselves had gone to college. They still had friends in Cairo who could help Humaid and Saleh and be there for them in case of an emergency. Abdullah called a friend of his there and asked if he could help Humaid and Saleh find a good apartment near Cairo University.

On September of that same year, Saleh and Humaid boarded a flight from Sharjah Airport to Cairo. It was not a very long flight. At 6 p.m., only three hours after takeoff from Sharjah, they landed at Cairo International Airport. They cleared customs in no time, collected their luggage and headed towards the terminal exit where Abdullah's friend, Kamal, was waiting for them with his son. Kamal welcomed them warmly and asked them if they had a comfortable trip. As they put their luggage in the car boot, Humaid and Saleh told Kamal they were too excited to even close their eyes for a second on the flight. Living for an entire year away from home was a huge step for them.

On the way, Kamal asked about Humaid's parents and enquired about their health. He informed Humaid and Saleh that he had rented a two-bedroom furnished apartment in the Garden City area for them. The apartment was about twenty kilometers from the airport, but because of traffic congestion, it took them more than two hours to reach it.

'Cairo is the most congested city in the Middle East,' Kamal said as they waited in the bottlenecked traffic. 'But you guys probably know that already.'

'Indeed,' Humaid replied. 'And with a population of more than twenty million, this is completely expected.'

Humaid and Saleh understood the magnitude of such traffic. Not even during the worst rush hour on Sheikh Zayed Road or the infamous National Paint Bridge bumper-to-bumper traffic congestion did they ever see anything like what they were witnessing that evening. Driving in Cairo would be a nightmare.

'*Um al-dunya ya Masr*,' Saleh added, beaming. *Egypt is mother of the world.* Reciting the famous Egyptian epitaph put a smile on everyone's face. Kamal and his son were very impressed with Saleh and appreciated his kindness and apparent love of their country.

To their pleasant surprise, Kamal told them that the apartment came with a maid who would arrive every morning to clean and cook for them and leave in the evening. Her name was Um Mohammed. He also informed them that the maid services were optional, but urged them to think with their hearts, because employing the services of Um Mohammed meant helping put food on the table for her children. Um Mohammed was a middle-aged, poor woman who cleaned houses to support her family. Humaid and Saleh agreed to keep her. In fact, they were happy to have her; she would help save them a lot of time and effort once they started their internship.

Garden City was one of the clean areas in Cairo, only one kilometer from their hospital. The apartment Kamal booked was on the second floor. It was spotless, neat and, as he said, fully furnished.

Um Mohammed was waiting for them at the apartment when they arrived. She greeted Humaid and Saleh, took their luggage to their rooms and offered to help them unpack, although they politely thanked her and said they would take care of that themselves. When Kamal and his son left, Um Mohammed prepared a light snack of tea and sandwiches for Humaid and Saleh before leaving for the night. She told them she would be back to prepare their breakfast the next day.

The next morning, Humaid and Saleh got up early. They heard Um Mohammed in the kitchen. She prepared a delicious spread of scrambled eggs with tomatoes, a generous serving of feta cheese, honey, white cream and *ful mudammas,* Egypt's most famous breakfast staple.

Ful mudammas lived to its notoriety of sitting heavy in the stomach, and it was famous for making people feel drowsy after eating it. Soon after he finished eating, Humaid yawned and stretched.

'Breakfast was absolutely delicious, Um Mohammed,' Saleh said, throwing himself on the couch and rubbing his tummy. 'But please, I beg you. Don't make all these dishes together again.'

Um Mohammed asked them what they would like to have for lunch. Humaid said he would be happy with any Egyptian dish she could prepare, as long as it didn't have fava beans.

'I think I had enough *ful* this morning to last me a life-time,' Humaid announced as he opened his wallet and took out a few banknotes and handed them to Um Mohammed for groceries. He was glad his dad had the presence of mind to exchange currency for him in Sharjah.

'There's a fresh vegetable and fruit market nearby,' Um Mohammed said, putting the money in her bosom. 'And I'll get you the best *basboosa* I can find for dessert.'

Humaid and Saleh showered and got ready for the day. They walked to Cairo University Hospital. Kamal was right. The hospital was less than a kilometer away from their apartment building, but it took such a long time to reach because it was very difficult to cross any of the streets safely. There were no proper pedestrian crossing areas, and people were crossing haphazardly and jaywalking all over the place. But before the day was over, Humaid and Saleh had already got used to the way people crossed the roads in Cairo and they learned how to swiftly squeeze between them to reach the opposite side of the road safely.

Upon arrival at the hospital, Humaid and Saleh met Ahmed, their old college friend, who was training at the hospital to become a surgeon. Humaid and Saleh were so happy to see him. They hugged him and thanked him for encouraging them to take this step, and for overseeing their registration at the hospital. Ahmed took them to the office of the University Hospital Director, Dr. Mehran, who was a close friend of Ahmed's father. He welcomed Humaid and Saleh and asked them about their plans while in Cairo.

'The university hospital's training program is flexible,' Dr. Mehran said. 'It's designed specifically to help new doctors navigate their interests and determine which specialty best suits their skills, be it surgery, general medicine or any other specialty.

'I want to become a surgeon,' Humaid said right away.

'And what about you?' Dr. Mehran asked Saleh.

'I think I prefer general medicine, but I might change my mind during my internship,' Saleh replied.

'And that is exactly why the first year of internship and training after graduating from college is important for all doctors,' Dr. Mehran declared, nodding his head.

Dr. Mehran called his secretary and asked her to bring the files he had arranged for Humaid and Saleh. The files contained detailed instructions on the upcoming twelve-month internship program. Humaid and Saleh were to work and train in General Medicine, General Surgery, Cardiac Surgery, Gynecology and Obstetrics, Neurology, Pediatrics, Ophthalmology and ENT.

Dr. Mehran went over the program with them as they sipped sweet tea served to them by an energetic office boy. When they were done, Humaid and Saleh thanked Dr. Mehran and excused themselves. Ahmed took them on a tour around the hospital.

Cairo University Hospital, one of the oldest hospitals in Egypt, offered almost all specialties. The main building was huge and consisted of seven floors. Led by Ahmed, Humaid and Saleh passed from one department to another and met the doctors who oversaw each ward. After completing a two-year internship at the hospital, Ahmed knew almost everyone there.

Ahmed left them around noon as he had to go to the operating theatre. Ahmed promised to try his best to be there the next day when their official internship was scheduled to start.

As they left the hospital, Humaid and Saleh decided to stop at the UAE embassy in Cairo to register their names. They wanted to acquaint themselves with the embassy, its staff and location, just in case something came up while they were in Cairo. The taxi driver knew where the embassy was located and took them there without asking for directions.

After passing through security at the Embassy gate, Humaid informed the receptionist that they were students. They were immediately ushered to the office of Mr. Al Hamed, who was in charge of Emirati student affairs in Egypt.

Mr. Al Hamed was from Abu Dhabi. He greeted Humaid and Saleh cordially and asked them about their internship and training, and how long they intended to stay in Cairo. He went ahead and provided them with a list of contact numbers, including a 24-hour emergency number.

'Two years have passed since the Egyptian revolution erupted,' Mr. Al Hamed said. 'It seems that things are quiet and under control now. However, security is not exactly perfect in the country,' he added, looking from Humaid to Saleh.

'There are terrorists on the loose and they won't hesitate to kill anyone who's not on their side. So, I can't stress to you enough the importance of being on your guard. Just be careful.' Mr. Al Hamed politely warned them.

'Heavens! I didn't know that,' Saleh exclaimed, taken by surprise.

'I don't mean to scare you,' Mr. Al Hamed said. 'But it's my duty to inform you of the big picture. Your safety is very important to us.'

Humaid and Saleh thanked him and went back to their apartment, where Um Mohammed had prepared lunch. The food was so tasty. Saleh finished everything on his plate and asked for more.

'Man, if you're not careful, you'll end up becoming a small elephant by the end of our internship here,' Humaid said, joking with him.

Um Mohammed was happy that they liked her cooking and wanted to know what they would like to eat the next day.

After washing the dishes, cleaning the apartment and doing the laundry, Um Mohammed said she was ready to leave for the day. However, Humaid, ever thoughtful and observant, asked her to take all the leftovers back home with her. She was extremely happy and grateful. She thanked him wholeheartedly as she packed the leftovers and left.

The next day after breakfast, Humaid and Saleh headed to the hospital, wearing their white lab coats. Safa Jamal, the administrator assigned to overseeing their training, was a beautiful twenty-three-year old Egyptian woman. She received them with a warm smile. She explained their responsibilities to them and led them on a tour around the wards in which they would be working.

Each year, Safa was responsible for around fifty new residents. She would follow their transfer from one department to another to make sure they attended regularly. She received monthly reports of their progress from the heads of each department, reviewed them and then forwarded them on to Dr. Mehran's office.

'If you're not comfortable in any department or if you want to train in another, just let me know and I'll see what I can do to assist you.' She said at the end of the hospital tour, smiling most of the time.

As was his habit, Saleh was itching to say something to lighten the atmosphere and make a new friend.

'Thank you for your support, but I want to say something unrelated to work if you don't mind,' he said to Safa.

'And what might that be?' Safa asked, smiling.

'You have a very beautiful smile,' Saleh beamed at her. Safa blushed, not expecting such a blunt comment. However, she recovered quickly and said, 'Thank you. But saying that doesn't mean you get any special treatment from me.'

The three of them laughed.

On their first day at the hospital, Humaid and Saleh had to train in the outpatient clinic. They had never seen such a crowded clinic before. The services rendered at the clinic were free; the cost of healthcare was subsidized by the Egyptian government. Consequently, poor patients didn't only come from Cairo, but also from the surrounding towns and villages. There were some very serious cases, such as advanced cancers, liver failures, kidney diseases, diabetes and hypertension. Liver diseases and cancers were very common in Egypt, as they frequently occurred as complications from Bilharzia, a disease caused by a parasite present in the Nile River. Bilharzia was mainly common among farmers and villagers. *The irony of the Nile,* Humaid mused. *As it flows from Upper Egypt, branches out into the Nile delta and then pours into the Mediterranean, it brings so much life to the country and its residents in one form, diseases and death in another.* Those with mild cases were prescribed medicine and sent home, while the very serious cases were admitted to the wards or rushed to the intensive care unit.

In the beginning, Humaid and Saleh just observed the consultant as he examined the patients, diagnosed them and prescribed their medication. Soon enough, they began examining patients under the care of their supervisor. After they were done with their assessment, they would run their diagnosis by their supervisor and the attending doctor to confirm it and ensure that the treatment they prescribed was the correct one.

The number of patients they treated on their first day at the outpatient clinic was probably ten times what they would have seen in a week in the UAE.

On weekends, or whenever they had free time, Ahmed would come visit them. Since Ahmed had a car and he was familiar with Cairo streets and burgeoning traffic, he would take them around to explore the city and its surroundings. On one weekend, they visited the old city where the architecture and sheer beauty of the old mosques, including Al Azhar mosque, one of the oldest in Egypt, took their breath away. They also visited the tombs of Sayyid Hussein and Sayyida Zainab, the grandson and granddaughter of Prophet Mohammed, as well as Al Azhar University, considered the oldest university in the world. The historic Citadel of Saladin stood on a mountain on the outskirts of the old city. It was built by the great conqueror, Salah Uddin, in 1176 AD.

They also visited Khan El Khalili, the well-known handicraft market. They strolled through the market, stopping at the different stalls and enjoyed a nice tea break at one of the market's many busy cafés. They chatted and reminisced about their college days in Sharjah and their common friends, as they sipped their tea and watched men play cards and backgammon and smoke shisha.

One evening, they decided to go on a scenic yacht tour up the Nile. As the yacht sailed, they enjoyed the night lights and the aroma of food from the many restaurants located along the riverbank. The sound of music drifted out to them from everywhere.

'This is magical,' Humaid said, appreciating and enjoying every second of the tour. They were lucky that night. The weather was mild and there was a light breeze in the air.

'On nights like this,' Ahmed said, 'one tends to forget the infamous Cairo smog.'

'Smog? What smog?' Saleh asked jokingly. 'Sweet dreams are made of these,' he sang.

'Who am I to disagree?' Ahmed and Humaid joined in.

On the yacht, they were served a buffet dinner—a fusion of Arabic and western dishes. At the end of the tour, happy and feeling over the moon, Ahmed drove them back to their apartment.

On other days, they would just head straight home after work, exhausted, but looking forward to Um Mohammed's food and yearning for the comfort of their own beds. Or, they would go to a restaurant recommended to them by Ahmed for its roasted pigeons or *mulukhiyya* with rabbit meat and rice, or simply stop at a street stall and try Cairo's delicious street food, especially *kushari*.

After two months of training in the outpatient clinic, Humaid and Saleh moved to General Surgery. Luckily, Ahmed was their supervisor there. He let them perform a number of surgeries. They started with minor surgeries that required local anesthesia, like the excision of abscesses or the removal of external tumors, and then moved on to more complicated surgeries like appendectomy (the removal of an inflamed appendix), splenectomy (the removal of a damaged spleen) and liver damage repair. They also performed surgeries on accident victims, which, they sadly noticed, came in all too often.

Saleh, who, unlike Humaid, was more interested in general medicine and not in surgery, would often excuse himself and leave the operating theatre. In fact, he preferred going to other wards in the hospital and, whenever possible, checking in on patients, just to escape being in the operating theatre. He became friends with several doctors, nurses and technicians at the hospital. It wasn't long before he perfected his Egyptian dialect and practiced it tirelessly with his new friends as well as with anyone who cared to hear him talk. At the hospital, everyone liked Saleh and stopped to chat and joke with him whenever they got a chance, high-fiving him and asking, 'What's today's joke, Saleh?'

Unlike Saleh, Humaid preferred to visit the hospital library and advised Saleh to take his internship seriously, instead of wasting his valuable time, as was Saleh's tendency sometimes.

The next phase of their first-year internship required them to spend a few weeks in the Neurology and Neurosurgery departments where they assisted in brain surgeries, as well as two weeks training in the Cardiac Surgery Department.

The Cardiac Surgery Department at Cairo University Hospital was considered the best in Egypt. For Humaid, it was fascinating to see first-hand how open-heart surgery was performed under general anesthesia.

After opening the chest bones and muscles, the blood was transferred to the heart-lung machine, which would then take over the function of the heart. Then the heart is frozen to four degrees centigrade to stop it completely. Once the heart stops beating, the repair work is done—be it the heart muscle or any of its arteries. After repair, the blood would be redirected to it again. As soon as the heart temperature is normalized, an electric current would be applied to restart pumping.

Having finished the assigned period at the Surgical Department, Humaid and Saleh moved on to the Gynecology and Obstetrics Department for two months, where they assisted during many successful births. Witnessing the miracle of birth stirred something fundamental inside their hearts. A baby's first scream as he took his first breath; new mothers crying tears of happiness to see and hold their babies after long hours of labor moved Humaid and Saleh to the core.

On one particular weekend, Humaid and Saleh wanted to visit the ancient pyramids in Giza located on the outskirts of Cairo. Ahmed didn't want to join them as he had already visited the pyramids several times, so he arranged for a guide to accompany Humaid and Saleh for two days, take them around Giza and explain the history of the pyramids to them.

Around 9 a.m. on the day of the trip to Giza, Humaid and Saleh found the guide waiting for them directly outside their apartment building. On the fifteen-kilometer drive from the apartment to Giza, the guide entertained them with stories about the pyramids and how no one could explain how they were built.

'The stones used in their construction were so large,' the guide said. 'It's almost impossible to conceive how they were carried to the top of the pyramids around 3,000 BC. However, a lot of secrets are constantly being unearthed, while many more still remain unknown.'

For Humaid and Saleh, it was quite exciting to enter the largest pyramid and see the tomb of Khufu in a hidden chamber.

After exploring the area around the pyramids, they hired horses and rode them around for an hour or so to discover the surrounding areas. Later, the guide took them to see the Pyramids of Saqqara.

After a long but exhilarating day, the guide drove them back to their apartment in Cairo. He arrived the next morning to take them to visit the Egyptian Museum in Cairo, one of the biggest and most important museums in the world.

After seeing the priceless treasures in the museum—mummies preserved for thousands of years, daunting statues, jewels and intricately decorated urns studded with precious stones, Humaid said to Saleh, 'I'm really surprised that so many Arabs visit Cairo but don't come here. Some don't even visit the pyramids. They're just interested in the nightlife and in shopping. How sad is that?'

The last part of their training was in less demanding departments. There, they got to examine and diagnose some very rare diseases not typically seen in the Gulf. Working in the Dermatology and ENT Departments felt like a piece of cake compared to the stress of working under pressure in any of the operating theatres. However, for Humaid, it was the adrenalin rushing through his body and the excitement he felt while working with a skilled team in the operating theatre that made all the difference and reaffirmed his decision to become a surgeon. He knew he had found his true calling in surgery.

By the time summer came to an end, they had completed their first year of internship and were now officially doctors. Each new intern had decided on his specialty at this juncture and could see his future clearly in front of his eyes. Humaid was set on becoming a heart surgeon. He knew that if he could accomplish that, he would be the first Emirati heart surgeon ever. Saleh had already made up his mind to become a Dermatologist. When Safa Jamal asked him why he chose that path, Saleh replied, 'You know, nobody dies at the Dermatology clinic.' She could not stop herself from laughing loudly.

Now that they had completed their first-year internship, they had time to visit some new places in Egypt. They took advantage of the free time they had and visited as many places as they could – from the summer resorts in Alexandria, Sharm El Sheikh and Ain El Sokhna, to Luxor and Aswan.

Still, there was so much to see but not enough time. Despite the oppressive summer heat, they decided to go on a three-day Nile cruise from Luxor to Aswan. That tour proved to be the finest and most enjoyable tour they went on in Egypt.

While sitting on their luxury cruise as it sailed up the Nile, they observed the beautiful views and farms on both banks.

When it came time for Humaid and Saleh to return to the UAE, they went to Cairo City Centre to buy gifts for their families. While they were in a leather shop, they heard a loud explosion in the distance, so loud that the windows in the shop shook. Humaid and Saleh and everyone in the store fell to the floor or ran for cover. When it was deemed safe for them to move, Humaid and Saleh quickly left and headed straight to their apartment. Later, Ahmed informed them that two terrorists had entered the largest church in Cairo and detonated explosive belts that were strapped around their bodies. They exploded themselves along with fifty or more worshippers.

'I just don't understand why anyone would kill himself and the people around him, including innocent children,' Humaid said, shaking his head in disbelief.

'These terrorists are brainwashed and act without thinking,' Ahmed said.

'The entire time we were here, nothing happened,' Saleh said. 'Now that we're about to go home, we almost got blown to pieces.'

'You're such a drama queen,' Humaid said to him, trying to lighten up the mood. 'The explosion wasn't even at the shopping center.'

'Well, it was close enough for the windows to shatter,' Saleh retorted.

'Seriously now, I don't get what these terrorists and the powers behind them believe,' Humaid continued. 'How can they call themselves Muslims? Islam believes in the sanctity of the human soul. The Quran spells it out clearly: *Whoever kills an innocent life, it is as if he has killed all of humanity, and whoever saves one soul it is as if he has saved all of humanity.* I just don't get it.'

'Neither do I,' Ahmed said, shaking his head. 'Neither do I.'

Chapter Ten
'A Marriage and a Death', Summer 2015

Humaid and Saleh brought a lot of luggage with them from Cairo to Sharjah. Their suitcases were full of souvenirs and gifts for their families. On their arrival to Sharjah Airport, they collected their luggage, cleared security and headed out to meet their families. Everyone was there: Humaid's parents and sisters, Saleh's parents, along with Saleh's two sisters and five brothers. Both families already knew each other.

Humaid and Saleh almost ran from the automatic door to kiss their parents' heads and hands and hug their siblings.

Maitha and Sara couldn't wait for Humaid to reach them. They ran towards him and he lifted them off the floor in a big bear hug.

'You have grown so much, *mashallah*,' he said, putting them down and looking at their faces. Both Maitha and Sara had indeed grown a few inches taller. They giggled when they heard that.

'I'm almost as tall as you are,' Maitha said.

'So am I,' Sara giggled as she stood on her tiptoes.

'What did you get me?' Maitha asked.

'And what did you get me?' Sara wanted to know as she grabbed Humaid's carry-on and started rolling it.

Saleh hugged and kissed his father's forehead and said something in his ear. That whisper, the almost imperceptible turn of Saleh's father's head towards Humaid's sisters and the smile and nod which followed were so subtle that no one noticed, not even his mother. But they were to change Saleh's life forever. Now that he had his father's blessing and approval, it was almost too hard for Saleh to hold his excitement.

'This weekend, Father, please,' Saleh urged his father as the two families were walking towards their cars.

'You don't think it's too soon, son?' Saleh's father said to him. 'You have just arrived.'

Nevertheless, when Saleh's father shook Abdullah's hand goodbye, he said, 'We would like to pay you a visit soon, Abu Humaid.'

'You and your family are welcome anytime, Abu Saleh. My house is your house,' Abdullah replied.

Once home, Humaid changed into his jalabiya and sat with his family in the living room sipping tea and chatting. He told them about his life in Egypt, the unforgettable experiences he and Saleh had there and the stellar training they were lucky to have received at Cairo University Hospital. Ever since the explosion took place, Humaid's family had been extremely concerned for his safety. They had heard about the suicide bombers in the news and immediately called Humaid to check on him every day until the minute he boarded his flight back home.

'Thank God you're safe and sound,' Afra said.

'And if I may add,' Asma jumped in, 'Extremely round. I think it's fair to say that you more than enjoyed Egyptian food.'

Still laughing at Asma's rhyming joke, Afra asked Humaid a question she had wanted to ask her brother since the day he arrived in Cairo. 'So, did you meet your dream girl there?'

'Humaid is getting married?' Maitha asked, her big eyes wide open in amazement.

'Hold your horses, girls,' Humaid laughed. 'First of all, as a rule of thumb, I will only marry an Emirati girl. And second of all, Miss Maitha, no. I'm not getting married. I sure am not ready to settle down.'

'But you're settled down now,' Sara said, innocently. 'You're back and you're sitting down and you're drinking tea. That looks settled enough to me.'

Humaid's mother hugged her youngest daughter and kissed her head. Pleased with her son's way of thinking, she said, 'Quite honestly, I've never met a girl more accomplished than Mona, and she's Emirati,' Asma added.

'And a doctor,' Afra conferred.

'So that's settled,' Sara said. Everyone laughed.

'Mona has completed her first-year internship,' Afra said. 'She's now working in the Eye Department at Dubai Hospital.'

'Great' Humaid said, impressed and proud of his college friend. 'Mona is an accomplished girl and any man would be lucky to marry her, but I meant it when

I said I wasn't ready to settle down at this point. I have a lot of plans for my future. Marriage can wait.'

'What do you have in mind for the future, Dr. Humaid?' Abdullah asked, still savoring the taste of the word *doctor* on his tongue. His son, a doctor. *Will I ever get used to it?* Abdullah thought.

'I want to become a heart surgeon,' Humaid replied. What he didn't share with his family was the bigger dream and hope he had been nurturing. Humaid didn't want to work at a hospital or a clinic. He wanted to travel the world to help those who were desperate for medical help. He aspired to help humanity. And he was restless to start.

For his second year of training, Humaid joined Dubai Health Department, the largest in the UAE with a Cardiac Centre. Saleh, more serious than ever about becoming a Dermatologist, chose to train in a hospital in Ras Al Khaimah. Both Humaid and Saleh wanted to be near their homes and families after a year of living away from them.

To gain more experience in other specialties before focusing on surgery, Humaid worked in the Trauma, Accident and Emergency Departments at Rashid Hospital, which was connected to Dubai Health Department. The administration at the hospital was very helpful and allowed Humaid to choose where he wanted to work and train first. He decided to stay in the Trauma Department for three months. There, he was required to stay overnight every third day. On such nights, he and other doctors would stay fully alert and on their feet throughout a 30-hour shift while handling an endless influx of patients. Most of the emergencies Humaid saw were caused by traffic accidents. It was very sad to see young people lose their lives because of careless driving.

He would also see children at the emergency room who were suffering from high fever. Understanding the irreversible damage that could be caused by a high fever, including, but not limited to, brain damage, Humaid would always consult the hospital's senior physicians when he had a child suffering from a high fever. Later in his training, when he became more confident, he relied on his own judgment and diagnosis and was rarely ever wrong.

The most depressing feeling Humaid had during his training at the Trauma Department was when a patient died on the way to the ER. Although all Humaid needed to do in that case was to confirm that the person was dead and write a death certificate, the loss of a life always left Humaid with a deep sadness but strengthened his determination to become a surgeon so he could help more and more people.

Two weeks after Saleh returned from Egypt, his father called Abdullah and asked if his family could come visit Abdullah's on Friday evening. Humaid made sure that he was off that day. He and Abdullah met their guests at the door when they arrived. They were equally surprised and happy to see that Saleh's two uncles and their wives were among the guests.

The women were ushered to the family's large living room by Maryam, Afra and Asma, while the men went into the majlis. After exchanging pleasantries over Arabic coffee and dates, Saleh's father cleared his throat and went straight to the reason of their visit.

'My family and I have come with a proposal tonight. We are here to ask for your daughter Afra's hand for my son Saleh,' he said.

Shocked, Humaid looked at Saleh. He felt blindsided by his friend. *You devil*, Humaid thought. All that time Saleh had fancied Afra and never even given the slightest hint that he liked or wanted her to become his wife.

'Saleh is like my son and our family will not find a better husband for Afra than him,' Abdullah said after a brief pause. 'We have known him since he was in elementary school. But Afra has the final word. I am sure you understand. Please give us some time to ask her. We'll come back to you with the answer in a few days.'

Even though Humaid's family had not been aware that Saleh's family was there to ask for Afra's hand, they had prepared a sumptuous dinner to celebrate the visit. Since both families were conservative, men and women ate separately. The women ate in the spacious dining room, while a nice spread was carefully laid out for the men in the garden. For the first time since they became friends, Humaid and Saleh didn't talk very much that night. They felt like they were treading on unfamiliar territory now. Humaid never thought that his best friend would one day marry his sister. *What does that make us now?* Humaid mused. *In-laws? Friends? Extended family?* He wondered what Afra would say and what turn his relationship with Saleh would take if Afra declined the marriage proposal.

After Saleh's family left, Humaid's family gathered in the living room. Afra didn't join them. She heard that Saleh had proposed to her and she felt shy and too overwhelmed. She wanted to be by herself to think about this sudden turn of events.

Abdullah asked Humaid about his opinion as he knew Saleh better than any of them.

'He's my best friend,' Humaid said, 'so I might sound biased. I've known Saleh almost all my life and, truth be told, there isn't a kinder and better person I would wish for my sister. I don't know anything bad about Saleh to report to you.'

Humaid was secretly glad that Saleh asked for Afra's hand and not Asma's. Saleh and his family were conservative, which was probably why he chose Afra, who cherished her Emirati culture and heritage and loved wearing the abaya, while Asma was completely different and tended to leave her abaya behind at home more often than not.

Everyone approved of Saleh, but the most important person in the equation was Afra. The decision was hers to make. Abdullah and Maryam raised their daughters well and empowered them with the freedom to express their own opinions and decide for themselves without fear. Even if Abdullah and Maryam liked Saleh and approved of him, they were not going to try to force Afra to marry him or try to sway her mind one way or another.

The next day after breakfast, Maryam went to Afra's room. Afra's face was flushed. She soon found out that Afra hadn't been able to sleep and had been up all night because she was excited and hesitant at the same time. She too believed that Saleh was a good man and would make a good husband. He came from a good family, was smart, good natured, had a sense of humor and was a doctor. He ticked all the boxes. Finally she told her mother that she accepted Saleh's proposal.

'And if he ever does anything that doesn't please you,' Maryam joked, 'Humaid will straighten him up.' Maryam hugged her daughter and congratulated her. 'I wish Humaid will want to copy his best friend soon and settle down,' she said. 'After all, Mona won't stay single for long.'

Back at the hospital, Humaid completed three months in the Trauma unit and moved on to the General Surgery Department at Rashid Hospital. This was the biggest surgical department in Dubai. There were almost thirty surgeons working there. Humaid had to spend three months working in General Surgery and Orthopedics. His duties included clinic and ward rounds in the morning with a team of consultants who were surprised to see for themselves how knowledgeable and efficient Humaid was when it came to surgeries. He could perform appendectomies, open abdominal muscles and excise gastric ulcers independently without the help of a senior surgeons.

One day, Humaid was called to see a new patient. It was a thirty-year old laborer who came to the ER complaining of excruciating stomach pain, mainly in his lower abdomen. Humaid examined the patient and found a hard mass under the tender area, indicating a long-term problem. He immediately consulted the senior physician on the floor and asked him to come examine the patient to confirm his diagnosis. It was decided that they needed to operate on the patient straight away. Humaid assisted in the surgery. When they opened the abdomen, it was full of blood. The surgeon used a vacuum to suck out the blood, revealing a large hole in the stomach.

It was clear that the poor man was suffering from a peptic ulcer, which was left undiagnosed and untreated for so long that it eventually burst open. Everything went wrong with the operation that day. The senior surgeon tried to close the hole, but it kept on oozing. The patient's pulse suddenly dropped. All the O negative blood, the patient's blood type, was depleted and there were no more units available at the hospital blood bank on that specific day. Soon, the patient's heart stopped beating. They tried to resuscitate him with a cardiac massage and electric shocks, but nothing worked. The Chief Surgeon announced the time of death.

This was the first time Humaid had seen someone die in front of him. He had handled dead bodies before and had dissected human cadavers in college, but this was different. He felt helpless and defeated and even responsible for the laborer's death. Unlike Humaid, the Chief Surgeon, although affected by the final outcome of the operation, looked at what happened objectively and assessed the situation practically.

'Don't beat yourself up, Humaid,' he said as they were taking off their scrubs and leaving the operating room. 'We did everything we could.'

Preparations for Afra's wedding were going at full swing. Afra and Maryam were busy buying Afra's trousseau—new dresses, new abayas, jewelry and shoes, as well as scheduling different fittings for the wedding dress and the other gowns. As was common in Emirati culture, the groom's family assumed all the expenses of the wedding, but Abdullah wanted to help somehow, so he took upon himself the responsibility of finding a good venue for the occasion and paid for it. Unlike some families who would burden the groom and his family for an exorbitant amount of money as a dowry, at times exceeding a million dirhams,

Abdullah didn't demand a dowry be paid for his daughter. He knew Saleh was newly employed and his father was not a very rich person. As long as Saleh was good to his daughter, money didn't matter.

Two days before the wedding itself, Saleh and Afra and their parents went to marriage court to sign the official marriage papers. The judge asked Afra if she was will-fully agreeing to marry Saleh. Afra nodded her head yes and signed the papers. Saleh and the witnesses signed too. With that binding contract, pronounced *milchy* in the UAE, Afra became legally Saleh's wife. The two families and their close friends gathered that night at Abdullah's house to celebrate the union in a small, intimate ceremony.

The big day came in January 2015. It was one of the happiest days for Humaid, as his best friend was marrying his dearest sister. Since it was a segregated event in line with UAE tradition and customs, the women's reception was held separately from the men's at a five-star hotel, while the men's reception was held at a well-known events venue near Sharjah airport.

There, the guests were greeted by Saleh, his father and uncles, as well as by Abdullah, Humaid and their male relatives. John, Rajan and Gibran, the groom's college friends, were there too. No one thought that Saleh would be the first one among them to tie the knot. They congratulated him and wished him a happy life.

'I can't believe that the runaway Bunny has finally been caught,' Rajan joked.

Saleh said as he hugged his friend. 'Are you back in the UAE for good?'

'No, Bunny. I came just to attend your wedding my dear friend. I'm finishing my internship in India.'

'Masha Allah', you look really good, Saleh,' Gibran said. 'I like your *bisht*. I like all the *bisht's* and *kondoras* I'm seeing here tonight,' Gibran added, making a sweeping gesture at the other Emirati men with their traditional clothes.

Saleh touched the golden trim of his elegant, black robe-like *bisht* and winked as he said to Gibran, 'I'll lend it to you when you get married, as long as you get married here in Sharjah.'

'Deal!' Gibran said happily.

Once all the guests were gathered at the women's reception, Afra, looking like a vision in her beautiful white dress with its long train and lace veil, walked into the hall, accompanied by songs and music. A *khaliji* singer and all-female band were hired for the occasion. They entertained the guests with their renditions of some of the most famous Arabic songs. Feasting, dancing and singing at both receptions lasted late into the night.

The men's reception was slightly shorter than the women's. When the guests started leaving, Saleh's male relatives headed out in a long procession of cars, honking their horns and blasting loud wedding songs with Saleh riding in a decorated car, towards the women's reception.

The women had already been informed that the groom and his relatives, as well as the bride's father and her other male relatives, were on their way. When the men entered the reception hall, the women parted to make way for them. Saleh climbed up the short steps to the stage where Afra sat on a beautiful red velvet chair trimmed with gold. She stood up as Saleh approached her. He lifted her veil and kissed her cheeks. He also kissed the foreheads of his mother and Maryam.

The bride and groom posed for photos alone and then with their families and best friends. While posing for a photo with Saleh, Humaid said, 'You devil! Is that why you wanted to become my friend? To steal my sister?'

'It's a win-win situation for me, you see,' Saleh replied. 'I have a best friend and a dear brother in you and a beautiful, smart wife in Afra. I am the luckiest man in the world.'

It was now time for the newlyweds to go to their private suite at a seaside resort between Sharjah and Ras Khaimah. Saleh's uncle had booked them a two-night stay there as a wedding gift, after which the new couple would fly to Switzerland for their honeymoon.

Chapter Eleven
Islamic Group in Syria , Winter 2016

Around nine in the morning, the same armed men from the Islamic group returned to the room. Despite the uncomfortable position he lay in all night with his hands tied behind his back, Humaid had managed to have some short bouts of sleep, although every joint and muscle in his body hurt. He couldn't feel his hands. The guards had wound the bands so tight around his wrists, almost cutting off his circulation.

One of the men untied Humaid. As the blood started to run through his veins, his arms hurt even more. The men offered him a bite to eat and a glass of lukewarm tea.

Humaid drank the tea in one gulp. When he was finished eating, the men tied his hands behind his back again and led him out of the room.

'Where are you taking me?' Humaid asked.

'To our Chief,' one of them replied gruffly.

They led Humaid to a pickup and sat him in the front seat between the two of them and started driving. Throughout the ride, the man on Humaid's right kept a gun pointed at him. Humaid was terrified. What if they hit a bump in the road and the gun went off?

'Our Chief is a just and God-fearing man,' one of the men said. 'Don't be afraid.' Humaid nodded. He didn't try to resist the men. He had no idea what they had planned for him. But whatever it was, he had a feeling they would not hurt him.

The car sped on empty streets winding between damaged houses. After a while, they passed stretches of green farms towards the town center and arrived in front of a large, heavily guarded building, which seemed to have been the municipality building in the past.

'ISLAMIC GROUP' was written on the front of the building in large, black block letters.

The men got out of the car and led Humaid between them, each holding one of his elbows. They entered the building and walked into a large hall where around twenty-five men were standing in various clusters with assault rifles and machine guns hanging from their shoulders. All of the men had beards and wore similar clothes emulating the early Islamic mode of dress. The men looked inquisitively at Humaid. One of them searched Humaid thoroughly to make sure he was not carrying any arms. There was nothing in his pockets as they were already emptied out by his captors the night before.

'The Chief is not here today,' a man who seemed in charge of the others said. 'His assistant, Abu Talha, will see you now.' He pointed at the door behind him and motioned for Humaid to go in.

'Untie his hands,' he ordered sharply when he realized Humaid's hands were still tied behind his back.

One of the two men who captured Humaid on the previous night untied him and led him by the elbows to Abu Talha's office. The second man followed directly behind them.

'*Al salamu aliykum*, brother,' the two men said to a bearded man sitting behind a massive mahogany desk.

'*Wa alaikum al salam*,' the man said as he got up and shook their hands.

Abu Talha was wearing the same type of early Islamic clothes, but his looked cleaner and newer. He too had a long black beard. Unlike the others, he seemed to take care of his appearance. His beard was combed and his manners were more refined. Or so it seemed.

'Are you Muslim?' Abu Talha asked Humaid.

'Yes, sir,' Humaid replied. 'I'm from the UAE.'

'You seem to think that just being from the UAE makes you a Muslim,' Abu Talha snickered.

'The UAE is a Muslim country, sir,' Humaid said, astonished that the man questioning him, presumably a Muslim himself, wasn't aware of it.

'Liar!' Abu Talha shouted at Humaid. 'I know everything about your country. Don't pretend you can teach me.'

Humaid was terrified. Abu Talha's expression had suddenly changed and he looked menacing. He seemed like a giant towering over everyone in the room.

'They tell me you're a doctor?' he asked Humaid.

'Yes, sir. I'm a surgeon,' Humaid replied. 'I was treating war injuries in the nearby village when the planes attacked.'

Abu Talha nodded. 'Are you Sunni or Shia?' he asked.

Humaid was taken aback by the question. No one had ever asked him that before. 'I'm a Sunni Muslim.'

'Good,' Abu Talha replied, satisfied. 'Sunni's are our brothers in Islam. We're fighting the Shia's and Alawites.'

Humaid didn't say anything. He had many Shia friends in Sharjah. He never felt that they were different from other Muslims.

Abu Talha scratched his beard in deep thought and asked, 'So you like helping fellow Muslims?'

'Yes, of course,' replied Humaid.

'Well, in that case,' Abu Talha said, 'we need a surgeon at our hospital. We don't have any good doctors or surgeons here at the moment. A lot of our brothers are dying from their injuries.'

'But, sir, I must go back to my work in Dubai. I only have—' Humaid started, but Abu Talha interrupted him.

'Shut up!' Abu Talha's loud voice rattled the ceiling fan. 'If you don't help your brothers, we'll charge you with treason.'

Humaid had no choice, so he thought it would be better to negotiate. '

'How long do you need me here?' he asked.

'As soon as we get another surgeon, we'll let you go,' Abu Talha said. Humaid felt helpless and trapped. He couldn't object. If he did, and if they charged him with treason, they would execute him in cold blood. Those men were ruthless. Human life meant nothing to them.

'Fine, sir,' he said to Abu Talha. 'But they've taken all of my money and passport,' he added, motioning to the two men with his head. 'May I please get them back?'

'You'll get your money back, but not your passport,' Abu Talha said. 'We'll give it to you when we're ready to let you go.'

'One more thing, please,' Humaid pleaded.

'What now?' Abu Talha was beginning to get irritated with Humaid. He didn't want to give in too much to him.

'My cellphone. Your men took it,' Humaid said. 'I need it. I have to call my family every day.'

Abu Talha thought for a second. 'Is that so?' But without waiting for an answer, he said, 'Fine. We'll give you back your cellphone for ten minutes every day to call your family, and only your family. Nobody else! And from now on, you'll call me brother, not sir. Understood?'

'Yes, brother. Thank you.' Humaid replied.

Abu Talha looked at the two men who remained standing the entire time without saying a word.

'Abu Wasim and Abu Samir here will take care of you. From now on, you're an official guest of the Islamic Group.'

Abu Wasim, who was originally from Jordan, and Abu Samir, who came from Iraq, led Humaid outside. This time they didn't tie his hands behind his back and didn't point a gun at him. The three of them headed straight to the car. Abu Wasim sat in the driver seat and indicated to Humaid to sit in the passenger seat next to him, while Abu Samir sat alone in the back. They no longer treated Humaid as a prisoner but as an esteemed guest, just as Abu Talha had instructed.

They drove Humaid to a guest house some kilometers away from where Humaid had met Abu Talha. The house was located on a farm and had a small river running behind it. The main hall was wide and had an oversized rug on the floor. There was a large sofa, love-seat and coffee table, as well as a dining table with six chairs. The kitchen was fully equipped, at least by Syrian standards. The house had three bedrooms, each one of them with a double bed, a dresser and two nightstands. The toilets were clean.

'This is going to be your house from now on,' Abu Wasim said. 'The only thing missing is a wife.'

'Do you want to marry now?' Abu Samir asked, half joking, half serious. Humaid thought they were joking, but they looked serious. When Humaid didn't reply, the two men laughed. Humaid had heard stories about Jihadi brides. He hoped that Abu Talha and his men wouldn't force him to marry to prove his loyalty to the Islamic Group.

Abu Samir and Abu Wasim returned Humaid's backpack to him. He checked it and found his wallet in it. There was nothing missing except his cellphone and of course his passport. Humaid told the men he was very tired and had a severe headache and wanted to take a nap.

'But you must eat lunch before you sleep,' Abu Wasim insisted as Humaid took a couple of strong pain killers from his backpack and gulped them with water.

'Fine. I'll eat,' Humaid said to avoid arguing with them, although he had no appetite.

Abu Samir went to the kitchen for a few minutes and came back with a large tray full of rice topped with a roasted half lamb. *It must have been kept in the oven to stay warm,* Humaid thought. He had smelled the aroma of food when they first walked into the house but didn't know where it was coming from. After placing the tray on the dining table, Abu Samir went back to the kitchen and returned with a large bowl of salad and another bowl of fruit. Humaid asked if someone else was joining them. The men shook their heads no.

'Bismillah. Let's eat,' they said and proceeded to eat.

Humaid ate a few bites, excused himself and left the table. He headed to the closest bedroom and threw himself on the bed and fell asleep right away.

It was late in the evening when he woke up with a jolt. At first, he didn't remember where he was. Then it all came back to him—Abu Talha, Abu Wasim and Abu Samir. He wondered if they had left him alone in the house. He tiptoed out of the bedroom and headed to the hall. Abu Samir and Abu Wasim were both snoring in the hall. Abu Wasim was stretched out on the sofa, while Abu Samir was sleeping on the love-seat. Both of them got up immediately when they felt Humaid approach.

'I'll make coffee,' Abu Samir said and headed to the kitchen. He came back a few minutes later with coffee and a plate of cookies.

The coffee tasted good. Humaid had felt the need for a strong cup of coffee all day. When they were done with their coffee and sweets, Humaid asked if he could take a walk around the farm to get some fresh air while it was still light outside.

'No problem,' Abu Wasim said, picking up his gun. 'Let's go.'

Abu Samir and Abu Wasim stayed a close distance behind Humaid as he walked around the farm where the house was built. The surrounding area was as beautiful as a postcard. Humaid could see a watch tower and a barbed wire fence in the distance.

'What's that there?' he asked, pointing in the direction of the barbed wire.

'The Golan Heights,' Abu Samir replied. 'They're under Israeli occupation.'

'And the watch tower is controlled by UN peacekeeping forces,' Abu Wasim volunteered the information.

'Are you not afraid of staying so close to the Israelis'? Humaid asked.

'Afraid?' They both laughed. 'Israelis are our friends,' Abu Samir said. 'They're protecting us. If the army's planes come anywhere near us, they hit them with missiles. If any of us gets seriously injured, we take him to the border and he gets treated free of charge on humanitarian grounds.'

'Humanitarian grounds?' Humaid asked, genuinely confused. 'Are you serious?'

'We don't joke,' Abu Wasim said. 'Anyway, it's getting dark and we have to get back to the house now.'

Once inside the house, they washed up, did their wudu and started praying in a group. Abu Samir, being the eldest, led the prayers. They had dinner after that, before going to the bed.

Both Abu Wasim and Abu Samir stayed at the house that night. They took turns watching the door of Humaid's room, not letting him out of their sight for a second. The next day after breakfast, Abu Samir gave Humaid a clean dark suit to wear. The style was not unlike the clothes he had seen the men of the Islamic Group's wear.

'You can't wear jeans outside,' Abu Samir said. 'This was mine but I don't wear it anymore.'

Humaid accepted the outfit and changed without argument. When he finished dressing, they drove him to the hospital. On the way there, he noticed that all the men he saw on the streets had beards and wore the same kind of traditional Islamic clothing. He didn't see many women outside, but those he saw were fully covered. Everyone seemed to be in a hurry. Everyone was clearly scared. There were bearded guards with machine guns on every corner.

The car stopped in front of a white building with a flag of the Islamic Group flying on it.

'This building was a hospital even before the Islamic Group liberated it from the Alawites and the infidels,' Abu Samir said proudly.

'Except for dividing it into two sections, one for men and one for women,' Abu Wasim added, 'we didn't have to make any changes to it.'

'We will be right outside,' Abu Samir said. 'Please don't try to do anything foolish. All exits are under constant surveillance. There are undercover guards all over the hospital and they won't hesitate to shoot you if you try to escape. Understood?'

'I won't try to escape,' Humaid assured them. *Where would I even go if I escaped?* He thought. *Not now. Not yet. I have to be careful and come up with a plan.*

'We really, *really* don't want you to get hurt,' Abu Wasim added, stressing his words.

'I said I'm not going to try to escape,' Humaid repeated, beginning to lose his temper.

Two doctors, two anesthesiologists and five nurses came to meet Humaid. All of them were male. Abu Talha was telling the truth. There were no surgeons at the hospital. The emergency room and the clinics were on the ground floor. Half of the first floor had been converted into an operating theatre and the other half into an ICU.

Humaid inspected the instruments and the equipment at the hospital and found them in good working condition. The theatre and ICU were well equipped for basic surgeries. The hospital staff looked extremely exhausted. It was as if everyone was working double shifts and not getting any rest at all. When they met Humaid, they shook his hand without smiling. There was neither joy in their eyes nor a feeling of pride or passion for what they were doing.

Humaid was put in charge of the accident and emergency department on the ground floor. He was given a room that had an examination table, a chair and a couch. The cabinets on both two sides of the room were fully stocked with bandages, surgical sutures, needles and medication.

For the first two days, Humaid saw many patients, although none of them were seriously ill. Some had cut wounds, while others came to the hospital with infections or acute abdominal pain as a result of overeating. Humaid diagnosed two patients with acute appendicitis and operated on them. Acute appendicitis surgeries were now easy for Humaid to perform as he had already done so many of them in the past. If a female patient needed surgery, he would go to the female side of the hospital and operate on her assisted by a female nurse and female anesthetist.

On the third day, Humaid heard a loud explosion not very far from the hospital. He jumped from his chair, but the rest of the hospital staff didn't show much emotion. They had become used to the sound of explosions and gunfire, which meant more casualties and more work for them.

Soon after, the Hospital Director came over and advised Humaid that one of the bomb factories had exploded. The hospital would be expecting many casualties and he should be ready. As soon as the Hospital Director finished his sentence, the sound of approaching sirens pierced the air.

Ambulances began arriving with the injured, followed by cars loaded with men covered with blood and debris.

'What happened?' Humaid asked one of the doctors.

'It seems they were making crude bombs and explosive belts when one of the bombs exploded,' the doctor replied, his voice devoid of emotion.

One ambulance brought a young man who had all of his limbs blown away. Another ambulance brought in a man with his head hanging on his chest. These two men had been standing closest to the bomb. They were dead on arrival.

Humaid instructed the aides to take the corpses to the morgue. Some of the injured were brought in with badly damaged limbs. All Humaid could do for them was stop the bleeding and amputate the limbs. It wasn't that there was no time for Humaid to perform vascular surgeries on them to save their limbs; the hospital facilities and operating room were not equipped for such demanding operations.

Humaid was shocked by the stream of injured arriving at the hospital. Among the injured were women, children and elderly people. When he expressed his astonishment, he was told that the bomb factory was camouflaged in a residential area. When the bomb exploded, the sparks ricocheted and the entire factory exploded, destroying the surrounding area and houses. Some houses collapsed completely. Their inhabitants were either crushed to death under the falling concrete or trapped under the rubble. Fortunately, the bomb storage itself was located in a different area. Had the factory stored all manufactured bombs in the same location where they were made, the damage and casualties would have been much worse.

With the help of other doctors and nurses, Humaid sutured the open wounds after removing all foreign bodies from them. The injured women were taken to the women's section straight away where female doctors treated them.

The final count that day was five dead, ten amputations and almost twenty major and minor injuries. Humaid went back to the guest house with Abu Wasim and Abu Samir later that day. Exhausted, he fell asleep immediately after dinner.

The next day was Friday. As soon as Humaid arrived at the hospital, he examined the blast patients to make sure they were improving. Everyone seemed in stable condition, and all he had to do was change their wound dressings.

At noon, when it was time for Friday prayers, all the men headed to the main Mosque; otherwise, they would be subjected to severe punishment. Humaid accompanied the other male doctors and nurses as they walked to the mosque. Inside, fighters and civilians occupied every inch. Humaid noticed that the fighters were from different nationalities.

Abu Talha was sitting in the front row, flanked by guards on both sides. Nearby, sitting on a wide chair facing the crowd at the mosque, sat a short, obese man who seemed to be in his late sixties.

'He is the head of the Islamic Group,' Abu Samir, told Humaid.

After the call for prayer, the Head of the Islamic Group read a written sermon. His voice was raspy and he seemed to find it hard to catch his breath. He was pale and looked quite unwell. When he was done delivering the sermon, he led the prayer a little faster than usual. Then he left the mosque with his fifty or so guards.

Humaid noticed that almost everyone was heading towards a park in the center of town. He and the other doctors followed, accompanied by Abu Wasim and Abu Samir. In the middle of the park, there were a few handcuffed and blindfolded men.

'They're criminals,' Abu Samir said and spat on the floor. 'Some of them will be hanged, some beheaded and some will have their limbs amputated. It depends on the nature of their crimes.'

There were also some fully covered women there in the middle of the square. They were charged with infidelity and were to be stoned to death. They were crying or shouting, saying they were innocent, begging for their lives to be spared. Hundreds of people had gathered to witness the execution. Humaid couldn't tolerate the cruelty of the entire spectacle. He couldn't understand why anyone would want to see another person killed, let alone enjoy the sight.

'Take me back to the house, please,' he said to Abu Wasim. 'This is too much.'

Abu Wasim shrugged. 'You better get used to it, doctor. There is at least one execution every Friday here.'

'God!' Humaid exclaimed. 'I save lives. I live to save lives, not to see them squandered away like this.'

'You better not let Abu Talha hear you say anything like that, doctor,' Abu Wasim said as he walked to towards the car with Humaid.

One relatively quiet evening at the hospital, a female nurse suddenly barged into Humaid's office.

'There's a woman in labor who's having complications and might not make it,' she said. 'The doctors in the women's section need your help, please.'

Humaid followed the nurse to the women's section. There, he was surprised to see Abu Talha pacing the floor, clearly under great duress.

'It's my wife,' he said to Humaid, holding him by the shoulders. 'You must not examine her or see her face.'

'How can I possibly treat a woman in labor if I don't examine her?' Humaid asked.

'All right. Okay then,' Abu Talha huffed. 'If it's absolutely necessary. She's carrying my son and must be saved.'

Humaid felt his feet turn to lead. The cruelty of Abu Talha's request was the antithesis of everything Islamic. *How dare such a monster even claim he is a Muslim?* Humaid thought. He felt such deep hatred toward Abu Talha and the false ideology he represented. But again, Humaid understood that he was their prisoner. Regardless of the house they allowed him to sleep in and the pseudo freedom his job at the hospital gave him, he was being held against his will. He didn't say any of that to Abu Talha as he looked him straight in the eye and said, 'God willing. I'll do my best to save them both.'

Inside, Humaid changed into a pair of clean scrubs and went to examine Abu Talha's wife. She wasn't screaming, just moaning nonstop.

'She's been in labor for fourteen hours,' the female doctor informed Humaid. 'She's completely dilated but can't push and the baby's not crowning.'

Humaid examined the patient's swollen abdomen. He could immediately determine that the baby was breech.

'How old is she?' he asked the doctor.

'Either fourteen or fifteen,' the doctor replied.

'That's probably why she's having complications,' Humaid said. 'She has a narrow pelvis.'

'What's the solution?' the doctor asked Humaid. 'If anything happens to the baby, we're going to pay the price.'

'Don't worry,' Humaid assured the doctor. 'A Cesarean will save both mother and baby. Just take her to the operating room and let the anesthesiologist put her to sleep.'

Once Abu Talha's wife was in the operating room and asleep, she was covered fully with sterile drapes, except for her abdomen. Humaid took a surgical knife and made an incision in the lower part of her abdomen. Then he made an incision in the upper swollen part of the uterus. Immediately, the head of the baby popped out. He put both of his hands under the baby's shoulders and pulled him out. He held the baby upside down from his legs and slapped his bottom gently. The baby gave a cry. Humaid handed the baby to the female doctor who was standing right next to him. She cut the umbilical cord and clamped the stump in two places.

Humaid turned his full attention to Abu Talha's wife. He started suturing the uterus first, then the abdominal muscles and finally the skin. When he was done, the operating room nurse took over. She cleaned the wound and bandaged it. Humaid left the operating room and removed his scrubs.

Outside, he found Abu Talha waiting for him.

'Both mother and baby are fine,' Humaid said.

'Praise be to Allah. It's a boy, right? The ultrasound said it was a boy,' Abu Talha said.

'Yes. A healthy boy,' Humaid replied. 'The mother bled a lot, but she will be ok. The long hours she spent in labor have—' but before he could finish his sentence, Abu Talha interrupted him.

'Thank God I have other wives. Talking of which,' Abu Talha rubbed his hands and with a lewd look in his eyes, asked Humaid, 'Do you have anything to help me, brother Humaid?'

Humaid didn't understand what Abu Talha meant, so he looked at him quizzically, but then it dawned on him that he was asking for an aphrodisiac.

'I'm a surgeon,' Humaid said, calculating his words carefully. 'If you think you have an operable problem . . .'

'Forget I asked,' Abu Talha fired away, interrupting Humaid again. 'Why are you still here? 'Go back to the men's section.'

After work as usual, Humaid found Abu Wasim and Abu Samir waiting for him by the car in front of the hospital.

'Abu Talha is very happy,' Abu Wasim said. 'Now that you delivered his baby boy safely, I am sure he will reward you and agree to whatever you ask for.'

Humaid almost regretted the last thing he said to Abu Talha. He decided to be more careful next time. He had to win Abu Talha's trust.

When they reached the house, Abu Samir gave Humaid his cellphone to call his parents.

'Ten minutes only,' he said to him.

Abdullah picked up after the first ring.

'Humaid, where on earth are you? When will you be back? Your mother and sisters are worried sick about you.'

'Soon, Dad. Soon Insha'Allah,' Humaid said, trying to sound like his usual self. He almost choked on his own words. He felt the tears come to his eyes and fought to hold them back, afraid that his father would sense something and get alarmed.

'Every day you say you're coming soon,' Abdullah said, almost angrily. 'When will this soon be? The group of doctors you travelled with are all back, except for you. What are you still doing there? If you don't want to be honest and tell me, then tell your mother. Here, she wants to talk to you.'

'Humaid!' Maryam's voice, choking with tears, rang in Humaid's ears. Hearing his mother's voice was almost too much for Humaid. He was afraid he would cry if he opened his mouth.

'Where are you, Humaid?' Maryam said. 'I don't know how much longer I can keep going like this. I'm so worried about you. The fear and anxiety are going to kill me.'

'Mama!' Humaid begged. 'Please don't say that. I'll be back very soon.'

'Promise?' Maryam demanded.

'I promise, Mama,' he said. Then he added, 'Insha'Allah.'

'You've never broken a promise to me, Humaid,' his mom said, a bit calmer, wanting to believe his promise.

'I promise, Mama,' Humaid said again.

After hanging up with his parents, Humaid was so upset he didn't have an appetite to eat. He went straight to bed, but he couldn't sleep. The thought of his family and friends and how free and happy he had lived back in Sharjah kept him awake. He missed his old life to the point of breaking.

Chapter Twelve
Sudan Medical Camp, Summer 2015

After their wedding, Saleh and Afra flew to Switzerland where they spent their honeymoon. Humaid missed them both. Even though he had all his family around him, Humaid missed Afra's presence terribly. He missed her liveliness, sense of humor, caring personality and willingness to help everyone in the family. However, Humaid wasn't the only one who missed Afra, everyone in the house did so as well. For Maryam, it was a bitter-sweet feeling. She missed her eldest daughter who was also her friend and knew that she wouldn't be living with them again. Nonetheless, she was also happy for her Afra and wished her all the best in her new life.

Maryam cried in silence. Her swollen eyes were the only telltale sign that she cried at all.

Humaid's work at Dubai Hospital was going smoothly. He finished the second year of his residency during which he trained in the different departments at both Rashid Hospital and Dubai Hospital. He was now more determined than ever to become a heart surgeon. A few months after Afra's wedding, he started his cardiology residency at Dubai Hospital. His main duties included making sure the patients in the ward were taking their proper medication and their vital signs were stable. When the attending doctor discharged a patient, Humaid would order the medication from the pharmacy and explain to the patient how to take it. Twice a week, he went down to the outpatient clinics with the entire team; and twice a week, he worked a 36-hour shift.

Humaid was still not permitted to perform any part of heart surgery by himself, as it was a highly specialized job. He had to gain the required skills first by attending a cardiothoracic surgery fellowship program at a recognized medical institute in Europe or the United States. However, Humaid made sure that he attended all the surgeries performed by his seniors, to assist and observe.

Feeling Humaid's enthusiasm, the surgeons would allow him to perform some minor steps of the surgery, such as suturing or closing a chest wound. Later, Humaid's consultant felt confident in his abilities and occasionally permitted him to excise a vein from the thigh region to be transplanted in the heart to replace the coronary artery. All this was carried out, of course, under the strict guidance of senior surgeons.

Humaid was keen on performing the main steps of heart surgery. He could hardly wait to be able to do so. Some of his colleagues told him about a charity organization in the UAE that helped perform heart surgeries in poor countries in Africa and Asia. Humaid found the number of the charity organization and called to find out more about their work and see how it could fit his aspirations and goals. The operator connected him to Mr. Qasim, who oversaw all the processes and logistics of organizing medical procedures, including heart surgeries, in poor countries. Mr. Qasim explained to Humaid over the phone that he was welcome to join the team of doctors and surgeons the organization periodically sent to poor countries. However, Humaid would need to bring his graduation certificate, a detailed account of his training up to that point and experience in the field of medicine, as well as a No-Objection Certificate from the director of the hospital where he worked.

Humaid gave considerable thought to joining the organization. The benefits were two-fold. He would be helping the poor, which he always wanted to do, as well as gaining all the surgical experience he needed.

One evening, he decided to discuss the subject with his parents. Afra and Saleh were back from their honeymoon by that time and they were also present.

Saleh had started working at the Dermatology Department in Al Qassimi Hospital in Sharjah, a few blocks away from the couple's new two-bedroom apartment. Afra continued her job at Sharjah Bank. Both Saleh and Afra looked very happy and settled into their married life.

As they were having dinner that evening, Humaid told his family that he wanted to go to Sudan to help poor people and perform heart surgeries there.

'What? Sudan?' Saleh asked, surprised. It was the first time he heard Humaid mention his interest in working there. 'Why Sudan?'

'It's been a dream of mine to help the poor,' Humaid said.

Maryam didn't say anything. She knew that if Humaid decided to do something, he would pursue it to the end. Abdullah asked for more details. He wanted to know if there were other doctors going with Humaid or if this was a personal adventure or in collaboration with a trusted organization. Humaid explained the role of the charity organization, which was supported by the Sheikh of Abu Dhabi and run by Red Crescent in facilitating the travel, and the humanitarian and medical missions involved. When they heard this, his family was satisfied.

'How long will you be there?' Afra asked.

'Two weeks,' Humaid replied, relieved and happy that his family was supporting him. He had passed the first hurdle.

The second hurdle was the Hospital Director, Dr. Salem Al Sayed. Fortunately for Humaid, he was understanding, and he appreciated Humaid's efforts. 'This is a noble cause and I don't mind giving you a No-Objection Certificate,' Dr. Al Sayed said right before he asked his secretary to type the NOC, stamp it, seal it and hand it over to Humaid.

'But there is a caveat.'

'And what is that?' asked Humaid.

'The two weeks would be at the expense of your annual leave,' the Director said.

'Oh, that's absolutely fine. I don't mind at all,' Humaid replied with a big smile.

Humaid's first charity trip was to Sudan. He arrived at Khartoum Airport and was received by representatives from another local charity organization. He stayed one night at a local hotel where he met other members of the organization.

The group was a mix of UAE, Sudanese, Egyptian and Pakistani nationals. The head of the group was a reputable heart surgeon from Jordan who used to work in Abu Dhabi. His name was Dr. Jihad. There were other heart surgeons and some fellows like Humaid. One of them was Rashid, a young Emirati doctor who had graduated from Al Ain College of Medicine and, like Humaid, was interested in becoming a heart surgeon. There were also a few anesthesiologists, nurses and technicians.

The group was informed that they would be working in a field hospital in a remote area of Sudan near the border with Ethiopia. This way their services would cater to a bigger segment of African population and reach out to other surrounding countries in need.

When it was time for the group to set out to their work location, they were transported in big convoy of jeeps and vans. Behind them were large, heavy trucks that carried equipment, instruments and tents, the biggest of which would be converted into a field hospital.

As the cars covered the distance, their wheels grinding on the uneven dirt roads, dust, oil, dirt and tar flew all around them. Humaid felt sorry for the laborers who were sitting on top of the trucks, accompanying them on their journey. They drove for many hours and passed through some of the most breathtaking topography Humaid had ever seen with the Nile on one side and the expansive African jungle spanning out on the other side.

After ten hours of almost non-stop driving, and as the scorching African sun was about to set, the convoy of vehicles arrived at the area where they were supposed to set up camp and a field hospital. The laborers unloaded the tents and the portable battery-operated lights. Another group started setting up tents where the group members would sleep, while others prepared a large campfire for the evening meals. At that stage of the journey, everyone was hungry and tired. The sandwiches and snacks they had on the way there were not enough to satisfy their hunger.

After eating the delicious barbecue that the laborers had prepared, the group members headed to their tents to sleep. There were no beds there, but each member was given a sleeping bag. Although a night on the floor in a sleeping bag was not the most comfortable way to sleep for anyone, they were too exhausted to notice and were fast asleep within seconds.

Most of the group got up very early the next morning as the sun was coming up. They could see the nearby villages and farmers working in the fields. The laborers began the task of setting up the tents, which were to serve as clinics, as well as two tents designated exclusively as operating theatres. The technicians helped install all the medical equipment. Humaid noticed that everyone in the group knew their job well. It was clear to him that it wasn't their first time setting up a field hospital and working in it.

The doctors started helping with the setup too, determining the position of the equipment and placement of the operating tables. Dr. Jihad, the Jordanian cardiologist, was supervising the work and making sure everything was in its place. Having worked at numerous field hospitals all over the world, his experience and vision were indispensable to the success of every operation and mission. Dr. Jihad, who was originally from Palestine, was in his sixties but appeared much younger. After receiving a scholarship from the Jordanian government to study in the UK, he achieved top ranking at the School of

Medicine where he studied and decided to follow his passion and become a heart surgeon. While studying in the UK, during his third year of college, he received news that his mother was sick. Her heart was failing. She was living in the West Bank at the time. He immediately returned to Amman but he required special permission from the Israeli authorities to cross to the West Bank. It took the Israeli authorities three days to grant him that permission; and by the time he arrived in the West Bank, his mother had already passed away. Even though Dr. Jihad couldn't be there to help his mother, the pain of losing her so unexpectedly motivated him to help those in need, especially in his capacity as a heart surgeon. It was also why he never married.

Humaid developed a very close friendship with Rashid and Dr. Jihad. Once the camp was set up and the field hospital operational, villagers started coming. Some of them were not sick at all, but the novelty and excitement of having a hospital nearby was enough to make them come and seek any kind of medical advice they could get.

The heart patients who needed surgeries were admitted to a temporary ward with twenty beds. The next day after breakfast, Dr. Jihad and the other Sudanese and Pakistani cardiac surgeons proceeded to operate on them. Both operating theatres were located near each other with the sterilizing rooms in between.

The field hospital was fully self-sufficient. Water was provided in large tanks. When the tanks were empty, the laborers would bring water from the nearby towns, the closest of which was about ten kilometers away.

In the beginning, Humaid and Rashid would just assist the surgeons by preparing the patients for surgery. Soon, they grew confident and started handling small parts in the surgeries themselves under strict supervision of the well-established and experienced heart surgeons. The main surgeons would repair heart valves or open blocked arteries. Such delicate procedures required the use of a portable microscope. After completing a heart repair, they closed the breastbone with wires which would stay inside the patient for rest of his or her life. After that, they stitched the surgical skin cut. A single heart surgery could last up to six hours.

Every day after sunset, as the outpatient clinics emptied out and the surgery patients were resting in the wards, the doctors sat around the campfire to chat. They discussed the various cases they saw that day and shared stories about their lives before the camp. Soon, they began to know more and more about each other. Only the drivers and laborers were paid for their services. The rest of the group volunteered their time and knowledge to help the poor.

Humaid would usually sit in the same circle with Dr. Jihad, Rashid and a couple of Sudanese doctors. He told them he was enjoying the camp and gaining valuable knowledge every day.

'If you're really interested in doing more charity work,' Dr. Jihad said to Humaid, 'Consider joining me next month in Jordan.'

'In Jordan?' Humaid asked.

'Yes,' Dr. Jihad replied. 'I'm heading there next to work at the Syrian refugee camps.'

'I didn't know that,' Humaid said. 'I mean, about the refugee camps in Jordan.'

'Oh yes,' Dr. Jihad sighed. 'There are over one million war refugees there and they're in dire need of help.'

'Count me in, Dr. Jihad,' Humaid said enthusiastically. 'I'll have to discuss this with my family first and run it by my hospital administration back in the UAE, but I don't see any obstacles there.'

After ten days of work at the field hospital, and after one hundred and fifty successful surgeries, the job of the group was done and they closed the camp. Everything was packed and loaded and within twenty-four hours, the group returned to Khartoum. During those ten days at the camp, Humaid was able to perform a few steps in various heart surgeries, as well as other emergency procedures that he was skilled at from previous experience.

Humaid and the group spent two days in Khartoum on this leg of the trip before they went their separate ways. Some of them, like Humaid and Rashid, headed back to their native countries. Others, like Dr. Jihad, went straight to another humanitarian mission.

Humaid was disappointed with what he saw in Khartoum, a city renowned for its educated and hospitable people. It was inconceivable to him how a city with so many resources was inordinately so underdeveloped. Although Sudan was one of the largest Arab countries with vast cultivable land and surrounded by water from the Blue Nile and White Nile, it was still importing basic food from abroad.

Sudan was amid political turmoil. The Arab Spring had not changed anything there, unrest in the country was palpable. Humaid had a feeling that the masses would rise soon to take that corrupt government down. The Islamic militants and terrorists in Sudan were getting stronger, and security was tight everywhere. Add to that the ongoing war in southern Sudan and you had a recipe for disaster. Politicians were fighting among themselves in the south. Refugees escaped to the north for their lives with the tattered clothes on their backs, creating one of the most catastrophic humanitarian crises in the world.

Chapter Thirteen
Amman Trip

Returning home to Sharjah felt so good – back to sleeping on a nice comfortable bed in a bedroom with air conditioning, a proper toilet and a shower, clean water and air. Humaid now realized how much comfort he was privileged enough to enjoy all his life, compared to the poor people in Africa. He thanked God a million times for his life. He felt he had taken those things for granted and realized their value only when they were not accessible. *Never underestimate the importance of living in a modern city with state-of-the-art healthcare facilities,* Humaid told himself.

Humaid's love for his family filled his heart and kept him focused and determined to succeed and make his parents and sisters proud. They were what mattered to him most. Sitting with them at the dinner table was the highlight of a long day.

Reports from and about Syria topped the news daily. Millions of refugees escaped to Jordan, Lebanon and Turkey. Some floated for weeks on unsafely overcrowded boats in a desperate attempt to make it all the way to Greece. Some of the refugees managed to escape to Gulf countries, including the United Arab Emirates.

Maryam, Humaid's mother, joined a charity organization in Sharjah to help refugees. She would share with her family heart-rending stories of suffering and atrocities as told to her by the refugees themselves. Everyone in the family was deeply moved by what they heard. Maryam encouraged her family to donate to the charity if they could. She told them the money would go directly to the families affected by the ongoing war in Syria.

'I guess charity runs in your family, Afra,' Saleh said. 'Back in college, your brother raised money to help an Indian student, and now your mother is collecting money for refugees.'

'It's all for a good cause,' Afra said, as she opened her purse, took her wallet out and put all the money she had on the table.

'Ah! I forgot you got your salary today,' Saleh joked. 'Hope you left us some cash for gas.'

'We'll put that on your card,' Afra said with a smile.

'I guess that will leave us with no savings for our children,' Saleh joked.

Humaid resumed his work at Dubai Hospital's Cardiology Department. His experience in Sudan made him more confident. His colleagues wanted to know more about what he did there. They were inspired by his stories. Many of them showed a keen interest in that kind of work, promising to look it up and volunteer if they could. He knew that some of them were just paying lip service and, even if they could, they would never leave their comfortable lives and high-paying jobs to go work at a field hospital in the middle of nowhere.

During his first week back at the hospital, Humaid was exiting the elevator on the ground floor when he ran into Farah. She didn't see him at first as she was busy talking to a couple holding a newborn baby.

'It's so nice to see you again, Farah,' Humaid said when the couple left. Farah turned in his direction.

'Humaid!' It was clear that Farah was pleasantly surprised to see her friend after all those years.

'You're wearing your white robe. Does that mean you work here?' Humaid asked.

'I was going to ask you the same,' Farah said. 'I'm a pediatrician now. I started here three weeks ago.'

'My God!' Humaid said, thrilled. 'I just came back last week.'

'We need to catch up,' Farah told him. 'Are you free now?'

'Even if I wasn't,' Humaid replied. 'I will always make time to catch up with you.'

As they headed to the coffee shop, Farah told Humaid that she worked for two years at Abu Dhabi Hospital where she had done her internship. She was now married to an Emirati man from Dubai and had moved to Dubai just recently.

'You got married?' Humaid asked.

'Yes, I did,' Farah said, absentmindedly touching the wedding ring on her finger as she walked.

'Am I the only one who didn't know that?' Humaid asked. 'Did my invitation get lost in the mail?

'I didn't know your address and when I managed to find it, you were out of the country, Humaid,' Farah explained.

'Ah! In that case, I will forgive you,' Humaid smiled. '*Mabrook*, Farah. I'm so happy for you.'

Farah enquired about their other friends. 'Are you still in touch with any of them?' she asked. 'Where's Saleh now?'

'That devil!' Humaid beamed. 'Bunny married my sister.'

'Really? How nice!' Farah was genuinely happy for Saleh. 'I guess my invitation got lost in the mail, too, right?'

Humaid laughed at Farah's wit.

'How about you?' Farah asked. 'Are you married?'

'No. Not yet,' Humaid replied, shrugging his shoulders.

'Fortunately, or unfortunately?' Farah asked with an inquisitive smile.

'Neither nor,' Humaid said. 'I'm still not ready to marry and settle down. I want to finish my postgraduate studies first.'

'*Mashallah*, Humaid. You're always thinking big,' Farah said. 'By the way, do you know that Mona works here now? She's an ophthalmologist.'

'Oh yeah!' Humaid said, feeling truly proud of his friends. 'My sister Afra mentioned that to me. I leave the UAE for two weeks and, suddenly, it's a class reunion at Dubai Hospital.'

When they reached the coffee shop, they found Mona there sipping herbal tea.

The three of them sat chatting about their different residencies and life for almost half an hour. It was like their old days at college.

'I ran into John during a conference in Bahrain last week,' Mona said. 'He works in Manama now.'

'What about the others?' Humaid asked.

'Well,' Mona said between sips of tea. 'Gibran decided to do his internship at the American University Hospital in Beirut. He's working there full-time now. However, Rajan moved back to Abu Dhabi with his wife.'

'Say what?' Humaid asked incredulously. 'Rajan too got married? What? Is there a race going on or something?'

'If it's a race,' said Farah, 'then I crossed the finish line five months ago. That leaves the two of you.'

'I have to head back to the clinic now,' Mona said, closing the subject.

'Why don't we make a point of meeting here on our breaks?' Farah asked as Mona gathered her things. They all agreed.

Humaid, Mona and Farah started meeting at the coffee shop regularly, sometimes with other doctors as well. That way, they got to know more and more of the doctors working at the hospital. Once again, it was a multinational atmosphere, like back in college. Some of the doctors were from India, Pakistan, Europe and others from Arab countries. The local UAE doctors were the minority, making up no more than twenty percent of the total workforce.

While sitting together alone, Humaid, Mona and Farah would always reminisce about their college days when the only worry they had was studying and passing their exams. They unanimously agreed that their college days were the best years of their life. They missed the events and the marathons as well as their study group.

Mona seemed more relaxed than she was during her college years. Her younger brothers and sisters were now in college. Her father was busy developing his business empire and had not yet taken another wife, but sooner or later, Mona knew he would.

Farah, who had been married for a few months only, seemed very happy in her marriage. Humaid told Farah and Mona about his internship in Cairo and about his experience volunteering in Sudan. They were amazed to find out how much experience he had gained in every specialty.

Aside from reminiscing about college and discussing hospital politics, their discussions often drifted to the conflict in Syria.

'Don't believe everything you read or hear in the media,' Mona said to him. 'The reality may be different.'

'I want to go to Jordan to help refugees there. That's the reality,' Humaid snapped, and then tried to control himself. 'People are fleeing for their lives and living on handouts, Mona. I don't need the media to tell me that. I'll go see it for myself.'

'One day in this lifetime, I hope to be able to do what you're doing, Humaid,' Farah said. 'I can see clearly why you don't want to settle down. Marriage would tie you down, literally. If it wasn't for that, I would have probably been booking my ticket to Jordan now. Who knows?'

'Or Sudan,' Humaid said.

'Or Sudan,' Farah agreed.

A few months later, Humaid received a call from Dr. Jihad. He wanted to know if Humaid was still keen on coming to Jordan to help the refugees.

'More than ever,' Humaid said.

'Well, then. There is no time better than the present,' Dr. Jihad said.

'Give me some time to make the necessary arrangements and I will get in touch with you right away,' Humaid told him.

As soon as Humaid hung up with Dr. Jihad, he called the Director's secretary and asked her if he could meet the Director as soon as possible. She told him to hold on for a second.

'If you can swing by in the next five minutes,' she said after a short pause, 'Dr. Al Sayed will be able to see you. He's stepping out for a conference in twenty minutes.'

Humaid didn't spare a second. He was at the director's office within minutes.

'He's waiting for you,' the secretary said. 'You have exactly seven minutes.'

'I won't be long,' Humaid said as he stepped into Dr. Al Sayed's office. The Director welcomed Humaid and shook his hand. He had grown to respect Humaid and admire his work ethic and selfless attitude. Knowing that Dr. Al Sayed was kind enough to see him at such short notice, Humaid immediately came to the point.

'Sir, I need two weeks off.'

'I beg your pardon?' the Director asked, taken aback. He didn't expect to hear that. 'You just got back, Humaid.'

Humaid explained his intentions to the Director and plans for doing charity work in the refugee camps in Jordan.

'Well, you must know it's very difficult for me to explain that to those higher-up, let alone convince them of this, Humaid. In fact, one of the subjects that was discussed recently was a plan to send several promising Emirati doctors to Europe or the USA for post-graduate studies on a full scholarship. Your name was on top of the list.'

'I promise you this will be my last request for unplanned leave. It's for just two weeks. Think of the exposure I will get there and the great experience,' Humaid pleaded. 'I appreciate the chance to work here, and I want to do what little I can to help the refugees. This is very important to me. Once I come back, I promise to jump at the scholarship. Just two weeks. That's all I'm asking for. Please?'

Dr. Al Sayed thought for a moment. He understood that Humaid had a point and he didn't want to upset him.

'Ok. Ok. Let me see what I can do,' Dr. Al Sayed said, wiping his glasses and readjusting them on the bridge of his nose. 'I have to run to my conference now. But I warn you, Humaid; this is the last time I will ever consider granting you an unplanned and sudden leave. Check with my secretary this time tomorrow to get my written leave approval. Two weeks,' he stressed, raising two fingers as he headed out with Humaid next to him. 'Not a day more.'

The next step for Humaid now was to convince his parents. He was preoccupied during dinner thinking of how to break the news to them.

'What's the matter, Humaid?' his father asked in a concerned tone. 'Did anything happen at the hospital?'

'No dad. Nothing happened at the hospital,' Humaid replied, trying to find the right way to broach the subject. He waited until they finished dinner and adjourned to the living room to have their tea before he mustered up enough courage to say to his father. 'I want to ask your permission and mama's to travel to Jordan for charity work.'

'Again?' Abdullah asked. 'You know you can do charity work here too. Ask your mother. Right, Maryam?'

'Why Jordan?' Maryam asked, curious.

'To help in the refugee camps,' Humaid replied.

'You're getting addicted to risky work,' Saleh, who loved having dinner at his in-laws, said. 'Why do you want to go to a war zone?'

'There is no war in Jordan,' Humaid wished Saleh would either keep quiet or at least support him. 'Mama,' he turned to his mother. 'You and dad taught me to help the poor and the needy.'

'But isn't it too risky to go there?' Maryam asked calmly. She didn't want Humaid to sense the fear gripping her heart. This wasn't a field hospital in Sudan. This was in a war zone. This was a bunch of ruthless mercenaries killing civilians in cold blood. For some reason, her son wanted to throw himself into the ring with all that bloodshed and mayhem. She had heard first-hand accounts from some of the survivors. Babies being ripped away from their mothers; children witnessing their fathers and uncles being butchered in cold blood, their sisters dragged away, raped and traded off like bags of rice. She'd seen the fear in their eyes and heard the screams of children waking up from recurrent nightmares of night raids, chemical attacks and gunfire.

'Jordan is very safe, Mama,' Humaid said. 'There is no war there. I'll be going with the same charity organization from the UAE. They would never throw me into a war zone.'

Abdullah was extremely worried, but by now, he knew that Humaid was meant to become a humanitarian. Trying to stop him would only make him miserable but more determined.

'Alright son,' Abdullah declared. 'If you want this, then I will not stop you, but your mother must also agree.'

'Mama?' Humaid pleaded with his mother. 'Please? If we don't help these refugees, who will? It was you who taught me to help the needy, Mama.'

Maryam nodded her agreement without saying a word. She was afraid she would cry if she opened her mouth to say anything.

Later that night, Abdullah woke up to find her sitting in bed, crying silently.

'You could have said no, Maryam. You know he would have never have gone against your wishes,' Abdullah said.

'And what about his wishes?' Maryam asked, drying her tears.

'He's tempting fate,' Abdullah said. 'I'm afraid that something will happen to him.'

'So am I,' Maryam moaned. 'But you know your son. The world is his operating theatre. He will not stop wanting to help as long as he knows there is someone in need of medical care and can't get it.'

The next morning, Humaid called Dr. Jihad and told him that he was ready to go to Jordan with him right away.

'Head to Abu Dhabi Airport on Saturday at ten in the morning,' Dr. Jihad said. 'We will be travelling from there.'

'You mean you're in Abu Dhabi now?' Humaid asked, checking the number Abu Jihad was calling from. 'Yes' Dr. Jihad said. 'I planned it this way so we could all get on the same flight.'

'I see,' Humaid responded.

'Don't forget to pack warm clothes and dress in layers,' Dr. Jihad said. 'Welcome aboard once again, Humaid.'

After he checked in at the airport terminal, Humaid met Dr. Jihad. He was with a group of around fifty doctors, nurses, technicians and other members of the Red Crescent and representatives of Abu Dhabi government including Mr. Qasim. They had already checked in a large number of parcels of medical supplies. The group boarded the Etihad Airlines flight to Amman. The trip was short, a little over two and a half hours.

At Amman International Airport, they were welcomed by members of the UAE embassy. The group was to spend two nights at a hotel in Amman.

They had only one free day. Humaid had never been to Amman, so he politely asked Dr. Jihad to show him around. Dr. Jihad knew the city like the back of his hand. He had lived most of his childhood there. It was where he had gone to school and college, fallen in and out of love, and dreamt of the world and what he could do to alleviate the pain and suffering of others.

'I left our village in the West Bank in 1945 and went to live in Jerusalem with my uncle,' Dr. Jihad told Humaid. In Jordan, we were provided with a shelter and food. Later, my uncle opened a small jeweler shop in Amman, similar to the one he had in Jerusalem only much smaller.'

The business was successful, but Dr. Jihad's uncle had never forgotten his house in Jerusalem, where he was born and where he lived until that point. He died at the age of ninety without ever setting foot in Jerusalem again. Dr. Jihad's cousins, four men and two women, were still in Amman. They were all married with children. However, on that particular morning in Amman, Dr. Jihad had no plans to see his relatives. After breakfast, he and Humaid hired a private taxi and set out to explore Amman.

Built on seven hills, Amman was a unique city. Dr. Jihad and Humaid first visited Citadel Hill, the highest hill in Amman. The Amman Citadel, which was the oldest site in Amman dating back to the bronze and iron ages, towered above the city. As they were walking around, Dr. Jihad explained the history of the Citadel and the surrounding areas to Humaid.

Later that day, the same taxi took them to the city center to see the Roman ruins. Dr. Jihad paid the taxi driver and let him drive off. He said that most of the touristic places were within walking distance. The Roman theatre looked out of place in the middle of all the modern buildings surrounding it. It was built in 138 B.C. and could hold 6,000 spectators. Humaid was astonished to learn that the Greeks and Romans built and ruled this city long ago.

After seeing most of the touristic sites, Dr. Jihad and Humaid were quite tired and hungry. They headed to Rainbow Street, a crowded shopping area with an endless array of restaurants. At Dr. Jihad's favorite restaurant, they ordered drinks and *mansaf* for two. It was the first time Humaid tried *mansaf*, a traditional Jordanian dish with meat, yogurt and rice. He loved it.

For dessert, they ordered *kunafa*. Humaid had eaten kunafa many times in the past, but nothing compared to the taste of this one.

'The food tastes out of this world,' he told Dr. Jihad.

'I'm glad you enjoyed it,' Dr. Jihad said. 'You won't get such tasty food in the camp tomorrow.'

Humaid swallowed hard and smiled.

Chapter Fourteen
Jordan Refugee Camp

Following an early breakfast the next morning, the convoy set out to the Emirates camp for refugees, located in Marjeeb Al Fahood, about eighty-five kilometers west of Amman near the city of Zarqa. The convoy consisted of ten vehicles, including four trucks carrying aid for the refugees and two military jeeps, courtesy of the Jordanian army. Eight armed soldiers rode in the jeeps for the protection of personnel, medical supplies and food.

The road to the camp was well paved and wide enough for cars to navigate on either side.

Humaid and Dr. Jihad sat together in the back of a comfortable Nissan four-wheel drive.

'This journey is much more comfortable than the one we took in Sudan,' Humaid said.

'Of course,' Dr. Jihad agreed. 'Jordan is a well-developed country and millions of tourists visit it every year. Did you know that the Emirates camp for refugees we're heading to is considered the most luxurious refugee camp, not only in Jordan, but in the world?'

Humaid nodded appreciating the information.

'It only takes in very needy families, widows, children and crippled men,' Dr. Jihad continued. 'You might be surprised to hear that it's only thirty kilometers away from the Syrian border.'

'Really?' Humaid exclaimed, making a mental note not to disclose that fact to his parents until he was safe and sound back in Sharjah.

'It's a safe place though,' Dr. Jihad said, as if reading Humaid's mind. 'The camp is protected by the Jordanian Army.'

It took them two hours to reach the gate of the camp. The entrance was guarded by armed soldiers. The guards opened the gate immediately as they were expecting the arrival of the convoy.

Once inside the camp, Humaid was very pleasantly surprised to see well-organized caravans lying on either side of the paved roads. The roads were muddy but that was because it had rained heavily the week before. There were vegetables and fruit farms all around the camp. The refugees were encouraged to work on the farms as most of them were farmers. Electricity and water were supplied from Zarqa. There was a recreational area and football field behind the management building. A little further away, there was a small hospital managed by the International Red Crescent and Red Cross Society.

Saif, the camp manager, was from the UAE. He was supported by Jordanian staff. One of them was from Zarqa; he was the most active man at the camp and seemed to know most of the refugees by name. Everyone called him Abu Adil. He helped the convoy unload the trucks and place the parcels and supplies in different storage rooms. The food was stored in air-conditioned units. The meat and chicken brought from Amman were placed in huge freezers and refrigerators straight away.

Humaid, Dr. Jihad and the other medical personnel and dignitaries were directed towards a well-furnished, heated waiting room connected to the management offices and were offered hot tea to warm them up. Humaid was beginning to wonder how cold it could get in Jordan during the winter months and understood why Dr. Jihad had advised him to pack warm clothes and dress in layers.

In the waiting room, Humaid made a quick call to his parents, informing them that the place was quite comfortable, very secure and there was nothing to be afraid of. He felt it best to leave out the detail about its proximity to the Syrian border.

Once they finished their tea, Abu Adil and his staff led everyone around the camp. There were caravans instead of tents or tarpaulin. Each caravan was converted into an accommodation unit with its own toilet and cooking facilities and was allotted to a family of four to six. The camp also had a recreation area with a small football field.

Finally, they reached the hospital. Humaid was glad to see how well organized and well equipped it was. There were clinics for different specialties, an accident and emergency department, a laboratory, X-ray rooms and even a dental clinic. The hospital also featured two operating rooms. The pharmacy received regular supplies of medicine. At that time, there were five thousand refugees in the camp made up of mostly women and children. The hospital was enough to address all their medical needs for the time being.

The accommodations for doctors and medical staff were located near the hospital. Humaid and Dr. Jihad shared a medium-sized room with comfortable beds. After a hearty meal at the staff restaurant inside the hospital, they returned to their room to get some sleep.

The next day, Humaid, Dr. Jihad and their team headed to the outpatient clinics right after breakfast. The senior camp doctor was there to go over the most severe cases with them and point out which ones, in his opinion, required surgery.

There were more than one hundred patients waiting at the outpatient clinic that morning.

Some of them were children who had lost their legs or hands in the war and needed further care and artificial limbs. Some had infections with clear signs of the onset of gangrene. Those patients were admitted on the spot. It was heartbreaking for Humaid to see so many injured children who, due to lack of medical care, would lose their arms or legs. He had never seen so many injured children. There were some elderly men as well who had complications from gunshot or bomb blast wounds.

Some children had heart problems and needed minor heart procedures. Dr. Jihad and Humaid could manage those cases easily and save their lives. There were women who had breast tumors, and a sample of the cells was taken during a biopsy procedure. The sample was then sent to the lab; and if diagnosed cancerous, the patient would then be sent to a major hospital in Amman for further treatment.

Dr. Jihad and Humaid saw only the complicated cases. The simple cases were managed by the other doctors.

There was a list of thirty patients who required surgeries. Dr. Jihad, Humaid and their team scheduled the surgeries in order of the severity of each case and spread out over a three-day period. First, they commenced with heart and lung surgeries, as they needed the most urgent care. On consequent days, they addressed tumors. They left the amputations and infected wounds to the end. At the camp, Humaid learned how to amputate limbs or do vascular grafts to save the limbs of patients. He also performed a couple of Cesarean sections as well.

The next morning, after finishing their post-surgery check-up rounds on the patients, Humaid and Dr. Jihad had free time to play a game of football with the camp children. Humaid was glad to see the children playing and forgetting their worries for a little while. Most of the children were orphans. While they were playing, one of the little boys fell and was not able to stand up. Humaid stopped the game and examined the boy who had gone completely blue and was breathing heavily. Humaid picked up the boy and rushed him over to the hospital with Dr. Jihad beside him.

'Can one of you run and get his parents?' Dr. Jihad asked the kids who were playing with them. A group of five boys rushed in the other direction toward the caravans.

'Is Basim going to be ok?' cried a seven-year old boy who looked pale with fear as he ran next to Humaid and Dr. Jihad.

'Is that his name?' Dr. Jihad asked.

'Yes, doctor. He's my cousin. His dad and my dad are brothers,' the boy said, wiping his tears with the back of his hands.

'And what's your name?' Dr. Jihad asked.

'Hani,' the boy replied, sniffling.

'Basim is going to be ok. No need to cry, Hani. He's in safe hands,' Dr. Jihad patted the boy on the head as they approached the hospital. 'I want you to stay here by the door. Ok, Hani? When Basim's mother comes here, please tell her we're in that room,' Dr. Jihad said, pointing to the ER. 'How old is Basim? Do you know?'

'He's ten,' Hani replied.

By the time Dr. Jihad walked into the ER, Humaid had laid Basim on the table and was giving him oxygen.

Basim's mother came running into the ER. She bent over her son, wanting to make sure he was alive.

'What happened to him? I can't lose him,' she cried. 'Please, doctor,' she turned from Humaid to Dr. Jihad and back to Humaid. 'His father died during the war. Basim and his sister are all I have left.'

Humaid asked the mother if Basim had any heart problems she was aware of.

'He was a little bluish when he was born, but later on, he looked normal,' Basim's mother said. She never took him to see a cardiologist as she thought that her son had an iron deficiency only.

'I suspect he has Teratology of Fallot,' Humaid said. 'It's a condition in which a child is born with four heart abnormalities. Babies born with this condition might show mild symptoms at first. The full onslaught of complications would manifest itself later in life.'

'Oh my God!' Basim's mother wailed.

'Don't worry, Um Basim' Dr. Jihad said. 'It's treatable.'

At that moment exactly, Basim opened his eyes and looked around. 'See, he's already feeling better. Aren't you Basim?' Dr. Jihad asked, a gentle loving smile wrinkling his kind face.

'Are you ok, sweetheart?' Basim's mothers asked, hugging him. Basim nodded.

After checking the oxygen concentration level in Basim's blood, Humaid and Dr. Jihad were satisfied that it was near 80. Normal was 95, but that was fine for now. Basim was admitted into the hospital so he could be observed over the next 24 hours and more tests could be run. His mother decided to stay with him.

Once they were out of earshot, Dr. Jihad voiced his concerns to Humaid.

'His condition looks serious,' he said. 'If he's not operated on soon, he will most certainly die.'

Humaid nodded. Jihad knew somebody in the main office of the International Red Crescent Society. He called and explained Basim's condition and how the boy needed immediate care.

Throughout the day, Basim looked fine, but he was still a little bluish. Dr. Jihad was very apprehensive. After another hospital round to check on the post-op patients, Jihad called IRCS again.

'I don't think the boy will make it if we wait until next week' Dr. Jihad said.

'The crux of the matter,' said the voice on the other end of the phone, 'is that there are only a few cardiologists in all of Jordan who can perform that type of complicated procedure on a child. In addition, all the ICUs are full. Don't underestimate the number of injured and dying people we get from Syria every day.'

Dr. Jihad and Humaid discussed taking Basim to the UAE. They knew that, up until that point, there was no proper pediatric cardiology unit in the UAE. They went to speak to Saif, the camp manager. Because of his history of humanitarian work, Saif knew where to find help. He picked up the phone and called someone in Germany who worked at an international charity organization.

A few hours passed before they received a call back informing them that the organization had arranged for a doctor to operate on Basim in Munich, free of charge. Immediately, they went to work, sorting out the logistics of getting passports and visas for Basim and his mother. Saif again had the solution. He called the UAE Embassy and explained to them the dire situation. The UAE medical counsellor asked for the IDs of Basim and Basim's mother, or at least scanned copies of their IDs to be emailed to his office.

Everything was arranged before the end of that day. 'There's a flight to Munich tomorrow morning and I want the child and his mother to be on it,' the counsellor told Saif over the phone.

'But a doctor has to accompany them, Your Excellency,' Saif said.

'Do you have a doctor in mind?' asked the counsellor.

Saif knew Dr. Jihad could not go as he had a Jordanian passport. He could start the ball rolling and ask Dr. Jihad to apply for a Schengen visa, but even an emergency visa might take anywhere from twenty-four to forty-eight hours. Basim didn't have that much time. Saif looked at Humaid.

'You're the only person who can go to Germany without worrying about getting a visa,' Saif said.

Humaid nodded. He and Dr. Jihad went to talk to Basim's mother and explained to her that Basim would get the best treatment in Germany and that they had to leave first thing in the morning. Basim's mother didn't know what to say. She was full of gratitude. She tried to thank them, but her words were mingled with tears and were incomprehensible. She hurried to her caravan and arranged for Basim's sister to stay with Hani's family.

Very early the next morning, an ambulance was arranged to drive Basim, his mother and Humaid to the airport. Inside the ambulance, Humaid, assisted by a paramedic, fixed an oxygen mask over Basim's face. They also connected him to a monitor to gauge his pulse, blood pressure and oxygen concentration in his body. Basim's mother sat on one side of Basim and Humaid on the other.

The ambulance sped all the way to the airport, its sirens wailing. A representative from the UAE Embassy was there waiting for them. He handed over Humaid, Basim's and Basim's mother's papers and visas. The airport security directed the ambulance to the plane. It was a normal flight, but the flight technicians had removed some of the seats at the back of the plane to make space for Basim's stretcher. Humaid and Basim's mother sat nearby.

Soon, the plane started taxiing the runway and took off. During the flight, Humaid constantly monitored Basim's vital signs, especially his oxygen concentration levels. If Basim's oxygen concentration fell, Humaid increased it at once by opening the cylinder valve. Basim's mother watched every move Humaid made. He would smile at her worried face often.

'I read a lot about angels in the holy book,' she said to Humaid. 'But it's the first time I actually see one in person. I believe now that they really do exist and live among us.'

'I'm not any angel, Um Basim,' Humaid said, shaking his head and securing the blanket around Basim's shoulders. 'I'm just doing my job.'

'I've seen so many people in Syria kill each other without mercy,' she continued, 'That I have stopped believing there were any good people left in the world.'

'The world is full of good people, Um Basim,' Humaid said as he sat down and fastened his seatbelt. 'It's because of them the sun keeps rising every morning.'

As they chatted during the flight, Humaid found out Um Basim had finished high school in Syria and before the war, she had started college. However, when the war broke out, their lives were turned upside down. Losing her husband was not easy, but she was trying to stay strong for her son and daughter.

'We had free schools and colleges in Syria,' she told Humaid. 'We owned a house and had farm land near Damascus. All medical treatment was free or at least very affordable. That's why I was furious when my husband joined the opposition party. It didn't make sense. I pleaded with him to come to his senses and think straight. Think of the children. But he was deaf to my pleas. He hid arms and ammunition in our house for the revolutionaries. One night, the army raided our house. They found the arms and the bombs in the basement, so they took away my husband and my eldest sons.'

Humaid was deeply affected by her story.

'My story is just one among thousands of similar stories,' continued Um Basim. 'We're just one family among so many other families who have been ripped apart and destroyed by this war.'

Five hours after takeoff, they landed at Munich Airport. As the plane was taxiing towards the terminal, Humaid saw an ambulance waiting for them outside. They exited from the rear door of the plane, close to the ambulance. There were a couple of immigration officers waiting for them. They went through their papers and stamped them immediately. Two Red Cross paramedics carried and secured Basim's stretcher inside the ambulance. Humaid and Basim's mother sat by his side.

One of the paramedics changed Basim's oxygen mask and tank and attached him to another monitor. Before the ambulance doors closed, a representative from the UAE embassy introduced himself and gave Humaid his contact number. Humaid told him that he wanted to go back to Amman soon after the operation was performed. The representative informed Humaid that there was a flight the next day at midnight and he could arrange a ticket for Humaid. Humaid thanked him profusely.

As the ambulance sped through the streets of Munich, Um Basim, who had never been to Europe, looked with amazement at the beautiful architecture and the vibrant cultural scenes unfolding in front of her eyes.

Soon they arrived at the Heart Centre of Munich University. It was still early in the afternoon and the head of the cardiac unit, Professor Koch, was there with his team of ten doctors and nurses. Professor Koch did not look very old. He must have been in his early fifties. Humaid had expected a doctor of his experience and caliber to be much older.

'Indeed, Dr. Humaid, your diagnosis is perfect,' Professor Koch announced after examining Basim. 'It is the Teratology of Fallot. We will be operating on him tomorrow morning.'

Fortunately for Basim's mother, there was an Arab female doctor in the team who explained to her everything about the surgery and informed her that Dr. Koch was one of the best child heart specialists in Munich. 'He has handled hundreds of similar cases,' she said in Arabic as she squeezed Basim's mother's hand reassuringly.

Basim was taken to a private room. He was conscious, but very pale. Um Basim, who had heard Humaid's conversation with the embassy's representative at the airport, pleaded with Humaid to stay for a few days after the surgery, but Humaid apologized and explained to her that he wasn't needed there anymore. On the contrary, a lot of people in the camp in Jordan needed his help. However, Humaid promised her that he wouldn't leave Germany until the surgery was performed successfully and Basim was out of danger.

Humaid was genuinely concerned about Basim. At the same time, he was eager to watch a new surgical procedure and see the latest surgical techniques in one of the best cardiac centers in the world. He approached Dr. Koch and asked him if he could observe the surgery from the gallery.

'Absolutely not,' said Dr. Koch with a serious face. 'You are to scrub in and join the operating team in the operating theatre,' he added with a smile. 'I wouldn't have you miss this for the world.'

Humaid booked himself a room at a hotel very close to the hospital. He woke up bright and early the next morning, had a quick breakfast and a strong cup of coffee and then hurried to the hospital. There, he scrubbed in and entered the operation theatre with Dr. Koch and his team.

Basim was already under anesthesia. The operation started smoothly. Dr. Koch opened the heart muscles exposing the abnormal hole in the ventricles called VSD (Ventricular Septal Defect) and closed it with a synthetic Dacron patch. Then he excised some muscles to widen the pulmonary artery. While operating, Dr. Koch explained his every step and the reason behind it to the other doctors as well as to Humaid. Once he was satisfied with the surgery, he sutured the heart muscles and diverted the blood back to Basim's heart.

The operation lasted four hours. After Basim's surgery, the incision was closed and bandaged, and he was wheeled to the ICU. As Humaid walked out of the operating room, Um Basim, who was pacing up and down the hall, rushed to him and asked, 'How is he?'

'Basim is fine,' Humaid replied. 'Alhamdulillah, the surgery went smoothly without any complications.'

'You're God's gift to me and my son,' she said as she held his hand between hers. 'I can't thank you enough. I'll pray to God to keep you safe and away from all harm.' Before Humaid could say anything, Um Basim bent down and kissed the back of his hand. Not expecting that, Humaid pulled his hand away quickly.

'Please, Um Basim,' he said. 'Don't thank me. I haven't done anything. You take care of yourself and Basim now. I must go check out of the hotel and head to the airport to catch my flight to Amman.'

They said goodbye and Humaid left. On his way out, he passed by Professor Koch who was walking towards his office.

'You don't look Syrian,' Dr. Koch told Humaid. 'And you don't look Jordanian. Where are you from?'

'I'm from the UAE sir,' Humaid said. 'You're one of my idols, Dr. Koch. I want to become as good a heart surgeon as you are one day.'

'Join us then and I will teach you all the tricks,' Dr. Koch said cordially. Once again, Humaid was reminded of how much younger Dr. Koch was than he had allowed himself to imagine.

'I would be honored to work with you here, sir; but at some point, I will have to go back to the UAE. There is a scholarship waiting for me there. Who knows? I might be lucky enough to come back here to further my education and learning.'

'Call me,' he said to Humaid as he shook his hand and gave him his business card. 'My secretary will make all the arrangements for you. But you will need to learn German before you join the hospital.'

'I will,' Humaid said. 'Danke schön.'

'Nichts zu danken!' Dr. Koch guffawed. 'I see that you're already making progress in German. Wunderbar! Wunderbar!'

At 11:45 pm, Humaid boarded a direct flight back to Amman and landed there early in the morning.

Chapter Fifteen
Back to Jordan, Winter 2016

Abu Jaber, the camp driver, was waiting for Humaid outside the arrivals terminal at Amman airport. As the car drove through the same roads back to the camp, Abu Jaber updated Humaid on the latest news. More refugees had come to Jordan in the past twenty-four hours.

'The war is getting more intense,' Abu Jaber said.

Abu Jaber was half Syrian and half Jordanian. His father was Jordanian and his mother Syrian. His maternal uncles and cousins were involved with different parties and sides.

'What you and Dr. Jihad are doing in the refugee camps is great, Dr. Humaid,' Abu Jaber said as he drove. 'But there are still people trapped inside Syria who need medical help and can't get it. The atrocities taking place all over the country are alarming. The stream of refugees escaping for their lives won't be stopping anytime soon if things continue the way they are. Those are the lucky ones who made it across the border alive. There are innocent people dying just because there are not enough doctors or nurses to treat them.'

'Are you able to go back to see your cousins, Abu Jaber?' Humaid asked.

'Yes, doctor,' Abu Jaber replied. 'But I don't only go back just to see them, I transport medical and humanitarian staff across the border.'

Humaid was quite impressed and touched by Abu Jaber's work and sacrifices. Deep in his heart, he wished he could also do something like him.

As soon as they arrived at the camp, Dr. Jihad gave Humaid an update of the patients he had performed operations on. Dr. Jihad looked tired. He didn't sleep at all the night before. Some of the new refugees arriving at the camp were in bad shape and a few of them needed emergency operations.

'There are still some cases of infected wounds and gunshot wounds that you'll have to manage alone,' Dr. Jihad said. 'I'm going to close my eyes for a few minutes.'

Humaid had slept on the flight back to Amman, so he felt well rested and energetic. He asked the nurse to bring in the serious cases first, people who had lost a lot of blood. He washed his hands and changed into a pair of clean scrubs.

For ten consecutive hours that day, Humaid performed one surgery after another. When he went to the caravan at around eleven that night, Dr. Jihad was just waking up.

'What time is it?' Dr. Jihad asked, rubbing his eyes. 'God! How long did I sleep?'

'For a few minutes,' Humaid said with a smile.

'Why didn't you send someone to wake me up?' Dr. Jihad asked, piqued after checking the time.

'Because you were right,' Humaid said, as he sat on his bed. 'I was able to manage all the cases by myself. Well, not all by myself. The nurses were absolutely efficient.'

'Any complications?' Dr. Jihad asked, still upset that his short nap had turned into a ten-hour deep sleep.

'There were no complications, so there was no point in disturbing you,' Humaid assured him.

After a very late dinner, Humaid went to bed while Dr. Jihad stayed up. He couldn't go back to sleep, so he tiptoed out of the caravan to go check on the patients Humaid had operated on. It wasn't that he didn't trust Humaid's skills and efficiency. He wanted to actually see Humaid's work to prove to himself that he wasn't wrong in trusting Humaid and believing in him. At the hospital, Dr. Jihad was surprised at how aptly Humaid had managed difficult cases without his help, especially at this stage of his training.

They had been in Jordan for only seven days, but so much had happened since their arrival. They had worked hard and performed many surgeries. During those seven days, Humaid had seen and diagnosed hundreds of patients and prescribed medication for them. Dr. Jihad saw great potential in Humaid and was proud to take him under his wing and help him realize his dream of becoming a heart surgeon.

In the morning, Dr. Jihad told Humaid, 'What do you think of a drive to Petra and Wadi Rum tomorrow? I think you deserve a rest and a bit of relaxation.'

'I say we go for it,' Humaid replied. Petra was on his bucket list, but he wasn't sure he would be able to visit there on this trip, so Dr. Jihad's suggestion was more than welcome.

'It's a three-hour drive from here,' Dr. Jihad said, thrilled that Humaid accepted without hesitation. 'I'm sure you'll love it there. There is nothing like watching the sunset at Wadi Rum and walking the winding alleys of the Rose Red City.'

The next morning, they were given a four-wheel drive jeep and was assigned the same driver, Abu Jaber.

On the way, they discussed different subjects. As usual, the situation in Syria was the main topic. Abu Jaber had first-hand news. Barrel bombs and chemical weapons were used. There were a lot of casualties inside Syria, but not enough doctors.

Humaid asked if they could go to help for a few days.

'Yes of course,' Abu Jaber replied, delighted that the young Emirati doctor was willing to go help his people. Others might have found it extremely daunting to even consider crossing the border to Syria. 'I can take you there. I know all the hidden routes. I'll stay with you and bring you back after two or three days.'

Dr. Jihad didn't take part in the conversation. He sat in the car and quietly stared ahead. He didn't want to influence Humaid's decision one way or another. Humaid was a grown man and he could make his own decisions. Dr. Jihad understood the dangers and risks inherent by the selfless and noble act Humaid seemed only too willing to perform. He did need Humaid at the camp in Jordan, but if Humaid wanted to go across the border to Syria, he wouldn't be able to stop him.

Dr. Jihad loved Humaid like his own son, and he didn't want him to put his life in danger. *But isn't this what I've been doing all my life?* Dr. Jihad thought to himself. He saw a lot of himself in Humaid when he was his age – the adrenalin rush of jumping into action, the dopamine level rising in his brain every time he saved a life and the thrill of getting the job done.

'Abu Jaber is a certified Jordanian tourist guide,' Dr. Jihad told Humaid when they reached Petra. 'He'll be able to explain the history of the place way better than me.'

'Is that so, Abu Jaber?' Humaid asked.

'Not better than Dr. Jihad,' Abu Jaber said, smiling. 'I don't think I can do anything better than you, Dr. Jihad. But it is true. That was my job before I joined the camp.'

Petra was a city carved out of giant stones by the Nabataeans in around 300 BC. The ancient city was so big that it was almost impossible for Humaid to see it all on foot in one day. Abu Jaber hired three mules to take them around. After the tour, they headed to a nearby town in Abu Musa Valley. Humaid bought a handmade leather jacket and some warm clothes to take with him back to the camp. Abu Jaber took them to a local restaurant where they ate the most delicious kebobs and shawarma Humaid had ever tasted. From there, they went to Wadi Rum and stopped to watch its legendary sunset.

On the way back from Petra, the topic of the war was opened up once again.

'I can go for the next two to three days, Humaid,' Dr. Jihad offered. 'You can take care of the patients in the camp.'

But Humaid, who really wanted to go inside Syria to get first-hand experience of what was happening there, said, 'Why don't I go this time and you go the next, Dr. Jihad?' He remembered Mona's words: *Don't trust the media. The reality may be different from what you think.*

'I have been thinking about this all day,' Dr. Jihad said, deciding to let Humaid know that the subject was weighing heavily on his mind. 'You are your parents' only son. Think about them. You are taking a big risk and they deserve to know.'

'But what will happen at the camp if a serious and complicated case comes into the hospital while you're away?' Humaid asked. 'I won't be able to manage it all alone. You must be present here.'

'Nothing will happen that you can't handle,' Dr. Jihad replied.

Humaid decided to put his foot down.

'I have made up my mind,' he said. 'If anyone is going to Syria, it's going to be me.'

Dr. Jihad gave in. He knew it was an argument he couldn't win. Humaid started discussing logistics with Abu Jaber, as well as the day and time they should leave. His eagerness was infectious. Humaid knew that he had only four days left before he was scheduled to return to the UAE to resume his work at Dubai Hospital.

It was decided that they would leave the next day under cover of the night.

'It's better to travel during the night when no enemy planes can see us,' Abu Jaber said. 'Don't forget to take your emergency kit and backpack with you and just a minimum amount of clothes, enough for three days. No suitcases please.'

The next day, late in the afternoon, after taking care of his patients, Humaid returned to his room. He tried to get some rest, but he couldn't sleep. He was too excited to close his eyes. This was going to be his first time in a war zone.

After the Isha prayers, Humaid packed enough clothes and his emergency kit in his backpack and leaned it against the wall. He sat on his bed to call his parents to tell them he was safe. They had nothing to worry about. He didn't mention anything to them about his impending trip. He talked to each member of the family and told them how much he missed them. It was Humaid's habit to call them every night, except when he had a long day. 'If I don't call you tomorrow or the day after, please don't worry. We're getting so busy here now, especially since it's almost time for me to head back,' he said to his dad, just to have an excuse in case he didn't have good reception in Syria.

When Humaid said that to Abdullah, he meant it. What he didn't know then was that the peril lying ahead of him was so much more bone chilling and life changing than the simple inconvenience of bad phone reception.

Chapter Sixteen
Escaping the Jihadists

There was that same dream again. He was walking on a quiet deserted beach. A hand, shapely and familiar, waved at him from beyond the cresting waves. Humaid started wading in the water to reach it. Suddenly, the beach seemed no longer deserted. Someone started pulling Humaid back. He didn't know who it was. He felt safer in the water. He could see the fingers now, slender and white, like tapered candles. He reached out and grasped the hand between his palms. It felt warm. He tried to look at the face, but it was shrouded by fog.

'Wake up!' Humaid heard Abu Wasim's voice, but when he opened his eyes, it was still dark outside, and he was alone.

Humaid's headaches had turned into severe migraines and were occurring more frequently. Humaid took two pills and went back to sleep. He woke up a little later than usual but felt better. However, this feeling didn't last long. He was still in bed when he heard the sounds of gunshots followed by rocket launchers. He ran outside his room and found Abu Wasim preparing breakfast.

'What's happening?' Humaid asked.

'We're now fighting the opposition Army,' Abu Wasim said as he flipped the eggs in the frying pan. 'They were our allies but now they're attacking us. They want to take this town. They know how strategic it is and now they want to take it. But don't worry. We know how to deal with them.'

Humaid paid attention to the sound of firing outside. It seemed far away. Maybe Abu Wasim was right and there was no reason to panic. Not yet.

After breakfast, Abu Wasim and Abu Samir drove Humaid to the hospital. He asked for permission to check in on Abu Talha's wife.

A nurse accompanied Humaid to the new mother's room. Humaid found her lying on her bed comfortably, her body and face covered. The baby was sleeping in a small cot beside her.

'How are you feeling today, sister?' Humaid asked, making sure he addressed her the way women under Islamic rule were supposed to be addressed.

'Alhamdulillah, doctor,' Abu Talha's wife replied. Humaid examined her C-section incision to make sure it had closed properly and was not infected. It looked perfect. Her pulse and blood pressure were normal. As Humaid was leaving the room, Abu Talha walked in.

'Al Salam Alaikum, brother,' Humaid greeted Abu Talha.

'Wa alaikum Salam,' Abu Talha returned the greeting hurriedly.

'I want to ask you something,' Humaid said. The baby started crying.

'Make it quick,' Abu Talha said, firing a look at his wife who immediately picked up the baby and started rocking him.

'I need to get back to the UAE,' Humaid pleaded. 'My mother is very sick.'

'Is that so?' Abu Talha replied angrily. 'You're worried about your mother and not worried about your brothers who are fighting and dying every day? Aren't you aware of what's happening outside now? No one told you? The faithless deceptive traitorous opposition army is attacking us. I need you now more than before. If I ever hear you say you want to leave, I swear to God I will hang you myself!'

Humaid's knees started shaking.

'Go back to work now' Abu Talha shouted, pointing his forefinger at the door. He slammed the door shut as soon as Humaid left.

Back at the men's section at the hospital, Humaid started seeing the new patients. There were many gunshot wounds that day. Humaid treated them all. He was glad that none of them required major surgeries. He wasn't sure he could perform those in his present state of mind. They received a few dead bodies too, casualties of the fighting outside. Humaid tagged them and sent them to the morgue.

The firing slowed down in the evening. *Who are these people?* Humaid thought. *They have a common enemy. They belong to the same religion and the same sect. They call themselves Jihadis, and yet, they kill each other? Why?* The only explanation he could come up with was: *they did it for land and money.*

It was shortly before midnight when he finished the last procedure. Abu Wasim and Abu Samir drove him to the house they shared. He asked for his cellphone.

'Ten minutes,' Abu Samir said as he handed Humaid the cellphone.

'I know,' Humaid replied piqued. 'Can I have some privacy, please?'

Abu Samir left the room, but Humaid knew he was spying on him from behind the door.

What am I going to tell them? Humaid wondered as he switched his phone on and scrolled down to see all the missed calls from back home. He was afraid they would be able to tell from his voice that something was wrong. Or he might tear up as soon as he heard his mother's voice. God! How he missed his family. It felt like he had gone for ages, not just eleven days.

Humaid switched the phone off and gave it back to Abu Samir.

'What?' Abu Samir asked. 'Is the battery dead?'

'No, I changed my mind,' Humaid replied. 'I don't want to call.'

'Suit yourself,' Abu Samir said as he put Humaid's cellphone inside his pocket. 'I'll go fix us something to eat.'

'It's too late for me to eat,' Humaid said. He was starving, but he had no appetite.

'You need to eat,' said Abu Samir, his tone softer. He felt bad for Humaid but didn't know exactly why he felt bad for him. Hamid was a prisoner, but he should at least appreciate the freedom and luxury they gave him. The Islamic Group needed a doctor to treat the mujahedeen; otherwise, they wouldn't be wasting their time and money on Humaid. *It's not my problem if he doesn't want to call his family*, Abu Samir thought to himself. *I'm just doing my job. I gave him his phone when he asked for it. I don't know why he changed his mind, but I can't tell Abu Talha that I let him go to bed hungry.*

Abu Samir went to the kitchen and heated rice and okra with beef stew for Humaid.

'Please eat,' Abu Samir said as he put the tray on the bedside table. The food smelled heavenly. Humaid realized that if he didn't eat, he would be too weak in the morning, so he ate a few bites, took a couple of pills for his headache and went to sleep.

He was in the middle of the same dream again when the door flung open and Abu Samir and Abu Wasim barged in.

'Wake up!' one of them said. He thought he was still dreaming, but Abu Wasim shook him.

'Get up! The Chief is not feeling well,' Abu Wasim said.

'Who? Abu Talha?' Humaid asked, rubbing his eyes.

'No man. It's the Chief,' Abu Samir replied roughly. 'Get up. You're needed there.'

'What time is it now?' Humaid asked as he got dressed quickly.

'Three in the morning,' Abu Samir said. 'Don't waste our time. *Yallah!* Move fast.'

'Are we going to the hospital or should I get my emergency kit?' Humaid asked.

'Get it,' Abu Wasim hollered. 'We're going to the Chief's house.'

Humaid grabbed his backpack, put his heavy leather jacket on, and followed Abu Wasim to the car. The engine was running and Abu Samir was already sitting behind the driving wheel.

'Sit in the back,' Abu Wasim ordered as he himself sat in the passenger seat next to Abu Samir. The car raced towards the Chief's house. Humaid couldn't see in which direction they were heading, but he knew he had never been to that area before. They drove for around fifteen minutes before Abu Samir picked up his walkie-talkie and ordered someone to open the gate.

The car's front lights shone on a huge metal gate in the middle of a twelve-meter high wall hidden behind a wall of tall trees. As the gate opened, Humaid could hear its rusty hinges turn on themselves. Judging from the sheer size of the building in front of him, Humaid guessed it must have been a former mansion with at least twenty rooms.

There were more than one hundred armed men guarding the house. They let the car pass and directed it to the main door. Abu Samir parked the car in front of the door, turned his head to face Humaid and said, '*Yallah!*'

But as soon as the three of them got out of the car, two armed female guards stepped forward. One of them pointed at Humaid and said in broken Arabic, 'Only the doctor can go inside.' Abu Wasim and Abu Samir didn't argue.

Humaid was accompanied by the two female guards. No one said a word. They took him to a large room and positioned themselves outside the door. Inside the room, the Chief was laying on a large bed, unconscious.

Humaid recognized the Chief from the Friday sermon at the mosque. There were about ten women sitting and standing around the bed, all of them had their face covered and some were crying loudly. Humaid wasn't sure if they were the Chief's wives or daughters.

Humaid thought he heard one of the women gasp. He stood there not knowing if it was safe to proceed and check on the Chief while he was surrounded by his harem.

'If you want me to treat the Chief, please step to the side or leave the room.'

Some of the women left reluctantly, while others seemed relieved to get a chance to leave the Chief's sick bed. They all left except one 'I used to be a nurse,' she said to the other women as they were leaving. 'I can help the doctor save the Chief.'

The voice, Humaid thought. But then he shook his head. He pulled out his stethoscope and his sphygmometer.

'I'm the Chief's fourth wife,' the woman who stayed behind said.

That voice! Where had he heard it before?

The Chief's blood pressure was dangerously low and his pulse extremely fast. After examining him, Humaid ascertained that the Chief had an enlarged heart and he wasn't getting enough oxygen. The Chief was breathing heavily. Humaid knew that it was the last stage of heart failure and the only thing that could save him was a heart transplant. However, for that to happen, the Chief would have to be transferred to a specialized cardiac center.

Humaid turned pale. If the Chief died, they would blame him and execute him.

'How long does he have?' the woman asked in that familiar yet unknown voice.

'Less than twenty-four hours,' Humaid replied.

Humaid's knees and hands were shaking. His own heart was pounding so loud he could hear it. He felt doomed. The Chief's men would never believe that he couldn't save their leader. They would think he killed him on purpose.

'Humaid!' said the woman. 'You don't recognize me?' As she said that, she glanced towards the door. When she was sure the female guards couldn't see her, she lifted her niqab off her face for a second.

'Mai?' *Mai Ashraf!!* Humaid almost screamed.

'Shhh!' Mai warned as she lowered her niqab and busied herself with adjusting the blanket around the Chief's chest, pretending to be talking to him just as one of the guards poked her head inside the room.

'Alhamdulillah,' Mai shouted to the guard. 'The doctor says the Chief will be ok. He's going to give him a shot now.'

The guard nodded and left the room to resume her position outside the door.

They're going to kill me if I don't save the Chief, Mai,' Humaid whispered as he tinkered in his backpack and pretended to prepare an injection for the Chief. 'And what on earth are you doing here?'

'It's a long story, Humaid,' Mai whispered. 'But you need to calm down now. Let's think rationally. We need to escape. We're both dead if the Chief dies while we're here.'

'I don't even know where we are,' Humaid said. 'How can we escape?'

'I've been planning this for the last two months. Just pretend you're treating him, ok?'

'Ok,' Humaid said. 'And then?'

'Give him the shot,' Mai said. 'Do whatever it is doctors do to look busy. Pretend you're trying to resuscitate him.

Mai opened the door and, pretending to be crying, called out urgently.

'Get the stretcher trolley from the second floor,' she pleaded, sounding convincingly concerned. 'The doctor wants to transfer the Chief to the hospital right away. Quickly! Move. You too. Go to the medicine storage unit and get all the oxygen cylinders you can find.'

As soon as the two guards left, Mai put her hand in the Chief's pocket and took out a bunch of keys.

'Hurry up, Humaid,' she said. 'Follow me.'

Humaid grabbed his backpack and followed Mai in the corridor. She unlocked a secret door under the staircase and they both crept inside it. Mai locked the door behind them quickly without making any noise. There was a big battery-operated torch attached to the wall inside. Mai switched it on and hurried towards a flight of narrow stairs going down, with Humaid at her heels.

They descended two flights of stairs to the basement. The exit door was locked. Mai tried a few keys. One of them worked. Her hands were shaking and her heart racing. She didn't care. She was getting out of there. She would rather get killed than return to the Chief. The door led to a long low narrow tunnel. With their backs stooped, Mai and Humaid almost crawled the fifty meters until the tunnel opened to an iron gate covered with leaves. Mai used one of the keys to open a large heavy old lock.

'Help me push the gate,' she said to Humaid. 'It's heavy.' Together, they pushed the door open.

Once outside, Humaid saw a military style Hummer parked a few meters away.

'Here,' Mai said, handing Humaid the keys. 'This one is for the car,' she said, pointing at the correct key. 'Let's get out of here.'

Humaid unlocked the car and they both got in. He tried to start the car, but it refused to start.

'Try again! Oh God! Please. Please. Try again. It has to start,' Mai cried. This was it. If the car didn't start, they would be dead for sure.

'*Bismillah*,' Humaid said and tried again while pressing down the gas pedal. The car started, with a rumbling noise. They heard the sound of motorcycles revving up close by.

'Which direction?' Humaid turned to Mai, not sure where to go.

'Just drive! Drive straight. Go this way.' Mai said as she turned her head to see if they were being chased.

The first gunshot hit the car less than two minutes later, followed by a tirade of gun shots, but fortunately none pierced the armored bullet proof car.

Humaid drove as fast as he could following Mai's directions. It all seemed so surreal – the moonlight, the armored car, Humaid and this friend, being chased by militants on motorcycles and jeeps with machine guns. Humaid felt he was playing a role in an action movie. He drove straight onto a sandy road. Someone shot directly at Mai. She screamed but the bulletproof windows protected her.

After chasing the Hummer for almost thirty minutes, the militants disappeared.

'It's a trap,' Mai warned. 'Don't slow down or stop. Keep on driving. Just keep on driving.' She was finding it hard to breathe. She couldn't sit still. She kept on turning her head to see if the militants were chasing them, expecting the Chief's men to appear any second and surround them.

Humaid drove for another hour. At some point, the sandy road turned into a muddy road, which led to a damaged paved road in desperate need of maintenance. A signboard pointing west had DAMASCUS written on it in Arabic.

'Follow the sign,' Mai said. She still couldn't believe she was free. She wouldn't be sure she was free of danger until they reached Damascus.

'Go faster, please,' she urged Humaid.

'How did you know about these escape routes?' Humaid asked her. He too felt a little reassured after seeing the sign pointing to Damascus. He realized he hadn't said anything for the past hour.

'He,' she said as she made a disgusted face, 'The Chief, wanted to make me happy. I was the youngest of his wives.'

'And the prettiest, I'm sure,' Humaid said. *Was it too soon?* As soon as he uttered the words, he wanted to bite his tongue.

'And the prettiest,' Mai smiled, leaning back in her seat. 'Once I gained his confidence, I asked him what would happen if we were attacked while he was away with the Mujahedeen. What would the women do? He showed me this route himself. He took me for a ride three times in this car just to make sure I memorized the road. I paid attention to every move, memorized the shape of each key, counted the steps it took to reach the staircase and the minutes it took to crawl out of the tunnel.'

'You saved our lives,' Humaid said.

'We're not safe yet,' Mai sighed. 'I'll know we're safe once we reach Damascus.'

Humaid drove for two more hours before Mai said, 'Turn into that orchard and park the car.'

'Why?' Humaid asked. 'Are we already in Damascus?'

'No, but if the army sees this truck, they'll know it's not theirs and they might hit it with a missile or a rocket from the ground or by plane.'

Humaid agreed. He turned into the orchard and parked the car under the branches of a fig tree. The branches were almost bare since it was winter, but that was the best he could find. They got out of the car. Mai pulled out a large bag from the trunk.

'What's that?' Humaid asked.

'Food,' Mai replied as she opened the bag. It was full of dried fruits, juice cartons and water bottles. Mai told Humaid there were thousands of dollars hidden in the car, but Humaid refused to take a single dollar from that dirty money. They walked deep in the orchard, as far away from the car as they could, sat under a tree and started eating.

'Do you want to tell me now how you ended up becoming the Chief's fourth wife?' Humaid asked.

Mai expression changed immediately, from excitement to sorrow as she remembered all the mishaps that had befallen her in the past few months. She started to cry.

'I'm sorry,' Humaid apologized, feeling terrible for making her cry. 'You don't have to talk.'

Mai dried her tears. 'It's ok. I don't mind telling you. It's just been so hard. Every time I think of the terrible chain of events that led to this; I feel so stupid.

My parents never saw eye to eye when it came to either living in France, the UAE or settling back in Syria. It all got quite bad after I graduated college. By the end of that summer, my mother asked for a divorce. She didn't even wait for the official divorce papers to come through before she packed up and left, taking my younger brother with her to Paris. Three months ago, my father said he wanted to travel to Syria for a few weeks to meet his father and other family members. My older brother and I went with him to Damascus. The war was already raging, but Damascus and the surrounding areas were safe. One day, my father took me and my brother in my grandfather's car to show us the village where he was born. Once we arrived at the village, Islamic militants attacked us. We got out of the car and raised our hands. My father told them we were civilians and Muslims just like them. They asked for our IDs. We didn't have any besides my father's UAE driver's license. They searched the car and found my father's old ID which my grandfather kept in the car. It was his ID from the days he did his military service in the Army. It must have been thirty years old, but they didn't care. They lined my father and my brother against a wall and shot them dead in front of me.'

By the time she reached this point, Mai was sobbing. She couldn't continue and rested her head on Humaid's shoulder. Humaid let her cry.

He knew there was nothing he could say to make her feel better.

'They tied me up and brought me to their Chief,' Mai lifted her head and continued after a few minutes. 'He saw me and couldn't take his eyes off me. I hated him with all my heart. How I resisted the urge to spit on his ugly lecherous face, I don't know! But I had to be smart. He was old and seemed frail and sick. I saw my chance. I offered myself to him. I told him that his men killed my family and I had no more relatives. I lied to him. I said I had always wanted to join the opposition. 'I only have one request,' I told the Chief. He smiled and asked, 'What might that be?' I said, 'Let me choose my husband from among your men.' The Chief was hesitant, but then he said, 'Choose.' So, I pointed at him. He was extremely happy. He already had four wives, so he divorced one right away and married me. If I didn't do that, they would have probably raped me or even killed me.'

'That was very clever of you,' Humaid said. 'Did he treat you well?'

'If your question is, did he rape me, the answer is, he would have, if he could. You saw his condition. His heart saved me. He would pop in whatever pills he could get his hands on, ask me to come to his bed, but he couldn't perform. I wasn't going to help him. You're a doctor. You know what I'm talking about.'

'And you're not a nurse,' Humaid smiled. 'The last time I saw you before today, you were receiving your graduation diploma in business.'

'That was a white lie,' Mai smiled, feeling a lot better that she finally opened up to someone about her ordeal.

It was almost noon when they got up to continue their journey to Damascus. Humaid made sure he had his backpack with him. It had his wallet with identification papers and some cash.

They walked for almost two hours, chatting about their friends and the good old college days, until the winter sun started setting. Mai, who had been forced to wear the niqab by her kidnappers, didn't want to have anything to do with it now that she was free. However, she reluctantly decided to keep her hair covered at least until they reached Damascus, just to be on the safe side.

Illuminated by the rays of the setting sun, Mai looked incandescent. Her face was golden brown and her long hair, escaping from under the hijab, reached her lower back. It had the same red streaks he loved. She looked so beautiful and innocent without her makeup and accessories.

'Can I tell you something, Mai?' Humaid asked, trying to catch up with Mai who was walking so fast trying to get to safety.

'Yes, you can,' Mai replied, turning towards him. 'But don't slow down please.'

'We used to call you *daloa* in college.'

Mai stopped, did a 180 degree turn and looked at him. 'You what?'

'Don't' get upset now,' Humaid cajoled her. 'Come on. You were *daloa*.'

Mai laughed and covered her mouth with her hand. 'We too had a name for you. We used to call you professor because you always walked around the university college with books in your hand.'

They were both laughing now.

Suddenly, the lights of a military jeep flashed in their eyes. They tried to hide but there was nowhere to hide. They were terrified. They thought the Chief's men finally caught up with them. The blood drained from Mai's face. They wanted to run but were afraid the military would shoot at them if they started running. Humaid held Mai's hand and said a prayer.

Chapter Seventeen
In Safe Hands

To their relief, the jeep belonged to the official Army. Two soldiers came out with their guns pointing at Humaid and Mai.

'Raise your hands above your heads,' one of the soldiers ordered.

'We're civilians,' Mai cried, suddenly not sure if the car belonged to the Army for real or if it was stolen by the opposition army or the Chief's men.

'This is a prohibited military zone. Why are you here?' the other soldier asked.

'We need help, please,' Humaid pleaded.

The soldiers patted them to make sure they were not carrying guns. The checked Humaid's backpack and his wallet.

'You're Emirati?' the first soldier enquired when he saw Humaid's ID. 'And you're a doctor? What on earth are you doing in a no trespass zone? We could have shot you.'

By then, Mai became more confident that they were not the Chief's men and not from the opposition army.

'We're running for our lives,' she said. 'We were taken prisoner by the fundamentalists and we managed to escape this morning.'

'Come with us,' the same soldier said. 'We'll get you to a safe place.'

Humaid and Mai sat in the backseat of the jeep, still holding hands. The jeep rolled towards the military camp. When they arrived, Humaid and Mai were led to the office of Colonel Nabil, the top guy on the base. The soldiers saluted the Colonel and briefed him about Mai's and Humaid's escape from the Jihadis.

'Is it true? You're an Emirati doctor?' the Colonel asked Humaid.

'Yes, sir. I am.'

'And you? Are you Emirati too?' he asked Mai.

'No sir, I'm Syrian. Humaid and I went to college together in Sharjah.'

'Hold on. Hold on,' the Colonel said. 'I need to sit down for this.'

Mai told Colonel Nabil her full name and told him her story. When she mentioned where and when her father and brother were executed, Colonel Nabil remembered the two bodies of a father and his son found a few months ago in a nearby village with gunshots in their heads. As Mai was telling her story, she was crying.

'Don't cry, Mai,' Colonel Nabil said gently. 'I remember that incident near Damascus. Those bastards will pay the price one day. I promise you they will.' He paused for a short while until Mai composed herself. 'We're going to keep you here overnight. Don't be afraid. You're not being held prisoner. It's safer for you here. It's just a technicality until we confirm your identities. I believe what you told me, but I must abide by the rules.'

Mai was given a room with a female soldier, while Humaid was given a room with Hussain, one of the soldiers who brought them to the camp. Hussain was a young recruit from Lebanon. He gave Humaid clean clothes and showed him where the showers were. Immediately after taking a shower, Humaid fell into an exhausted asleep. He woke up at the sound of *adhan* for fajr prayers. He found Hussein already awake.

'Can I go to the mosque to pray?' Humaid asked.

'Of course,' Hussein replied. 'I'll come with you. My instructions are not to leave you alone for your safety.'

After prayers, they headed to the mess hall for breakfast. The food was already laid out on a large table. Hussain told Humaid to pick up a tray and join him. They sat at a table with other soldiers. Humaid was astonished at the different nationalities that were sitting at the table with them. Humaid ate his food quietly without speaking to any of the soldiers.

'You looked surprised to see so many Lebanese and other foreigners here,' Hussain said when they were back in their room. 'Am I right?' he asked.

'You're right,' Humaid said. There was no point in hiding the obvious. 'I was pretty surprised.'

'We've been allies for the last twenty years. Our pact requires us to protect each other in the face of an external attack.'

Humaid didn't say anything for some time. He sat on his bed and thought about all the strange inconsistencies he had witnessed in Syria.

'I spent two weeks between the opposition army and the extremists,' he said to Hussain. 'Each side is convinced they have a valid reason to initiate fighting and keep at it. You are all Arabs. All Muslims. You all pray and bow to the same God. Why on earth do you kill each other? Why can't you solve your differences peacefully?'

'Easier said than done, doctor,' Hussain said, as he shined his shoes. 'It all sounds good, but in reality this is not how things work.'

'You know who benefits from this war you're fighting?' Humaid asked. All the fear and anger bottled up inside him for the past two weeks was rising to the surface. 'Foreign powers. They sell you weapons. They train you and stand by and watch as you kill each other. You lose your families, your homes. My God! You're losing your country!'

Hussain stared at Humaid; the expression frozen on his face.

'I'm sorry,' Humaid said. 'I didn't want to vent like that on you. You don't deserve this.'

'No. No,' Hussain said. 'Don't be sorry. Everything you said is true, but there is no going back, doctor.'

'Why?' Humaid asked.

'I'm just a private in the army,' Hussain said as he tied his boots. 'I follow orders. The powers that be say march, I march. When the powers that be say shoot, I shoot. Anyway, Colonel Nabil wants to see you at twelve.'

Humaid's clothes were hanging on a peg in the room. They had been washed and pressed. Humaid changed and headed with Hussain to see the Colonel. He found Mai there already.

'We've confirmed your identities. Her uncle,' Colonel Nabil said, motioning with his head towards Mai, 'is a high-ranking officer in the Ministry of Health and that's why you're not going to be charged for trespassing and entering Syria illegally.' He said the last part as he pointed his forefinger at Humaid. 'Hussain will take you both to Mai's uncle's house in Damascus tomorrow morning.'

Humaid and Mai could not believe their luck. They thanked the Colonel and kept on thanking him until he said, 'Enough! Off with the two of you before I change my mind.'

Humaid and Mai walked out of the office and headed to a bench a few yards away and sat down, still feeling they were in the middle of a dream and afraid they might wake up.

Humaid told Mai about his job at Dubai Hospital. 'You know Mona and Farah?' he asked.

'Weren't they part of your entourage?' Mai smiled.

'Yes, they were,' he replied, smiling. 'They work at the same hospital with me, but in different departments. Farah is a pediatrician now and Mona is an ophthalmologist.'

'I think I remember them,' Mai said. 'Are they married?' Mai didn't know why she asked, but now that she asked the question, it was too late to take it back.

'Farah is, but not Mona,' Humaid replied.

'Do you like her?' Mai asked. 'Isn't she the one meant to snatch you, professor?'

'I'm still not sure if Mona is the right girl for me,' Humaid said on a serious note. 'My family likes her though.'

'You're both Emiratis. You're both doctors. And your family likes her. Does her family like you?'

'I don't know.'

'Well, I'm sure they do,' Mai said. 'So, why not? I can't see why Mona isn't the right one for you.'

'I'm interested in doing charity work. I still want to specialize. I will be travelling a lot to refugee camps. I don't know if I will survive or get shot the next time I travel.'

Mai placed her fingers on his lips.

'Don't say that, Humaid. You won't get shot or killed. You're a good man and you want to help others. Our God will protect you. I hope that one day I will be able to do something like you.'

'If there's a will, there's a way, Mai' Humaid told her.

'I need to get my life back first,' Mai said. 'There is so much that I need to sort out before I can stand on my own two feet again. But I will. I will stand strong and I will give charity work a serious thought. I promise you.'

The sun started to set. They said good night to each other and headed for their rooms.

'See you tomorrow,' Humaid said.

'See you tomorrow,' Mai echoed.

When Hussain went into the room, Humaid asked him if he could have a phone to call his parents. Hussain offered him his mobile.

'Here. Call them.'

Humaid dialed his mother's number first. She replied immediately. 'Who's this?'

'Mama, it's me,' Humaid said, almost in tears.

Maryam couldn't believe her ears. 'Humaid? Is that you?'

'Yes, Mama. It's me. How are you? How's dad?'

'Oh my God! It's you!' Maryam exclaimed. 'Where have you been? The country is up in arms searching for you.'

'I'm alright, mama. It's a long story. I will tell you everything when I see you. I just want you to know that I'm safe.'

'Come back, Humaid,' Maryam pleaded. 'Please come back already.'

'I'll be there in a few days. I promise.'

'Abdullah!' Humaid heard his mother call his dad. 'It's Humaid.'

His father came on the line. 'Humaid! Where are you?' Abdullah asked anxiously.

'I'm near Damascus with some friends. I'll be heading to Beirut in a couple of days max and then back to the UAE. If it makes you feel any better, call me tomorrow on this number.' Humaid looked at Hussain as he said that. Hussain nodded ok.

'Ok, son,' Abdullah said. 'Everyone is here. They want to talk to you.'

'Not now, dad. Please,' Humaid said. 'Tell my sisters I love them. I can talk to all of them tomorrow. I promise. I will call you and talk to everyone then.'

'Ok, son. Ok. Please stay safe.'

'I will.'

Humaid hung up. He gave the cellphone back to Hussain and thanked him.

'So, you're a surgeon?' Hussain asked. Humaid nodded.

'You look too young to be a surgeon,' Hussain said.

'Really?'

'Where did you study medicine?'

'At the College of Medicine at Sharjah University.'

'You have a College of Medicine in the UAE?'

'We have five or six Colleges of Medicine in the UAE.'

Hussain started asking about the UAE, its people and how they were living. Humaid knew why he was asking all of these questions. They were told that Emiratis were all rich, live in luxury and have no brains.

After answering Hussain's questions, Humaid said, 'Ok now. It's my turn to ask you about yourself.'

'Well,' said Hussain. 'My mother is from Aleppo. My father is from south of Lebanon. I was born in Syria, but I lived most of my life in Lebanon. That's where I went to school. My father joined the resistance during the 2006 war with

Israel. He got killed there. I joined the resistance so my father's death wouldn't be in vain. Becoming a martyr like my father doesn't scare me. My older brothers are still in Lebanon.'

'What about your mother?' Humaid asked.

'She too is in Lebanon now,' Hussain replied.

'Do you have relatives in Syria?'

'Yes,' Hussain said. 'My maternal uncles and cousins. Some of them died in Aleppo in 2011. Some are still there and living in very harsh conditions. They suffer daily attacks.'

Humaid and Hussain stayed up late talking and went to sleep for a few hours after the fajr prayers. When they woke up, Hussain went to the camp and brought a four-wheel drive car. He was in his military uniform. There was another heavily armed soldier with him. Humaid sat on the back seat. He wondered if Mai was coming with them in the same car or if she would be riding in another one.

'We're going to pick Mai up from the other side of the camp where the female soldiers are stationed,' Hussain said, as if he could read Humaid's mind. They found Mai waiting for them there. She opened the passenger door on the other side of the car and sat beside Humaid. Four more heavily armed soldiers got in the car near the main gate.

'It will take us two to three hours to reach the center of Damascus,' Hussain advised Humaid and Mai as he turned his head around to face them. 'We'll be taking a lot of detours to avoid militants and danger zones.'

Humaid and Mai nodded. The two of them prayed silently for a safe drive to Damascus. Mai sat with her head bent down, not looking outside. She looked scared and vulnerable. Humaid looked at her and remembered the first time he met her in the college parking lot. She was a completely different person then. In college, she was so lively, confident, assertive and fearless. But now, she looked pale, worried, frail and depressed. She had clearly lost weight. Her beautiful eyes, once filled with sparks of energy and purpose, looked empty and sad.

Mai didn't utter a single word the entire way. Whenever the car passed broken walls, destroyed houses or signs indicating a past or current presence of the Islamic army, her face changed color.

They entered Damascus after a few hours and their car headed straight to Mai's uncle's house. They found her uncle, his wife and their children waiting for them. As soon as Mai got out of the car, she ran to her uncle's arms. They hugged for a very long time, both of them crying.

When her uncle finally let go of her, she hugged everyone else. Mai pointed at Humaid and said, 'This guy saved my life.'

'Not true,' Humaid said as he shook her uncle's hand. 'Mai is the one who saved my life. I put myself in a very dangerous situation and ended up imprisoned by the Islamists.

If it wasn't for Mai's quick thinking and ingenious planning, the Islamists would have killed me for sure.'

Humaid wanted to stay at a hotel, but Mai's uncle refused.

'My house is big enough to accommodate you, doctor. We would be offended if you turned down our Arab hospitality.'

Humaid was initially hesitant, but Mai intervened. 'Don't be stubborn now, Humaid. Stay. Just for one or two days until you get a passport to return to the UAE. Also, no hotel will let you check in without a passport,' she smiled.

Humaid accepted the invitation. The officers refused to stay and insisted they had to drive back to the camp right away. Humaid, Mai and her family thanked them and said goodbye.

Chapter Eighteen
Explosion in Damascus

Humaid woke up the next the morning to the sound of a gentle knock on the door. A housemaid opened the door and brought coffee to him in bed. She told him breakfast would be ready in the dining room in thirty minutes.

The two-story villa was massive. The bedrooms were located on the first floor, except for the guest bedroom, where Humaid spent the night. It was on the ground floor and had direct access to the garden. Mai's uncle had four sons and one daughter. His eldest son's name was Basil, so everyone called him Abu Basil.

When Humaid walked into the dining room, he found the family already there, except for Mai. Um Basil, her aunt, told him that Mai wasn't feeling well and would be eating breakfast in her room.

During breakfast, Humaid told Abu Basil that he would like to return to the UAE as soon as possible.

'You will, Humaid, but it's a little more complicated than you think,' Abu Basil said. 'You don't have your passport with you and the UAE embassy in Damascus has been closed for months. I'm trying to find some backdoor routes to smuggle you from Syria to Lebanon. Once your reach Beirut, the UAE embassy there will arrange everything for you.'

'I am really sorry,' Humaid said. 'I had no idea. I really don't want be an inconvenience to any of you.'

'Don't say anymore, please,' Abu Basil said. 'After everything you and Mai went through, you are family now.' He turned to his older son Basil, 'Why don't you take Humaid around Damascus today and show him our beautiful city.'

'Did you know that Damascus is known as the City of Jasmine?' Um Basil told Humaid.

'What a beautiful name,' Humaid said. 'I didn't know that, but we refer to it as Al Fayhaa.'

'That too,' said Um Basil. 'The fragrant city.'

'And then tomorrow,' Abu Basil said to Humaid, 'you and Basil can head to Beirut in my official car.'

When they got in the car, Basil asked Humaid, 'Is there any special place you'd like to visit in Damascus?'

'Yes, please,' Humaid said. 'I'd love to go to Al Hamidiya Souq. I went there with my family around ten years ago and I still remember it like it was yesterday.'

'Al Hamidiya Souq it is then,' Basil said smiling, as he revved the engine.

Humaid noticed that the streets in Damascus were much less crowded than they were the last time he visited the city with his family. Back then, Damascus was a crowded, bustling city. It was totally the opposite now. Some streets looked eerily deserted.

Even the city center was much less crowded than he remembered. Humaid and Basil reached Al Hamidiya in less than thirty minutes instead of the hour it normally took from Mezza district where Mai's uncle lived. Spread out over an approximately 600-metre long street covered by a ten-meter tall metal arch, Al Hamidiya Souq had hundreds of stalls and kiosks. Since no vehicles were allowed to enter during shopping hours, Basil parked his car directly outside the entrance to the market; and he and Humaid continued on foot.

In Al Hamidiyah Souq, almost everything one would need was on sale – clothes for all ages, bed sheets, blankets, jeweler, carpets, fresh foods, spices, souvenirs and furniture. Remembering that his mother and sisters bought a few cotton products made in Syria the last time they visited the Souq, Humaid thought it was a safe bet to buy them more. He also bought a suitcase and a carry-on.

Since he had very few of his clothes with him, Humaid bought some more for himself. He was surprised that everything he bought at the Souq totaled less than 200 dollars.

'The currency lost almost 90 percent of its value,' Basil told him. 'Shop owners are desperate to sell their products. Hardly anyone shops at the Souq anymore. That's what war does to a country. It doesn't only kill people; it destroys the country's economy as well.'

There were a lot of children begging on the streets or offering to polish shoes for just a few coins.

'Some of these children came from other cities where the war is still raging,' Basil told Humaid. 'They should be going to school, but look at them. An entire generation has been lost in this war. Who knows what they'll grow up to become, provided they live long enough to make it to adulthood? Criminals? Terrorists?' Humaid felt his tongue was tied. He just nodded at Basil's comments without saying anything. The abject misery of those children tore him apart. He no longer wanted to shop. How could he indulge in the luxuries of cotton and debate currency value when he saw hungry children begging wherever he looked? So instead, he and Basil crossed the market's narrow streets and headed to Umayyad Mosque.

Umayyad Mosque, known as the Grand Mosque, was built in the seventh century. Before Islamic rule, Damascus was ruled by the Romans for hundreds of years. There were a plethora of archeological sites in Damascus, including churches, temples and old baths. After visiting the mosque, Humaid and Basil went out to see other sites. When they arrived near Sayyidah Ruqayya Mosque, they heard the call for prayer.

'Shall we go in to pray?' Humaid asked.

Basil hesitated.

'This mosque is managed by the Shiites,' he said. 'You don't mind praying there?'

Humaid smiled. 'Is it a different God from the God in the Sunni Mosque?' he asked. Basil understood.

They walked inside and prayed together with the others. After praying, they left the mosque and started walking towards their car. Humaid put his suitcase and shopping bags in the trunk.

'Let me take you to a nice local restaurant for lunch,' Basil said. There was nothing Humaid loved more than local food, so he didn't object. Basil drove to a traditional restaurant in the town center. The restaurant was situated on the second floor of a building overlooking a roundabout.

They chose to sit on the balcony. Basil ordered a few plates of traditional *mezze* and grilled meat and rice for the main course. Locals like to drink fresh fruit juices and the kind of juice they drank depended very much on the season. Since it was the season of the pomegranate, they ordered pomegranate juice. Humaid and Basil chatted as they sipped the delicious juice, sampled the appetizing mezze and watched the traffic down below.

While eating their lunch, Humaid noticed a very old and dirty car parked on the other side of the roundabout. There was something strange about the car. Just as he was about to point it out to Basil, there was a loud explosion. The same car that Humaid had just suspected looked out of place exploded. Humaid and Basil fell out of their chairs. Pomegranate juice spilled all over their clothes and their food scattered around them. Humaid saw the pedestrians near the car be violently projected into the air while other women, men and children, fell to the ground, some bleeding and screaming, some motionless. Within seconds, they heard police and ambulance sirens heading in their direction.

Basil was so shaken that he couldn't get up by himself. Humaid helped him stand up and made sure he wasn't injured. Humaid, who was by now used to such explosions and to seeing horrific injuries, sat back in his chair and tried to assess the situation.

'We must leave right away,' Basil said. 'There may be a second explosion.' He quickly paid their bill and ran down the stairs two at a time. The street was full of spectators. Humaid pulled Basil through the crowd and guided him to their car. Luckily, they had parked it a few blocks down the road. Otherwise, the blast would have definitely damaged it.

'I don't think I can drive,' Basil said to Humaid, handing him the car keys. 'I'll give you directions back to the house.'

When they arrived home, they found everyone including Mai, waiting for them outside. The family had heard about the explosion and tried to call Basil. Um Basil screamed when she saw their clothes covered in a red-colored substance.

'It's just pomegranate juice, Mama,' Basil said.

'Why didn't you pick up?' she cried, hugging her son. 'We must have called you a hundred times.'

'I didn't hear the phone ring,' Basil said as he pulled out his cell phone and saw all the missed calls and messages.

'That's normal after an explosion,' Humaid told him. 'We were so close to it that our hearing must have been temporarily affected.'

Relieved that no one was hurt, everyone went inside the house to hear from Basil and Humaid about what happened. Mai didn't say anything the entire time. She just sat there with a blank expression on her face. In a few minutes, she quietly went back to her room.

'You can leave for Beirut tomorrow morning right after breakfast,' Abu Basil told Humaid over dinner. Once again, Mai didn't join them for dinner that evening. 'I have made all the arrangements for you.'

Humaid thanked him for everything. After dinner, he excused himself to go to his room and call his parents.

'I can hear it in your voice,' Abdullah said to Humaid over the phone. 'You sound upbeat. This time you're definitely coming home.'

'Insha'Allah, Dad,' Humaid said. 'Can you please inform the Embassy in Beirut that I will be there tomorrow?

'Don't worry, son,' Abdullah said. 'The ambassador, Mr. Al Rashidi, is my friend. I'll call him now.'

Humaid then talked to his mother, sisters and Saleh.

'I have great news for you when I see you, Humaid!' Saleh said.

'What is it?' Humaid asked, eager to hear any piece of good news after all he had been through.

'Not a word until you land here,' Saleh replied.

Humaid packed his new clothes and gifts in the suitcase he had just purchased from the souq. When he was done packing, he went to sleep. In the morning, as he got out of bed, he saw Mai sitting in the garden all by herself. He wanted to have a word with her before leaving Damascus, so he brushed his teeth, changed his clothes and went out to her. Even though Mai saw him, she didn't move or smile.

'Good morning, *Daloa*,' Humaid said trying to make her smile.

'Good morning, Humaid,' Mai said almost inaudibly, her eyes fixed on the ground. It was as if she was avoiding eye contact with him.

'Is everything alright?' Humaid asked her, but she didn't reply. 'Look at me, Mai,' he said. When she did, Humaid saw tears in her eyes.

'How long are you going to stay like this?' he asked. 'Keeping to yourself. Not talking to anyone. Staying in your room all the time. The Mai that I know is a strong woman. You need to pull yourself together.'

'I don't know what to do, Humaid,' she cried. 'I don't know where to go from here. Sometimes, I don't even know what to think. My mind is a blank. I have lost all feeling, all emotion. I don't know what to believe anymore or who to believe in.'

'Do you want to come back with me to the UAE?' Humaid asked her. 'You need to be away from the trauma of war to recover and concentrate on healing.

You might even find a job there. Who knows? Or if you want, you can go to France and live with your mom for the time being.'

'I don't know,' Mai said, holding her head in her hands and shaking it right and left. 'I don't know. I feel broken. It's like I've lost the ability to make any decisions. I have not yet absorbed the shock of losing my father and my brother. You'll never be able to imagine what I went through after they were killed. The humiliation I was made to feel. Those monsters. How they—'

Mai couldn't continue. She was sobbing and trying to catch her breath and not raise her voice. 'I feel so dirty, Humaid. So unworthy. I don't know. I can't possibly explain to you how it feels. I can't.'

At least she's talking and not holding everything inside her. That's the first step towards healing, Humaid thought.

'Take your time,' he said to her. 'Focus on yourself. But remember, you are worthy and you are not dirty. Never let anyone tell you otherwise. You and only you know what's best for Mai and one day, you will decide for yourself what to do.'

'Thank you,' Mai said, drying her tears. 'I needed to hear that. I just need time by myself to decide.'

'Point taken,' Humaid said. 'I'll leave you now. God knows when we'll meet again, but we will meet Insha'Allah.'

'Insha'Allah,' Mai said with a faint smile. 'Come have breakfast with us at least,' Humaid urged.

'I'm not hungry,' Mai said.

'I won't push you, but you do need to eat, Mai. You're looking so frail.'

'I will eat. I promise. But not now.'

'Goodbye, Mai,' Humaid said, as he shook her hand.

'Goodbye, Humaid.'

Humaid headed back to his room, collected his luggage and proceeded to the dining room where the family had gathered. After breakfast, he said goodbye to everyone, thanked them and left.

Basil couldn't come with Humaid as he hadn't recovered from the shock of the blast. A marked official car was waiting for Humaid outside the house with a private chauffeur.

On his way to the border, Humaid wondered about the sudden change in Mai's behavior. He remembered reading about psychological trauma in college. Its effects could appear long after the initial shock. Mai could be suffering from

PSTD 'Post Stress Traumatic Disorder.' If left untreated, it would lead to severe depression and anxiety and require a prolonged period of psychiatric treatment.

At the border with Lebanon, the driver asked Humaid to stay in the car and went inside the immigration building. He was there for about fifteen minutes. Humaid kept on praying, hoping they would let him cross and not complicate things for him.

'All clear,' the driver announced as he came back with a few stamped papers. 'We can cross now.'

Humaid breathed a sigh of relief. Now, for the first time since he got in the car that morning, he looked outside the window and enjoyed the beautiful mountains and the phenomenal landscape of the Levant around him. The view was breathtaking. No wonder Lebanon was known as the Switzerland of Middle East. Once the view of mountains ended, Humaid could see the city of Beirut and the Mediterranean Sea below them.

Chapter Nineteen
Lebanon and the American University

Once they reached Beirut and Humaid saw the UAE Embassy, he took a deep breath of relief. He couldn't believe that he had reached his destination without any trouble. He had experienced so many accidents, injuries and shocks that it seemed like a miracle for him to have this part of journey unfold smoothly.

Located near the cornice, the off-white, two-storey building housing the UAE Embassy had heavy security. As Humaid's car approached the building, an armed guard stopped them a short distance from the main gate. He asked them to open the car boot. He searched it and checked the underside of the vehicle for explosives using a mirror and a metal detector.

They were then allowed to proceed and park in the enclosed embassy parking lot.

At the entrance, another security guard in a black suit and dark glasses stopped them. Humaid introduced himself and showed his Emirates ID. Humaid collected his luggage from the car, thanked the driver and said goodbye to him.

Humaid asked if he could leave his luggage at the reception desk and the guard replied yes. That done, Humaid followed the guard to the elevator and went with him to the second floor. They got out of the elevator and went to a large room with a beautiful view of Ramlet Al Baida beach. Mr. Al Rashidi, the UAE ambassador, was sitting behind a large table, facing the sea. As soon as he saw Humaid, he got up from his chair and welcomed him.

'Thank God, you're here safe and sound,' Mr. Al Rashidi said as he shook Humaid's hand. 'Have a seat. Make yourself comfortable,' he added, pointing to a sofa by the table.

'Thank you, Sir,' Humaid said, sitting down.

'What you did was not only risky, Humaid, it was absolutely mad,' the ambassador told him, shaking his head. 'Going to Syria is extremely dangerous. Didn't you know that?'

'I'm sorry things turned out the way they did, sir, but I went there with good intentions. I wanted to help those who couldn't get medical assistance. It's just that one bad thing led to another.'

'Yes, yes,' the ambassador said. 'Your father explained everything to me. I need to issue you a temporary passport so you can exit Lebanon and fly safely back to the UAE. Don't worry, son. I'll have your passport ready within two days. Just leave a copy of your ID here. Your father already faxed me a copy of your passport. We have booked you a room in the Four Seasons Hotel, not far from here. An embassy car will take you there. Meanwhile,' the ambassador warned Humaid, 'stay in Beirut. Don't go to the north or south of Lebanon for God's sake.'

'I won't, Sir,' Humaid replied meekly.

'And don't stay out late at night,' Mr. Al Rashidi added. 'There have been a few terrorist car bomb explosions here too.'

Humaid nodded, thanked the ambassador for his thoughtful advice and for everything he did for him, and left.

When he settled into his hotel room, Humaid, who was starving at this point, ordered himself lunch from room service. He changed his clothes, filled the bathroom tub with warm water and took a bath, a much-needed treat after all the hardships he had been through. While in the tub, he called his family from the hotel's bathroom phone. Maryam and Abdullah were elated to hear his voice and know he had finally arrived in Beirut safely. Humaid spoke with everyone, including Saleh.

'What with everything you've been up to so far, Humaid, I am beginning to think you're a nut job,' Saleh said.

'You're not the only one,' Humaid said, smiling.

'How are you though, really?'

'I'm fine, Bunny. Do you remember Gibran from college?' Humaid asked.

'Of course, I do,' Saleh replied. 'I even have his contact details. I'll give them to you now if you want.'

After eating his lunch, Humaid took a long nap. When he woke up, he made himself a strong cup of coffee and sat on the balcony of his room. He noticed that Zaitona Bay was close to his hotel. He thought of going out for a walk, but then decided against it after recalling Mr. Al Rashidi's advice to not go out late in the evening.

Humaid had visited Lebanon two or three times with his family and knew the country very well. He loved Beirut's architecture, layout and clean streets. Beirut was built on the hills overlooking the Mediterranean Sea. Less than a couple of hours drive from Beirut lay the most spectacular snowcapped mountains, making Lebanon the only country in the Middle East where one could ski on real snow and swim in the sea all on the same day.

Known around the world for delectable, savory cuisine, Lebanese people didn't only know how to cook; they were friendly, hospitable and easy going people. One of the main things Humaid loved about Beirut was its weather, which was rarely too harsh. Sitting on the balcony of the hotel sipping his coffee, he had a feeling of peace and calm surge through him, something he hadn't felt in ages. The phone rang so Humaid went inside to answer it.

'How are you, boss?' It was Gibran.

'Gibran!' Humaid exclaimed. 'I was waiting for Saleh to give me your phone number to call you. How did you know I was here?'

'Piece of cake,' Gibran laughed. 'Saleh called me and told me you were at the Four Seasons Hotel. So, I called the hotel and they transferred the call to you. How long will you be in Beirut?'

'Two days,' Humaid replied.

'Let's get together, man,' Gibran said. 'I'm busy tonight, but I'll free my schedule for you tomorrow. Why don't I pick you up at 10 in the morning and take you around Beirut?'

'Sounds like a plan to me,' Humaid said.

Humaid was enjoying his breakfast in the hotel dining room the next morning when Gibran arrived. The two men embraced, genuinely glad to see each other.

'So, what brings you to Beirut and for a very short time, Humaid?' Gibran asked.

'It's a very long and complicated story, Gibran. I don't think I can finish it all in one day.'

'Well,' Gibran said. 'You can fill me in while we're driving. Where would you like to go first?'

'Byblos,' Humaid said without hesitation. 'Last time I went there with my family, we stayed for a very short time, so I couldn't see it properly.'

'Byblos, here we come,' Gibran said as the two of them walked out to the car.

Byblos, also known as Jubail, was about forty-five kilometers from Beirut. However, because of the traffic congestion, it took more than two hours to reach there.

'Let's start by why you are in Beirut,' Gibran said as he tried to man oeuvre his car in the heavy traffic.

Humaid started with his first visit to the refugee camp in Jordan and how he entered Syria illegally to help at the hospital run by the opposition party, only to get kidnapped by extremists, and how he ended up working at their hospital too. He told Gibran about finding Mai at the Chief's house and how they escaped together, how they were picked up on the road to Damascus by the official army, about the explosion in Damascus and how Mai's uncle arranged for him to cross safely into Lebanon.

'And here I am now,' Humaid concluded.

'Wow!' Gibran exclaimed. 'All of that in two weeks or so?'

'I lost count of the days while I was in captivity,' Humaid said. 'I even lost hope of ever getting out.'

'Look at the positive side, Humaid,' Gibran said, as he signaled and merged right, edging closer to the Byblos exit. 'You're here now, safe and unharmed.'

'Alhamdulillah,' Humaid said.

'You're brave, Humaid. To volunteer to go to Syria at a time like this takes guts. But quite honestly,' Gibran added, 'you're crazy. I do work at a refugee camp in Lebanon, but I would never want to risk my life unnecessarily by crossing into Syria itself. Going to a war zone is a suicide mission.'

Humaid smiled without commenting.

They arrived at the ancient city of Byblos before noon. The 7,000 year old city with its ancient seaport was inhabited throughout history by Egyptian Phoenician Greeks and Romans. Their ruins could be seen throughout the city. Perhaps the best-preserved structure in Byblos was the Fort of Byblos, which was built by the Crusaders who used it as a launching pad to attack and occupy Jerusalem.

'Some people mistakenly think Lebanon is a new country without ancient history,' Gibran said. 'Even Beirut itself has roots that go back as far as 3,000 BC. The Roman Forum in central Beirut dates to the first century AD.' Humaid was surprised to hear that.

After visiting the fort, they went to a nearby handicraft market where Humaid bought a few souvenirs. Later that afternoon, they decided to eat at a restaurant near the fort overlooking the Mediterranean. They ordered seafood, a specialty in Byblos.

On their way back to Beirut, they discussed politics, current regimes and the economic implications of the war in the Middle East in general, and Lebanon in particular. Lebanon's economy was very badly affected by the war in Syria.

'We used to depend on each other,' Gibran said. 'So many businesses have had to shut down because of the war. The tourism industry has been hit hardest. No one wants to visit countries engaged in any war.

The involvement of the Lebanese resistance in the war has ruined our image as a neutral country.' Gibran came from a Sunni family who strongly opposed politicians from the opposition party.

'The problem with you Lebanese,' Humaid said, 'is that you're all from the same country, but you hate each other. Sunnis hate Shiites and Shiites hate Christians. Christians hate the Druze and the Druze hate all. All of you live in one country, but every sect lives in its own cocoon. Lebanon will only prosper if all of you are united and start working for your country instead of for your sect. This is my opinion. I hope you don't mind me saying that,' Humaid looked at Gibran to see if he offended him.

'Not at all, Humaid. You're absolutely right,' Gibran said.

The conversation shifted again to Syria.

'There is a discussion on Syria at the American University of Beirut tomorrow,' Gibran added. 'Would you like to go?'

'Yes, I'd love to,' Humaid replied. 'It's always better to hear different opinions on any subject.'

As they returned to the outskirts of Beirut, the traffic became more and more congested. In Beirut, they parked the car and walked around the Solidaire area which was built after the prolonged Lebanese civil war. Humaid noticed a lot of visitors from the Gulf, including Emiratis sitting outside restaurants, smoking shisha or enjoying Lebanese cuisine.

Humaid and Gibran found an outside table at a nice café and ordered fresh juice and shisha. Humaid used to smoke shisha in the UAE but never got hooked on it. However, that day, sitting there with Gibran exchanging small talk and enjoying the scenery, Humaid didn't mind the shisha.

As it got dark, Humaid asked Gibran to take him back to the hotel.

'Be ready tomorrow,' Gibran said as he dropped him off. 'The discussion at AUB starts at eleven in the morning.'

'Come have breakfast with me here at eight thirty,' Humaid invited Gibran. 'And we'll head from here.'

'I will. Good night, Humaid.'

'Good night, Gibran. Thank you so much for today. See you tomorrow.'

When Gibran arrived at eight thirty in the morning the next day, he found Humaid waiting for him at the hotel dining hall. They enjoyed a leisurely meal, sipped their coffees and left the hotel around ten to give themselves time to find parking at AUB and good seats at the lecture hall.

Considered the most prestigious university in the Middle East, the American University of Beirut was built on a hilltop overlooking the Mediterranean Sea. It was spread out over an area of six acres.

Gibran parked the car and they headed to the main building. They passed through security and their IDs were checked. Once inside, Gibran said, 'We still have forty minutes before the debate. Let me show you around.'

AUB campus was among the most beautiful campus Humaid had ever seen. The mixture of old and new buildings blended harmoniously throughout the campus. It was a fully self-sufficient-city on its own. Each college had its own building. There were dormitories, libraries, supermarkets, restaurants and even a small hospital within the campus. AUB had its own football stadium, an Olympic-sized swimming pool and a large private beach.

Humaid and Gibran walked around the campus and strolled between the green fields and the fragrant cedars. When it was time for the discussion about Syria to start, they headed to a large historical building and went to the main lecture hall.

The hall had around 700 seats; almost all of them were filled. Humaid was not expecting such a large crowd. He saw Syrians, Lebanese, European and Americans in the audience. At exactly 11 am, the speakers—two politicians, one European and the other American; two dignitaries from the UN and two AUB political science professors—walked onto the stage and introduced themselves.

After a short introduction on the region, the number of dead and injured, the discussion commenced. The panel discussed the economical and geopolitical impact of the war on Lebanon and the entire Middle East.

Before they opened the floor for Q&A, the panel addressed the United Nations Humanitarian services and the economic support they were providing to refugees, as well as the UN peacekeeping efforts to bring all sides to an acceptable solution to end the war.

The Q&A lasted for almost an hour. Some people in the audience were for the war and some argued vehemently against it. Humaid was itching to say something. He finally raised his hand. The moderator pointed at him. Humaid rose from his seat.

'I am a doctor from a Gulf country, Humaid said. 'I lived with the opposition forces, extremists and the government forces for the last few weeks.'

Everyone turned towards Humaid and paid attention to what he was saying.

'Each side is convinced they have a valid reason to fight and defend their principles,' Humaid continued. 'Each side says it's sick of this war and wants peace. Most of them are Muslims and believe in the same God and pray in the same way. Why are they killing each other then?' Humaid asked. Without waiting for a reply, he continued, 'I believe it's because of the long-term hatred between them. If external powers don't supply arms and training to either party, they will have nothing to fight with. Instead of supplying arms, Arabs, Europeans, Americans and Russians must push all sides to sit and discuss their differences. If that gets accomplished, ninety percent of the problem would be solved. Let the people of the land solve their own problems. War is not the solution.'

Most of the audience clapped in agreement.

'Let's close our debate with this beautiful message of peace,' the Lebanese moderator announced, on their way outside, Gibran clapped Humaid on the back and said, 'What you said there was truly thought provoking and showed real leadership. I think you should be elected as their president. If they do so, their problems would be solved forever.'

They both laughed.

'Where to next?' Humaid asked.

'Al Hamra Street,' Gibran replied. 'You cannot come to Beirut and not stroll along Al Hamra.'

They visited some new shops on Al Hamra Street, where Humaid bought a couple of suits and a few shirts for himself.

Walking along this vibrant, famous street had always been a rewarding experience, even during the bad economic situation. After Al Hamra, they headed to the Rouche, the corniche of Beirut, and arrived at Sakhra, with its two huge rocks protruding out of the sea. One of the rocks was an inverted U-shape through which sea water flowed.

Humaid and Gibran found a restaurant overlooking the Sakhra and sat there. They were soon joined by a group of Gibran's friends. The discussion soon turned to the war.

'Can we please change the subject?' Humaid pleaded. 'I'm sick and tired of this argument.'

One of Gibran's European friends said, 'I don't understand something. Why do you Arabs want to solve your differences with violence? Why can't you sit like civilized people and solve them peacefully? Don't answer me now, please. Think about this when you go back home tonight.'

'Okay,' said Gibran. 'Let's change the subject and order shisha for everyone.'

They smoked shisha and ordered Lebanese mezza and other dishes. After eating, Humaid said goodbye to everyone and left with Gibran. At the hotel parking, Humaid announced, 'Most probably, I will be leaving tomorrow, so let's say goodbye now.'

Gibran got out of his car and the two friends hugged goodbye.

Chapter Twenty
Psychiatric Therapy

It was nine o'clock in the morning when the phone rang in Humaid's hotel room.

'Your passport is ready,' Mr. Al Rashidi said when Humaid picked up. 'You can travel anytime you want. There is a direct flight on Air Arabia today to Sharjah Airport if you want to fly on it.'

Humaid thanked the ambassador. 'Yes, sir. I want to travel as soon as possible. This afternoon is fine.'

'Okay,' the ambassador said. 'I'll send the embassy PRO to pick you up at noon and take you to the airport.'

Humaid was overjoyed. Right after hanging up, he called his family and informed them of his arrival time. Everyone, especially his mother, was exhilarated to hear the news.

Humaid started packing right away. He went down to have breakfast and made a quick call to Gibran. He too was happy for Humaid. Gibran asked Humaid if he would consider coming back at some point to help in the refugee camps in Lebanon.

'Call me when the time comes,' Humaid said. 'I'll definitely consider it. Goodbye for now.'

Humaid checked out of the hotel and waited for the embassy car. When the car arrived, the driver helped Humaid with his luggage. The embassy's PRO handed Humaid his temporary passport and all the papers he would need to show at immigration. He accompanied Humaid to the airport and left only after he had his passport stamped.

Humaid was ecstatic to be going home. He had been away for more than a month. He had really missed his family and the peace and warmth of his own country.

After going through passport control at Sharjah airport, Humaid rushed to collect his luggage. His entire family was waiting for him at the arrival terminal. They were all crying tears of joy to finally see him. His mother hugged him and didn't want to let go of him. He kissed her forehead and his father's. After hugging everyone, they all got into the three cars they had come with and drove back home.

Once home, Humaid changed his clothes and joined his family in the living room. They couldn't wait to hear everything about his experience in Syria and Jordan. But especially in Syria.

Humaid told them most of the story, leaving out some of the very upsetting, brutal details. He told them about Mai and how they both helped each other escape and how her father and brother were killed, and finally how her uncle helped him leave Syria. Everyone felt sorry for Mai.

'I have two pieces of good news to share with you today,' Saleh said. 'Afra is pregnant.'

Humaid and everyone else congratulated Afra and Saleh.

'And what is the second piece of good news?' Humaid asked.

'This,' Saleh said as he took out a pair of metal handcuffs from his pocket. 'This is for your feet, Humaid, so you'd never leave again on another dangerous risky mission.'

'I don't think we need the cuffs,' Maryam laughed. 'I'll keep Humaid's passport in the safe in my room. It will be there until I let him travel again.'

'And when that happens, it has to be a safe place where there is no war,' Afra added. 'Or Saleh's handcuffs will have to be put to good use.'

Everyone laughed. After dinner, Humaid went to his bedroom. He was so excited to be back home that he couldn't sleep. Finally, when he did, he dreamt about the bomb blasts and the casualties he had seen in Syria. He woke up in the middle of the night and couldn't go back to sleep. He thought about his job, when he should return to it, and how he would need to explain to the Hospital Director why he was held up in Jordan. He didn't feel ready to go back to work, so he decided to give it some time until he felt strong enough to face everyone.

His head throbbed with the same splitting migraine pain he had suffered in Syria. He took a couple of tablets, tossed in bed for hours, and finally managed to drift into a fitful sleep until midday.

In the evening, Maitha and Sara asked Humaid if he would play Scrabble with them. He tried, but he couldn't concentrate on the game. They teased him about the silly mistakes he was making as he played, but his mind was elsewhere. Everyone noticed how distracted Humaid was, but they figured it must be because he was mentally exhausted after his ordeal.

Afra and Asma were busy discussing the price of a garment they both liked and the date of a party one of their friends was holding in a week. Humaid couldn't tolerate their talk. Suddenly, he snapped at them.

'You don't have anything else to talk about? Do you know how people are living in this world? Some of them have no food to eat and you are thinking about parties, expensive bags and clothes?'

Still fuming, Humaid got up and went back to his room, leaving everyone stunned. Humaid had never spoken that way to his sisters before.

Abdullah and Maryam were also shocked by Humaid's unexpected bout of anger. He was usually the epitome of calm. Later, Humaid himself was upset by the way he raised his voice at his sisters. He remembered Mai and how her depression had affected her outlook on the world. He suspected that the way he was feeling was a result of the psychological trauma he had experienced in Syria. He knew that those effects would not appear immediately but would start manifesting themselves after some time had elapsed between the initial phase of shock and the end of his tribulations.

After dinner, Humaid took permission to go to his bedroom early. The headache was back. He took a couple of tablets again, knowing very well they should not be taken more than once. He slept for a while and had a nightmare that he was back in the village with the Islamic Army wearing clothes covered in blood with more blood splattered all around him. In the nightmare, a Jihadi fighter held a sword and swung it in Humaid's direction. Humaid screamed and woke up. Maryam and Abdullah came running from their room. They found him sitting in his bed, sweating and shaking.

'What happened?' Maryam asked. 'Are you okay?'

'I'm fine Mama. It was just a bad dream,' Humaid said.

'I'll stay with you until you go back to sleep,' Maryam said. She sat on the bed next to Humaid and put her arms around him and began reciting surah from the Quran to ward off evil and bad dreams. Abdullah waited a few minutes until he was sure Humaid would be okay, then went back to his room.

Maryam couldn't go back to sleep even after Humaid did. It was very unsettling for her to see her son in such an unstable condition. The last time this happened to Humaid, he was ten years old suffering from a high fever. She stayed with Humaid in his room all night and only left when the sun came up.

Maryam and Abdullah were alone at the breakfast table. They discussed Humaid and the changes they had witnessed in him. They were extremely worried about him.

'I think we must find a psychiatrist and let him help Humaid,' Maryam suggested. Abdullah agreed.

'I know an excellent psychiatrist,' he said. 'Dr. Sami. He will take good care of our son.'

'But how can we convince Humaid?' Maryam asked.

'Leave this to me,' Abdullah replied. 'I'll convince him. I'll arrange an appointment as soon as possible.'

When Maryam heard movement in Humaid's room, she prepared a breakfast tray and took it to him.

'Good morning, son,' she said. 'Do you feel better now?'

Humaid nodded. 'Yes,' he said in a weak and unconvincing voice.

Maryam left his room and asked Abdullah to go talk to Humaid.

'How are you, son?' Abdullah asked.

'I'm fine, Dad.' It was as if he knew what his father was up to.

'I want you to know that you and I are friends,' Abdullah said, sitting on the edge of Humaid's bed. 'I would never want you to feel that I am just your father. We have always spoken to each other very frankly, right?'

Humaid nodded. 'Yes, dad. I'm just very confused right now. I don't know what's happening to me.'

'Your mom and I don't know the best way to approach this and how to deal with the situation.' Abdullah said. 'But we do think you should see a psychiatrist.'

At first, Humaid hesitated. He thought about it for some time.

'Okay, but this should be confidential,' he said.

'Don't worry,' Abdullah assured Humaid. 'No one else besides your mother and me will ever know about it, unless you tell them. Dr. Sami is a friend of mine. He has a private clinic in Sharjah and he has an opening this evening.'

That same evening, Abdullah accompanied Humaid to meet Dr. Sami. It was a long time since Abdullah had taken his son to a doctor. When they arrived at the clinic, a nurse took Humaid's blood pressure, pulse and temperature and then directed him to Dr. Sami's office. It was not a typical doctor's room. It was furnished like a sitting room in a house. There was a sofa and round table in front of it. The side walls were decorated with paintings of natural landscapes in light colors. Soft music emanated from speakers built in the ceiling.

Humaid felt relaxed right away. Dr. Sami himself was an extremely pleasant person. He was of medium height, about fifty-five years old and had a smiling face. He welcomed Abdullah and Humaid, invited them to sit down and offered them something to drink. He himself sipped from a glass of cold water and sat on a wing chair facing them.

'How can I be of help, gentlemen?' he asked.

Abdullah introduced Humaid and told Dr. Sami that his son was a doctor and was planning to become a heart surgeon.

'This is wonderful,' Dr. Sami exclaimed.

'Humaid worked for a few weeks in the refugee camps and has just returned. But he seems to have changed. He's been having nightmares and recurring migraines and a short temper.'

'Abdullah, why don't you leave us for an hour?' Dr. Sami said. 'We'll discuss this like two doctors. We'll dig deep until we find the root of the problem. Won't we, Humaid?'

Humaid nodded and Abdullah left the room.

When they were alone, Dr. Sami asked Humaid about his family, his education and how long he'd been practicing medicine.

'Why don't you make yourself comfortable and tell me the whole story,' Dr. Sami said. 'Make sure you don't leave out any small detail and tell me what happened in the last month.'

Humaid started with the history of his visit to Jordan, Syria and Lebanon. He gave him full details of all the events, he had been through. Dr. Sami listened attentively and only spoke when there was a point that needed clarification. Humaid told the doctor about his bouts of anger and the nightmares he'd been having. When he was finished, Humaid felt as if a heavy burden was lifted off his shoulders.

'What you're feeling and experiencing is a result of the extreme shock you have suffered recently,' Dr. Sami said. 'This is normal. You put yourself in this mess and now you're the only person who can get yourself out of it. I will prescribe medication to help you handle the stress, especially in the beginning. Take it for no more than four weeks, six weeks max, and then we'll gradually stop the medication altogether. I don't want to scare you. You're a doctor, so you know if you continue taking the pills, you might get addicted to them.'

Humaid understood and nodded.

'You'll get over this, Humaid, and you'll be completely fine.'

Humaid took the prescription, thanked the doctor and left. Abdullah was waiting for him outside.

After a few days, the medication kicked in and Humaid started feeling much better. He started spending more time with his family in the evening and playing more with his younger sisters. His headaches became less frequent. He regularly took the medication Dr. Sami had prescribed for him.

Ten days after his arrival, Humaid decided to return to his job; the most difficult thing was meeting the Director and trying to explain to him the reason for his delayed return.

On his first day back at Dubai Hospital, Humaid headed straight to the Director's office. He was surprised to find Dr. Al Sayed very understanding and supportive. He didn't give Humaid a hard time or grill him for overstaying his two-week vacation leave. Humaid found out later that Saleh and Abdullah had paid a visit to the Director a few days earlier and explained Humaid's predicament to him.

'When do you want to return to work?' Dr. Al Sayed asked.

'Today if possible,' Humaid said, hoping that he had not misheard the Director.

'Today, it is then,' Dr. Al Sayed said. 'My secretary has your papers ready. Just sign them and go join your team. They're waiting for you.'

The Cardiac Surgery Department was located on the first floor. Team members and the head of department usually met before starting their rounds. As soon as they saw Humaid, they went to greet him. They wanted to know what took him so long to come back. Humaid didn't want to tell them what happened to him, so he only told them that he was so busy at the camp that he had to delay his departure.

'Let's go,' the head of the department said. 'Our patients are waiting for us.'

They got up and entered the Cardiology In-patient Department. There were about twenty-five patients there, mostly men, some women and a few children. Dr. Halim, the senior specialist, explained the history of each patient and the doctors examined them.

By mid-afternoon, they had seen all the patients. Each doctor shared his opinion about the different cases they saw. In the past, Humaid would actively participate in the discussion. He would examine the patients and render his suggestions. However, Humaid was a different person that day, as he hardly spoke the entire three hours it took his team to complete their rounds, and he didn't examine any patients. His mind seemed to be in another place, not concentrating on what the doctors around him were saying. Whenever he tried to examine a patient, he remembered pictures of the casualties he saw in Syria, so he stopped and let another doctor finish the job.

As the team gathered for lunch at the hospital cafeteria, Halim asked, 'What in the world is wrong with you today, Humaid?'

'It's just my headache,' Humaid said, albeit unconvincingly. He saw Farah and Mona from a distance but didn't try to approach them. In fact, they came to him and they shook hands. Humaid didn't respond as warmly as he usually did. He replied casually to their enquiries and sat in his chair. Farah and Mona looked at each other, perplexed.

'Humaid, did you know that Mona got engaged,' Farah announced.

'Congratulations, Mona,' Humaid said, forcing a smile. Farah and Mona left and headed back to their table.

Humaid returned home late that afternoon. He joined Maryam and Abdullah for tea. They asked him about his day.

'It was okay,' Humaid said, nothing more. Maryam had prepared his favorite *karak* tea. Humaid took his cup and started sipping the tea slowly.

Maryam and Abdullah discussed different subjects as usual, the current political situation in the Middle East, and economic and social conditions around the world. When Abdullah shifted the conversation towards the situation in Syria, Humaid got up and said, 'I'm tired. I think I'll go lie down in my room.'

Maryam got upset with Abdullah.

'I told you not to discuss this subject while Humaid is around. He wants to forget what he faced there, not to be reminded of it daily.'

Abdullah nodded. He knew it would take some time for Humaid to become fully normal again. He wondered if Humaid would ever be the same. Dr. Sami had told him that psychological trauma sometimes took a longer time to heal than physical trauma. Abdullah made sure Humaid kept his weekly appointment with Dr. Sami. He would drive Humaid to the clinic himself. Other times, he deliberately let him go on his own.

On his next visit, Humaid told Dr. Sami about his changed attitude at work. He was the only person to whom Humaid could confide. Dr. Sami would either say it was normal and Humaid would get over it very soon, or he would increase or decrease the dose of his medication.

After each visit, Humaid felt lighter and better. He would join his family and chat with them, even laugh and joke.

When they enquired about Mona one day, Humaid told them she was engaged to one of her cousins.

'What?' Afra exclaimed. 'See? You lost her. Believe me, she still loves you. If you want to marry her, I'll talk to her and Saleh will talk to her father. We will convince her to break off the engagement.'

Humaid was silent for some time, then he said, 'Afra, my dear. This is life. God plans everything and he has planned it this way. Marriage is both luck and destiny, as the famous saying goes. Don't try to change it by force. I'm not upset. I wish Mona all the best in her life. She has suffered a lot. I'm sure her cousin is the right person for her. I heard he has agreed to live with them in her father's house. This way, they can take care of her brothers, sisters and father as well.'

Disappointed, his family changed the subject.

Chapter Twenty-One
Language School in Munich, 2017

Days merged into weeks and weeks into months. An entire year had passed since the day Humaid returned from Syria. He was almost back to normal at home and at work.

At home, there was an addition to the family, Jamal, Afra and Saleh's baby. At six months old, he was beginning to crawl and recognize everyone. Humaid would pick him up and play with him any time he saw him. Maryam liked to taunt Humaid, saying, 'If you were married, you'd have one of your own.' Humaid would smile and change the subject. He was not ready to settle down.

He was still on medication, but not taking as much as he was when he first returned. The time period between pills was much longer now. He'd only take one of Dr. Sami's pills occasionally to feel more focused or grounded.

Lately, something was tugging at him, a vague feeling that he was supposed to be somewhere else. *I should go back to camps to help the poor;* he would catch himself thinking more often than not.

At work, things were also returning back to normal. Humaid started participating in meetings. He presented papers and discussed scientific breakthroughs. He went back to spending time with Farah and Mona at the hospital cafeteria.

Farah already had a baby girl. During one of their coffee breaks, Mona and Farah urged Humaid to tell them what happened in Syria. He had tried to avoid the subject, but gradually he told them the entire story, including Mai's tragedy.

'Mai? The same Mai, you used to call *Daloa*?' Mona asked.

'Yes,' Humaid replied. Both Mona and Farah were extremely affected by what Humaid told them.

'Is there anything we can do to help her?' Farah asked.

'I don't know. It's all so complicated. But I promise to let you know if I can think of something,' Humaid replied, touched by his friends' generosity and compassion.

Dr. Sami had told Humaid that when he started talking calmly about his ordeal, it was a sign he had already overcome the shock. Humaid started to focus his thoughts on his postgraduate studies, so he decided to speak to Dr. Al Sayed.

Humaid approached Dr. Al Sayed and explained to him that he was ready to pursue his postgraduate studies. Again, Dr. Al Sayed was very supportive and told him it was the right time for him to go for it.

After discussing the subject with his colleagues and parents, Humaid decided that Germany was the right place for his postgraduate studies, so he contacted Dr. Koch and his secretary. They sent him forms to fill out and asked him to send a copy of his diploma and a detailed outline of his experience at various hospitals and clinics.

A week after sending all the required forms, Humaid received a letter of acceptance from the Cardiac Centre at the University of Munich. On the same evening, he informed his family about his plans. Everyone was sad that he would be leaving them for three to four years, especially Maryam and Abdullah. However, they understood it was essential for his future to have a specialization.

'You have to promise us you're not going to go to Jordan or Syria again,' Maryam demanded.

After a short pause, Humaid promised. Maryam knew that Humaid always kept his promises.

'The flip side is that we know where we will be staying in Munich when we go there next time,' Saleh said. 'Make sure you rent a big place to accommodate all of us.'

'Don't listen to him,' Afra laughed.

'I will make sure there is enough space for Jamal at least,' Humaid smiled, picking up and cooing. 'I am going to miss him.'

Early in the morning one hot summer day, Humaid said goodbye to his family. Saleh and Abdullah took him to Dubai Airport. Maryam didn't go because she did not want Humaid to see her cry.

The flight to Munich took six hours. Upon arrival, a representative from the university came to welcome Humaid. He told Humaid the university had booked an apartment for him not far from the hospital. He drove Humaid to the apartment and gave him the keys.

During his first few days in Munich, Humaid felt homesick, but he soon managed to overcome this feeling by immersing himself in his work. He visited Dr. Koch.

'You'll have to study German for six to ten months, depending on your progress,' Dr. Koch told him. 'Once you become proficient in the language, you can start your actual post graduate courses.'

Dr. Koch's secretary took Humaid to the German Language Institute, which was located inside the same university.

The Language Centre at Munich University was one of the oldest and most well-known centers in Germany. Using unconventional, modern techniques to teach the language quickly and effectively with the help of gadgets, computers, microphones and performances, Humaid began with basic speech and writing. There were around thirty students in his class, most from the Middle East including Turkey, Syria and Iran, as well as some Europeans and Americans. They had five teachers who took turns teaching them, headed by Sophie, a twenty-five-year-old German teacher. Sophie was tall and had a fair complexion. She asked the students to introduce themselves and tell the class where they came from. The students introduced themselves in English.

After a few weeks, the class started speaking basic words in German, at least in the classroom. Sophie was very professional, but it was clear to everyone that she had an unfriendly attitude towards Arabs.

'Arabs are not serious,' she told her students once, making it sound like a casual comment. 'They only come here to have girlfriends.'

Most of the Arab students felt that Sophie didn't give them enough teaching time, as compared to students of other nationalities. Humaid somehow found out that Sophie was Jewish.

One afternoon, Humaid went to the university cafeteria for lunch. He noticed Sophie sitting alone at a table. He carried his tray and headed straight to her and asked, 'May I join you?'

Sophie looked at him and said, 'If you wish.' They ate in silence at first until Humaid said, 'It's a nice sunny day.'

'It is,' Sophie replied, showing no interest in carrying on the conversation. Humaid was not used to anybody talking to him in such a cold manner.

'Miss Sophie,' he said firmly. 'I don't know why you have such a bad attitude towards Arabs and Muslims.'

'I don't,' Sophie snapped.

'It's very obvious and everyone in class has noticed,' Humaid snapped back. Sophie's facial expression changed.

'If you must know, then I too have a question for you. Why are all terrorists Arabs or Muslims? And why do you want to kill all Jews?' Sophie glared at Humaid as she put her fork and knife down on the table.

Humaid was ready for this. 'Are all Germans angels?'

'No,' she replied.

'The Nazi Germans killed millions of Jews during the Second World War. Even now, there are still some Germans who hate Jews, just because of their beliefs, and yet I don't see you hating Germans.' Sophie kept quiet so Humaid continued. 'There are a lot of Arabs who have Jewish friends. If you read history books, you will come to know that Arabs saved Jews from the Greeks when they attacked Jerusalem in the fifth century and protected them from the Crusaders later. When Muslims ruled Spain, Romans were killing Jews, blaming them for killing Jesus. Most of the Jews in Europe took shelter in Spain because they found peace there under Islamic rule. Some Arab rulers even had advisors and ministers who were Jews. Did you know that, Miss Sophie?'

Sophie didn't reply.

'We Muslims believe in all of the prophets that you believe in and consider you as people of the Book. I know many Palestinian Muslims who are married to Jews.'

Surprised, Sophie asked, 'Then why do they want to kill Jews in Israel and want to destroy the only country we have?'

'I have to say that your information is faulty. We don't want to kill anybody. In Palestine, it's a completely different situation,' Humaid replied. 'Palestinians and Jews used to live in peace in the same country until the Imperialists came and brought the Zionists with them. They killed so many innocent Palestinians and forced millions out of their houses and villages. Some Palestinians took shelter in neighboring countries. Some became refugees in their own country.'

'This happened more than seventy years ago,' Sophie said. 'Now Israel is the only Democratic country in the region. So why fight and destroy it?'

Humaid laughed. 'Democracy? Do you know that Israeli rules for Jews are different from the rules they have for Palestinians? If you read Israeli laws impartially, you'll find out it's an apartheid country.'

'That's a lie!' Sophie said.

Humaid looked up the *Israeli Law of Return 1970* on his phone and held the screen to Sophie to read, *Any Jew, born anywhere in any part of the world is entitled to Israeli Nationality even if he or she was not born in Israel.*

'Is this not a racist law?' he said. 'Why are the same laws not implemented for Palestinians, even those born in Israel?'

Sophie kept quiet for a while.

'What is the solution in your opinion then?' she asked.

'There are hundreds of resolutions passed by the UN. There are also international laws. Israel is a member of the UN. We can take these resolutions and laws and build on them. War, violence and extremism will not solve the problems. Peaceful talks and negotiation will.'

Both Humaid and Sophie agreed on this point.

From that day forward, everyone noticed a change in Sophie's behavior. She spoke to everyone in the class respectfully, especially Humaid.

Humaid was quite happy with his progress in learning German. He started communicating with German people in their native language.

Germans did not like foreigners to speak in any other language while they were in their country. If you spoke their language, they would open up to you and become more friendly and helpful.

After classes, Humaid usually called his family; online video chatting meant they could also see each other. Maryam and Abdullah were satisfied that Humaid had adapted to living overseas. Humaid was also in regular contact with Saleh, Ryan, John and Gibran. Gibran told him he volunteered regularly at the refugee camps in Lebanon. Every time they spoke, he would ask Humaid if he would like to come and perform heart surgeries in the camp. Humaid wished he could, but he had to finish his postgraduate training first. He also tried to call Mai, but there was never any response from her; and she never called him back.

After six months, Humaid completed his language course requirements. He was a fast learner. Sophie was very happy with his progress and provided him with a certificate of completion. He was ready to join his training with Dr. Koch.

Dr. Koch and Humaid chatted in German for the first time. 'You finished your course two months earlier than anyone expected,' Dr. Koch said to Humaid. 'The new batch of students for training will join us after the winter holidays, so you are free to enjoy your stay in Germany and tour around or go back to your country until then.'

Humaid thanked Dr. Koch and said, 'Great. I will see you after the winter holidays then.'

Humaid was not the type of person to sit around and do nothing. He bought a used BMW sports car and started exploring the areas around Munich. He visited other German cities like Frankfurt, Berlin and Stuttgart. He was amazed to see the division of East and West Berlin after the Second World War, and how they were united now. He also visited some natural spots like Baden-Baden, the Black Forest and the lakes of Germany. He toured some of the nearby Austrian regions, including the city of Salzburg and Zell Am-See, and was intrigued by the sheer number of lakes and rivers there as well as the large number of ski resorts. It was the most beautiful area he had ever seen. After two weeks of enjoying Germany and the surrounding areas, Humaid returned to Munich and was thinking of returning to the Emirates to see his family. He fell asleep while looking up flights.

Chapter Twenty-Two
Back to Egypt and Sudan

The mobile phone ringing on the table near his bed disturbed Humaid. He checked the time. It was 4 am. He wondered who was calling him that early in the morning. He tried to ignore it, but the phone kept on ringing. Humaid was very sleepy and had great difficulty opening his eyes.

At first, Humaid was tempted to ignore the call. The name of the caller and the phone number did not show up, so he felt he was under no obligation to answer. But then he thought, *what if it is an emergency, regardless if I know the caller or not? I better answer.*

'Hello?' he said, resting the phone on the pillow and dreaming of the moment the call would end so he could rest his cheek right there and go back to sleep.

'Humaid? This is me. Jihad,' Dr. Jihad's voice sounded both urgent and happy to have finally managed to get Humaid on the line.

'Dr. Jihad!' Humaid replied, rubbing his eyes and sitting in bed. 'I hope everything is alright?' Then he added with a gentle reproaching tone, 'You know I'm in Munich. It's 4 a.m. here.'

'I'm sorry, Humaid. I honestly didn't know,' Dr. Jihad apologized. 'I'm in Abu Dhabi now. We're in the process of organizing an emergency medical camp for Sudan, but nobody wants to go there, with the revolution, strikes and unrest gripping the entire country.

'Oh my God!' Humaid replied. 'What can I do to help?' When Humaid asked the question, he didn't actually think Dr. Jihad would ask for his help. He thought Dr. Jihad was merely venting, expressing his despair to a trusted friend who might suggest a logical solution to the pressing problem at hand.

'I am alone in all of this. All I have is one Pakistani cardiologist, Dr. Farooqi. Remember him? He was with us the last time. Sudanese doctors in the country are also participating in strikes so I can't count on their help. I'm not sure at this point how many of them will be able to join us there.'

It dawned on Humaid then. He almost heard the question before Dr. Jihad asked it.

'Can you please come for a week?'

There it was, the question Humaid saw coming with his peripheral vision. He could suppress the longing he had in his heart for action and the unyielding nagging to get up, shake off sleep and start planning.

'Let me see,' Humaid said, putting both feet on the ground and pulling out his calendar on his iPad. 'I'm free for ten days come Saturday. I was thinking of going back to Sharjah to see my family,' he said. He had even bought the round-trip ticket.

'I can skip that,' Humaid continued, trying to block out the image of his mother's disappointed face as well as the disappointment his last-minute-change of plans would create for his family. One day they would understand.

'I must go to Cairo first, though, and then to Khartoum,' Humaid told Dr. Jihad.

'Thank you, Humaid,' Dr. Jihad said, sighing with relief. 'I will forever be grateful to you. You always step up to the occasion and never fail to deliver. We'll meet at Khartoum Airport three days from now. Exactly three days, ok? I will make sure to schedule my flight from here, as well as the team's flight, to be close to each other.'

Humaid hung up and, understandably, sleep had disappeared from his eyes. He brewed himself a strong cup of coffee and switched his laptop on to search for flights. There was a flight to Cairo early next day, so he booked it. However, he was not able to find a connecting flight to Khartoum with a 48-hour layover in Cairo, so he called Ahmed.

'Hello, my friend,' Ahmed beamed on the other line. 'Long time no see!'

'You know how it is, Ahmed,' Humaid said.

'I've been extremely busy. I'm calling you from Munich. I plan on stopping in Cairo tomorrow for a couple of days. I'm on my way to help with an emergency medical camp in Sudan. Can you possibly book me a flight to Khartoum from Cairo? For some reason, I couldn't do it online.'

'I sure can. What time and what day would you like to travel?' Ahmed asked. Humaid gave him the details of his itinerary and hung up. Two hours passed before Ahmed called back.

'I can understand why you couldn't book a flight online, but I got everything sorted out for you,' Ahmed said reassuringly. 'The unfolding unrest in Sudan has caused most of the flights to be cancelled. You're such a trooper, leaving the safety of Munich to throw yourself into the uncertainty of what's going around in our neighboring country. Anyways, I found you a flight to Khartoum in three days. Will that work for you?'

'Perfect,' Humaid said. 'Yes, please go ahead and book it. I'll see you tomorrow then. Are you free?'

'I will make myself free for you my dear friend,' Ahmed said.

'Great! Thank you so much, Ahmed. I'll go online to book my stay in Cairo. Any recommendations?'

'Casa Ahmed is always open for you,' Ahmed said. 'Don't even think about booking a hotel.'

'Your generosity is greatly appreciated, Ahmed, but I have to turn your offer down. I'm sure you understand.'

'In that case, I will book you a hotel. Leave it to me.'

Humaid only packed a small carry-on bag and his backpack. As soon as the flight landed at Cairo International Airport and the doors opened, he rolled his carry-on and hurried out. Ahmed was waiting for him outside. The two friends were genuinely glad to see each other. They hugged warmly and, as they walked to the parking lot where Ahmed's car was waiting, they updated each other about their latest news and plans.

Ahmed expertly maneuvered his car through Cairo's famously crowded streets with their traffic bottlenecks. It felt like Deja vu once again to Humaid. He had missed the beautiful city where he and Saleh had lived for over twelve months when they set off on their first-year medical internship.

After updating Humaid on his progress at Cairo University Hospital where he was now a senior surgeon, Ahmed added that he was planning to travel to the UK for his fellowship.

'And when will that be?' Humaid asked, excited for his friend.

'Very soon,' Ahmed replied. 'But that's not all. I want to share with you some very exciting personal news.'

'Tell me,' Humaid said, swiveling in the passenger seat to see Ahmed's face.

'I'm engaged,' Ahmed said, a big smile brightening his face. 'Didn't you notice?' he added, lifting his right hand off the steering wheel and showing Humaid his ring.

'Wow! Congratulations. That is indeed some excellent news,' Humaid said. 'Who's the lucky girl?'

'Do you remember the beautiful tall girl at the hospital? Safa Jamal?' Ahmed replied.

'I sure do,' Humaid said. 'Who can forget Safa's smile.'

'Yeah, that Safa,' Ahmed concurred.

'You've done well, man,' Humaid said. 'She's a wonderful, kind person. She was hands-on and helped me and Saleh a lot during our internship.'

Entering a newly developed area about 15 km from the airport, Ahmed parked the car near a modern ten-storey building.

'I live here,' Ahmed said, unbuckling his seatbelt and opening the door to get out of the car.

'Come on,' Humaid protested. 'I thought you booked me a room in a hotel.'

'I cannot let you stay at a hotel while I have an empty apartment in my city.'

'You really don't have to do that,' Humaid said, still sitting in the car.

'But I really want to do that,' Ahmed said. 'So, are you going to just stay in the car, or do you want to come see my place?'

'Fine. Thank you, Ahmed. I owe you big time,' Humaid said as he stepped out of the car.

'You owe me nothing. Give me that,' Ahmed ordered, reaching for Humaid's carry-on.

Humaid slung his backpack over his shoulder and followed Ahmed to the building. They took the elevator to the third floor. Ahmed unlocked the door to his apartment.

'This is nice, Mashallah,' Humaid said as his eyes took in the beautifully decorated living foyer and the exquisite modern furniture in the living room.

'Thank you. I feel blessed,' Ahmed said, leading Humaid to one of the bedrooms. 'It helps when your dad is in real estate development. It's a three-bedroom apartment. My father bought it for me.'

Ahmed switched on the light revealing a spacious, elegantly furnished room with a four-poster, wooden bed and large windows.

'This is your room,' he said. 'Get comfortable. I need to go to the hospital now, but I'll be back in time for dinner.'

'Okay,' said Humaid as he put his backpack on the dresser. 'I'll shower and take a nap to be fully energized for the evening.'

After his shower, Humaid changed into a pair of pajamas and went straight to bed. He slept soundly for a few hours. When Ahmed arrived in the evening, he found Humaid in the living room watching a black and white Egyptian film on television.

'How do you feel about a nice dinner at an outdoor restaurant?' Ahmed asked as he put his briefcase on the console and took off his jacket.

'That's a splendid idea,' Humaid said, switching the TV off and getting up. 'I'm ready.'

'Let me just change and we'll leave right away. I'm starving,' Ahmed said as he headed to his bedroom. 'I'll be right back.'

For dinner, they headed to a cozy restaurant that offered outdoor seating and served legendary barbecue and fresh juices. Throughout their delicious repast, Ahmed and Humaid reminisced about their college days and the year Humaid spent training in Cairo. There was lot to catch up on and so little time. Humaid informed Ahmed of his training, his humanitarian work in medical camps, as well as his horrifying experiences in Syria. Ahmed was quite sympathetic and touched, learning for the first time of the extreme hardships Humaid had suffered while in captivity.

After they finished their meal, the two went a leisurely stroll along the Nile and then headed back to the apartment.

'I'll take you to meet Dr. Mehran tomorrow,' Ahmed said. 'And we can have lunch with my future wife later on. Okay?'

'I can't wait to see Safa again,' replied Humaid. 'Good night, Ahmed.'

'Good night, Humaid.'

After breakfast the next morning, Ahmed and Humaid headed to Cairo University Hospital and entered Dr. Mehran's office.

'Welcome back, Humaid,' Dr. Mehran said, as he rose from his seat to shake Humaid's hand. 'How are you? And how's Dr. Saleh and your family?'

'Sir, everyone is well and happy,' Humaid replied. 'Saleh is married now.'

'Great!' Dr. Mehran said. 'How about you?'

'I'm doing my fellowship in Munich as a cardiac surgeon,' Humaid said.

'This is wonderful indeed,' Dr. Mehran said with admiration. 'I wish you the best of luck, Humaid.'

After their short meeting, Ahmed and Humaid went to Safa's office. When she saw them approach, her face lit up with a big smile.

'Look who's back!' Ahmed said.

'What a wonderful surprise,' Safa said, shaking Humaid's hand. 'Ahmed said he was bringing a friend with him to lunch but refused to tell me who it was.'

'Shall we go?' Ahmed said. 'It's still early for lunch, but we can have some refreshments until we're hungry enough to eat.'

'Mabrouk, congratulations on your engagement,' Humaid said as they walked out of the building. 'You are two of the most amazing people I've ever known and you sure are the perfect fit for each other.'

'You are extremely kind,' Safa said as she held Ahmed's hand, with a big smile still on her face.

Ahmed had taken the day off to be with Humaid. For lunch, they headed to one of Cairo's most elegant restaurants on the Nile known for its roasted pigeon and homemade rice pudding. The waiter guided them to a table on the restaurant terrace, where they spent an hour enjoying a hearty, delicious meal while chatting and watching the boats, called *dahabiyas* go by. Dahabiyas sailed up and down the Nile, rowed by sailors wearing traditional Egyptian *jellabiya*'s, some of them singing folkloric songs with the wind carrying their deep melodious voices to Humaid and his friends.

'I haven't been this relaxed in ages,' Humaid said.

'Come back and work with us and we can have more days like this,' Safa said to Humaid with a big smile, as the waiter placed three chilled crystal bowls of rice pudding in front of them.

'Where else would you find roasted pigeon this delicious and rice pudding this sweet?' Ahmed added, scooping a big spoonful of ice pudding and offering it to Safa.

After lunch, Safa headed back to the hospital while Ahmed and Humaid strolled for a few minutes on the riverbed to digest their food, before heading to a quiet café overlooking the Nile and ordering tea.

'There's only one flight at 3 a.m. tomorrow morning to Khartoum. I tried to get you on a later flight, but there is simply none.'

'No problem at all,' Humaid said. 'I'm used to it by now. I can sleep during the flight.'

That night, Humaid went to bed early and was up at midnight. Ahmed drove him to the airport.

'You're not leaving before promising me you'll take good care of yourself, Humaid. I don't want anything to happen to you,' Ahmed said.

'Nothing will happen to me Inshallah,' Humaid replied.

'And I want you to give me your word that you will be here at my wedding.'

'You bet I'm going to be here for your wedding,' Humaid assured Ahmed. 'After all, I drank from the Nile and whoever drinks the Nile'.

'Will always return to it,' Ahmed finished the old adage and high-fived his friend.

When Humaid arrived at Khartoum International Airport, he found Dr. Jihad waiting for him on the tarmac.

'Don't be surprised,' Dr. Jihad said. 'I have clearance to meet you here. Come. Sudan Red Crescent has made all the necessary arrangements. We'll leave for the camps from the airport in two hours. Everyone is waiting for you.'

After a short break and a wholesome breakfast at the airport VIP lounge, Dr. Jihad, Humaid and the accompanying support staff headed to a convoy of four-wheel cars and set off to the camp. It was basically the same support staff from before, with the noticeable absence of a few surgeons and anesthetists.

The long line of cars and trucks drove on the same uneven dirt road. They arrived at the same spot after an entire day of driving. The medical camp was set up and organized just like the previous time. For everyone, including Humaid, nothing was new.

There were the same tents for sleeping and the same sleeping bags.

The next morning, the group went about their work as usual. After setting up the tents for clinics and operation theatres, they started examining the patients. On the second day, they started operating on those patients requiring surgeries. This time around, Humaid performed more surgeries. He was more confident and more secure about his steps and all the procedures he executed. Dr. Jihad and the other surgeons trusted him and let him perform the surgeries without interference as they took care of other pressing work at the camp.

After seven days of intensive hard work, the camp was disbanded after it was announced a resounding success. Humaid had planned to return to Cairo and then to Munich as soon as possible. This time, however, since it wasn't safe to stay in Khartoum, he proceeded straight to the airport. The Red Crescent had already arranged for Humaid to fly to Cairo and, after two hours back to Munich.

During his last trip to Sudan, Humaid sensed the pending revolution. Its scorched scent, blood-soaked cry for help, throat-drying angst and desperate dreams permeated the air. This time, the Sudanese doctors informed him that the long anticipated Arab Spring in Sudan had already started. There was no place safe enough in Sudan.

Chapter Twenty-Three
A New Friendship

Back in Munich, Humaid started his training as a cardiac surgeon at Munich University Heart Centre with Professor Koch. The center treated children as well as adults. Professor Koch had more than thirty cardiologists on his team. Some were still under training, while others had already acquired their certification. Humaid's immediate supervisor was a female German Cardio-Surgeon named Professor Christiana. There were two other trainees with Humaid, one from Saudi Arabia and a female surgeon from Syria; both had already completed two years of their training.

As he started working, Humaid gained more and more experience with the German way of administering treatment to patients, the way diseases were investigated and when to finally decide to use the knife. The first year, Humaid mainly observed procedures and prescribed treatment after receiving approval from his seniors. In the operation room, he was only allowed to assist during surgeries. While assisting or during hospital rounds, he didn't hesitate to ask questions if he noticed the doctors approached the patients in a different way from what he was used to.

Humaid decided not to tell anyone in Germany about his surgical experience in the various medical camps and about his ordeal during the war in Syria. He told himself he was there to learn not to boast about his past. However, everyone at the hospital soon realized that he was an intelligent person and a fast learner. Sometimes during hospital rounds, even Profession Koch would turn to Humaid and ask, 'What do you think of our approach to the treatment of this patient, Dr. Humaid?'

This made some of the junior doctors a little jealous, but Humaid always tried to keep a low profile and make friends with everyone, including the nursing staff.

One day, he was having lunch alone at a café on the university campus when he heard someone ask in English, but with a German accent, 'May I join you?' Humaid lifted his eyes from his plate to see Sophie, his German language teacher, standing in front of him and smiling.

'If you must,' he said with a smile. They both laughed as Sophie pulled up a chair and sat down facing Humid.

'So, you already joined the hospital, Dr. Humaid?' she asked.

'Yes,' Humaid replied. 'That's why I'm here. What about you? Have you taught more Arabs or Emiratis?'

'I sure did,' Sophie said after taking a sip from her soft drink cup. 'Now don't start fighting with me again. I'm treating them quite well.'

'Thank you, Miss Sophie,' Humaid said graciously. 'You are very kind, but you were misinformed previously.'

The two of them chatted for a few minutes in German and would switch to English only when Humaid had some difficulty remembering a word or the correct conjugation of a certain verb. They almost forgot the time until eventually their lunch time period came to an end and they had to go to their separate jobs.

They ran into each other quite often after that day, either at one of the hospital or university cafés or at other restaurants on campus. At first, Humaid thought it was no more than a coincidence since the German Language Department was not far from the hospital. However, then he began wondering if those seemingly accidental meetings were purely by coincidence or possibly consciously planned in a way to make Sophie's lunch and break hours and the places she frequented synchronize with his.

He didn't mind Sophie's company. To the contrary, she was fun. Most of the time, they talked casually about work and, later on, they discussed more personal matters. Sophie was an only child. Her mother was Jewish, but her father was not. He walked out on Sophie and her mom when Sophie was five. When she was a child, Sophie loved her father. His sudden disappearance scarred her for life.

Sophie was curious about Humaid's family. She asked him detailed questions about how they lived and what they did. She was frank with Humaid and told him that she envied him the blessing of having a big family where everyone loved the other and lived harmoniously together.

'I talk to my mother once a week, sometimes once a month, but just for few minutes,' Sophie said, shrugging her shoulders in a defeated way. 'After five minutes on the phone, we run out of things to say to each other.'

One day, as they were having lunch together, Sophie wondered to herself: *How come he never asks me out on a date? Will he ever ask?* Finally, when she could not take it anymore, she said, 'Humaid, do you like my company?'

Humaid was startled by Sophie's question.

'Of course, I do,' He replied, feeling the blood rise to his face. 'That's why I sit with you so often.'

'Then why don't you invite me for dinner?'

Humaid was stunned and it showed. He took a second to collect his thoughts before saying, 'I'd like to, I guess, but I don't know where I can take you. I don't go to bars or discos and I don't drink alcohol. I doubt that you would enjoy an evening out with me.'

'So where do you go on your days off?' Sophie asked, intrigued.

'Well, I have some friends at Munich Islamic Centre,' Humaid replied. 'I usually go there to pray and end up dining with them.' Then he added quickly, 'Sometimes I go to the theatre but not that often.'

'Wunderbar!' Sophie exclaimed in German. 'I have been meaning to visit the Islamic Centre for a long time, but I didn't know if I would be welcome there.'

'You would be welcome, Sophie,' Humaid said emphatically. 'If you're interested, I can take you there, but you'll need to wear—' Humaid paused, trying to remember the word for *modest dress* in German.

'I know. Don't worry. I'll do that,' Sophie announced.

'I'm off this coming Friday,' Humaid said. 'I know you work on Fridays, but I can pick you up after you finish at the Language Institute and take you there.'

'It's a deal,' Sophie beamed. 'Or can I say it's a date?'

'I'm not sure, Sophie,' Humaid said, careful not to hurt Sophie's feelings. 'Let's take it a day at a time.'

On that particular Friday when Humaid pulled up at the Language Institute, he found Sophie waiting for him by the gate. Humaid took a deep breath and felt relieved when he saw Sophie wearing a loose dress reaching below her knees. He was driving his sports BMW. He stopped the car next to Sophie, got out and opened the passenger door for her.

'Nice car,' Sophie said, clearly impressed, as she sat in the passenger seat and the automatic seatbelt seamlessly slid across her body. 'When did you buy it?'

'A week after I finished my German language course,' Humaid replied. 'It's just that you never got to see it because we always met at the university cafés.'

The Munich Islamic Centre was located outside the city center area. The complex consisted of a mosque, a restaurant and community meeting hall. When they arrived, Humaid took Sophie directly to the community meeting hall. He had already warned her that some men refused to shake hands with women and that she should not be upset about it.

At the Community Centre, Humaid introduced Sophie to his friends. Most of the women wore long dresses or loose pants and long-sleeve blouses, their hair neatly covered under their scarves. They clustered in groups and chatted cheerfully. There were also lots of children of different ages. Humaid introduced Sophie to some of the families. Everyone greeted her warmly, even after knowing that she was not a Muslim.

After that, Humaid introduced Sophie to Sheikh Mustafa, the manager of the Islamic Centre. Sheikh Mustafa was originally from Turkey. He was around fifty and had a long thick white beard. He greeted Sophie warmly. Humaid told him that Sophie was Jewish.

'That makes her a believer like us,' Sheikh Mustafa said. 'We too believe in Moses and Ibrahim and Isaac.'

Sophie was pleasantly surprised to hear that.

'I have a lot of questions about Muslims and Islam,' she said to Sheikh Mustafa. 'Humaid has already told me a lot, but there is still more I want to know.'

'Sister, I know most of the questions you have,' Sheikh Mustafa assured Sophie. 'But it's almost Isha prayer time. I'll give you some very short books in German. Read them first and then come back to me anytime you're free. I'll give you as much time as you want. These books will answer most of your questions.'

Sophie thanked Sheikh Mustafa when he gave her the book and promised to take him on his word and call him later. As the call for prayer resonated from the high minaret, Humaid left Sophie with some women in the community meeting hall and went to pray.

Once prayers were finished, everyone got together in the community hall, including Sheikh Mustafa. Dinner was served. It was Sophie's first experience eating halal food.

'Jews have kosher food, while Muslims have halal food. Interesting,' she told Humaid. 'Isn't it interesting that Halal and kosher meats are slaughtered in the same way? Surprising how close our religions are.'

They ate and said goodbye to his friends and headed back to Humaid's car. When they arrived at Sophie's apartment, Humaid got out and opened the passenger door for her. As she stepped out, Sophie asked Humaid if he wanted to come upstairs for a cup of coffee or tea. Humaid hesitated. He remembered his father's advice: *you will face lots of temptations. If they're against your beliefs, just say no and walk away.*

'I am not ready for this now, Sophie,' he said. 'It's not who I am.'

Sophie, clearly upset, said, 'No problem, Humaid. Suit yourself. Good night.'

'Good night,' Humid replied.

For Humaid, the days passed very fast in Munich. He was busy most of the time. Before he knew it, it was summer. Medical trainees in Germany got four weeks of vacation every year. Humaid divided his weeks equally: two for his summer vacation and two for his winter vacation. He informed his family that he would have a two-week holiday in July and was eager to see if they wanted to come to Germany and spend the time with him.

'I'll show you around. The weather here is fantastic,' Humaid told Abdullah and Maryam over Skype.

'I can't see why not,' Abdullah said right away.

'Yes!' Maryam and the girls exclaimed. 'We're going to Germany.'

The entire family went to visit Humaid in Munich, including Maryam, Abdullah, Asma and Maitha even Afra, Saleh and baby Jamal. Humaid rented two large adjacent apartments just outside of Munich and a nine-seater van to accommodate all of them. He was determined to make their trip a memorable one.

And it was. Humaid drove his family around as they toured a number of ancient castles, unique German villages and some of Germany's most well-known landmarks. Most of the places were within driving distance. Humaid and Saleh would drive most of the time.

'German ladies are really beautiful,' Saleh said one day to Humaid. 'Did you meet anyone special?'

Humaid smiled and didn't reply.

'If you don't like them, no problem, just introduce them to me,' Saleh said and turned his head to look at Afra who was sitting right behind him.

'I can hear you,' Afra said as she pinched his neck. 'You want to spoil my innocent brother?'

'Sorry, my queen. I was just joking.'

Throughout their stay in Germany, the family enjoyed the trips with Saleh entertaining them, while Humaid did his job being their tour guide.

The two weeks passed in the blink of an eye and, soon, it was time for the family to return to Sharjah. Humaid drove them to the airport in the van.

'I'll be home in December,' he told Maryam as he hugged her goodbye at the departure terminal. 'I have two weeks off then and I have every intention to spend them with you.'

After dropping his family off at the airport, Humid felt depressed. Their absence left a deep void in his heart and life. But it helped that the next day was a work day at the hospital. Once he started working, he forgot all his worries. He busied himself preparing a presentation for the next weekly meeting at the hospital. Time went by very quickly.

After their visit to the Islamic Centre, Humaid and Sophie continued to meet, occasionally at the university restaurant or café. They would spend the time amicably discussing various topics and ended up developing a strong plutonic relationship. Sophie informed Humaid that she visited the Islamic Centre a few times and met with Sheikh Mustafa. As time progressed, she realized that having Humaid as a friend was so much better than severing a friendship because of different relationship she had wrongly imagined. Training at the Cardiac Centre went very well. Humaid learned a lot about surgeries and perfected his skills. He also saw and assisted several complicated cases and surgeries. Time flew by and it was already December. The streets of Munich, its shopping malls and parks lit up with colorful lights. The Christmas tree on Marienplatz was already set up and decorated with thousands of lights. It stood mighty and tall, towering above everyone's heads. Humaid was eagerly waiting for his winter break to travel back home.

While looking up flights online, he received a call from Gibran.

'We're in extreme need of a surgeon in the refugee camps here in Lebanon,' Gibran said. 'It's snowing in Beirut now and on the mountains around it. There are so many refugees in the camps who are freezing to death. Please, try to come, just for one week if you can. If you want to help, this is the right time.'

Humaid was silent for a few seconds thinking it over. 'Okay, Gibran, I'll come. Luckily I am free for a few days.'

Humaid started to plan his trip immediately. He booked his flights to Beirut and from there to Sharjah.

He started to pack his belongings, not forgetting his medical supplies, which would most certainly be required in the camp.

Humaid informed his parents that he would stop in Lebanon for a few days and then come home to Sharjah. He did not mention the refugee camps.

Chapter Twenty-Four
Back to Lebanon

The Middle Eastern flight touched down on Beirut Airport runway in the early hours of the morning. The airport was almost empty, except for the passengers on the flight from Munich.

Humaid collected his luggage, cleared immigration and customs and exited the airport. An airport taxi was available in front of the exit door. He told the driver, 'Four Seasons Hotel, please.'

It took just fifteen minutes to reach the hotel. The roads were almost empty. Humaid got out of the taxi, paid the driver and walked to the hotel's reception. He had already booked the room in advance. The receptionist upgraded him to a room with a sea view.

Humaid carried his heavy backpack, pulled his suitcase and went to his room. He changed into comfortable clothes, dropped onto the soft comfortable bed, and sent a text message to Gibran: *I'm at Four Seasons, room 515.*

Humaid pressed the send button, closed his eyes and fell asleep. Late In the morning, he was awakened by the ringing of his phone on the bedside table. He answered.

'Yes?'

'It's me, Gibran! I am downstairs at the reception.'

'Gibran. Don't you sleep in the morning, man?' Humaid asked sleepily.

'What morning? It's noon my dear.'

'Really?' exclaimed Humaid. 'Give me a few minutes to shower and I'll be down with you. Grab a coffee.'

After showering and getting dressed, Humaid went down and found Gibran waiting for him. They embraced affectionately.

'Let's go for brunch,' Gibran suggested. Humaid agreed.

They walked outside to Zaitona Bay, which was only five hundred meters away. While eating egg burgers and fresh juice, Gibran briefed Humaid about the recent political and economic situation, which was not much different from what it was the last time Humaid was in Beirut.

'How was Germany and your training there?' Gibran asked. Humaid explained to him that he had finished the German language course and his first year of training at the Heart Centre of Munich University.

'So, you speak German now?'

'Ja,' Humaid replied in a German accent.

Gibran smiled. 'We are free to go around today. But we need to leave for the refugee camps very early tomorrow morning. They have lined up a lot of cases for us.'

'No problem,' Humaid said. 'I've been waiting for this and I'm enthusiastic to restart my mission in the camps. What time should we be there?'

'Six in the morning.'

They walked around at the nearby Solidaire shopping area, but did not buy anything. They visited an area where a historical mosque stood side by side next to a very old church, proof that the old generations were more tolerant than the new. They decided to turn in earlier than usual, wanting to be fully rested and ready for the long day ahead of them.

Humaid got up at five the next morning, showered, prayed and got dressed. He went down to the dining area and had a full breakfast. He made sure his medical and first aid kits were in his backpack.

Gibran arrived exactly at 6 a.m. Humaid got in the car and Gibran started driving towards Baalbek near the Lebanese border. The highway skirted the mountains and went through the valleys. There was snow on the mountains and on the roads. It was a very cold morning. Gibran put the car heater on to make the trip more comfortable. He and Humaid removed their heavy coats and placed them on the back seat. It took them two hours to reach the entrance to the camp.

Baalbek lay in a valley surrounded by snow-capped mountains. It was most definitely set to experience another harsh winter. The refugee camp in Baalbek was the largest refugee camp for Syrian refugees in all of Lebanon. Approximately 350,000 refugees were living in the camp, which was managed by UNHCR and the Red Cross.

The camp was divided into different areas with basic health facilities. The housing consisted of tarpaulin tents, which did not protect the refugees from the harsh winter and rain. The camp had one big central hospital where critical cases were treated. The hospital was surrounded by almost one hundred makeshift health centers for administering basic healthcare. Most of the staff were volunteers.

As soon as they arrived, Gibran and Humaid went directly to the main hospital. The building had only one floor, but it was spread out over a large area of land. They headed to the administration office where several doctors and nurses were waiting for them. Dr. Hashim and Nurse Fatin, who oversaw the hospital, greeted them warmly and invited them to have breakfast with the staff. After they had coffee and a light breakfast, Dr. Hashim informed them that they had several war injuries at the camp.

A few of them required immediate surgery, while others needed suturing. There were children who needed heart and lung surgeries as well as some patients who required abdominal procedures.

Gibran assured the other doctors and staff that he and Humaid would take care of all the serious cases, including the heart and lung cases. Dr. Hashim was relieved and thankful since they did not have any heart surgeons at the camp. He asked Nurse Fatin to accompany Gibran and Humaid to the cardiology department to determine which patients they would operate on that day.

Gibran and Humaid followed Fatin. They saw the adult patients first. They conferred among themselves and decided which patients they should prioritize that day. After that, they passed through a small passage near the morgue to reach the pediatric ward. Humaid noticed two small bodies covered up to their chins with white sheets on steel tables. They were aged around five or six. Their faces were pale and expressionless. As he passed, Humaid touched one of them.

'My God, they are dead!' Humaid screamed, his hand trembled in shock.

'They went outside the camp last night,' Fatin told him, 'and froze to death. It's heart breaking. Every day we receive bodies of dead children. They die sometimes because the heaters in their tents stop working or they go out searching for food.'

Will God ever forgive humanity for the death of these innocent children? Humaid wondered.

Humaid and Gibran went to the operating room and began their work. It was ten in the evening before they were finally done for the day. Some of the very serious cases were transferred to the American University Hospital, which had the best cardiac surgery center in the Middle East. By 10:30pm that night, exhausted and ready to change out of their scrubs and head back to Beirut, Fatin came running towards them.

'Dr. Humaid! Dr. Gibran! I know you guys are very tired, but we have a young teacher who's very ill. She seems to have pneumonia and her ECG is irregular. Can you please take a look at her? She was just brought in from the camp health center.'

'No problem,' Gibran said.

'We'll examine her, Fatin,' Humaid added.

Fatin led them to the intensive care unit near the emergency department. As they entered the room, Humaid almost froze on the spot.

'Oh my God!' he exclaimed, his heart beating fast. 'I know this patient. She was my college friend. Her name is Mai Ashraf.'

Gibran also recognized Mai. She was unconscious, her breathing rapid and shallow. Her temperature was high and her chest was full of fluid. Mai's heart was beating faster than normal.

Gibran put an oxygen mask around Mai's face as Humaid injected her with Atropine to support her heart.

He asked Fatin to give her intravenous fluids. Humaid selected a fourth generation cephalosporin antibiotic, which he had brought from Germany and injected it into the IV line. He also injected another medicine to reduce her temperature and remove the fluids from her chest.

Mai needed to be observed for six to eight hours to see if she was improving. Humaid was afraid that if the treatments they administered were not successful, Mai would not survive.

He told Gibran to return to Beirut, as he would have to work the next day.

'I'm staying here tonight,' he told Fatin and asked her to bring him a chair. She brought him a comfortable reclining chair with a pillow and a blanket.

Humaid stayed up all night, regularly checking Mai's temperature, pulse and ECG. After three hours, she started showing signs of improvement and her temperature began to come down. Her breathing became deeper and her heart rate regular.

Humaid was not aware he had dozed off. He didn't feel the sunlight pouring through the window.

The first thing he felt was the warm and soft touch of a palm resting on his left hand which he had flung on the bed. He saw that Mai was awake and looking at him. Her face was still pale, but she was smiling. She pressed his hand.

'Am I dreaming or is it really you?' Mai asked in a weak voice.

'Maybe I'm the one who's dreaming, Mai,' Humaid said, lacing his fingers with hers. 'You gave us such a scare last night.'

The door opened and Nurse Fatin came in with fresh eggs, cheese, milk, and coffee.

'Enough talking,' Fatin said. 'Please eat something. There is more than enough for two here. If you want to go back to Beirut, Dr. Humaid, we can arrange transport for you right away. If you want to stay, we have accommodation for doctors here. You are more than welcome to stay.'

Mai looked at Humaid, her eyes silently pleading with him to stay. 'I'll stay,' Humaid said. 'I don't mind going to the doctors' accommodation now to shower and close my eyes for a couple of hours. Meanwhile,' he looked at Mai, 'I want you to have this delicious breakfast and rest. I'll be back to check on you soon, ok?'

'Ok,' Mai smiled.

Fatin called a younger nurse, gave her a key and told her to show Humaid to his room. Humaid thanked her and followed the nurse. The room was small but warm and comfortable. Folded neatly on the bed were clean towels and a pair of hospital pajamas. Humaid took a shower and put the pajamas on. He could not sleep for some time. Lying in bed, he stared at the ceiling and wondered why God kept on bringing Mai and him together again and again. He finally drifted off into deep sleep.

There was that same dream again. He was wading in the Gulf. The same deserted beach and the same smell. The same hand with long slender fingers pulled him out of the water. He looked at the face and!

There was no fog this time. The face was crystal clear. 'I know this face, I know who she is,' Humaid said in his dream.

His eyes shot open suddenly. He did not realize how long he had slept, he got dressed quickly and went back to see Mai at the hospital. He found her sitting in her bed enjoying a bowl of hot chicken soup.

'Did you get a good rest?' she asked him smiling.

'Yes,' he replied while holding her wrist to check her pulse. 'What about you? Do you feel better?'

'I do, much better,' she replied.

Humaid kept quiet for some time. Words were refusing to form on his tongue. He did not know what to say or how to start. He wondered if it was too soon to say what he wanted to say. Finally, he made up his mind.

'Mai,' he said. 'I want to say something to you. Something I should have said to you a long ago.' He held her hand. 'I love you, Mai, and I cannot imagine my life without you. I have loved you since the first time I met you, but I didn't realize it. I loved you more when we met in Syria, but I kept denying it.'

Mai let her spoon fall to the floor. Humaid's words had taken her by surprise. She couldn't believe what she just heard.

'Are you sure Humaid?' she asked. 'Maybe all you feel is pity for me because of my ordeal. If this is what it is, then please leave me alone. I am quite happy here. After you left Damascus, I wanted to make something of my life, so I decided to help the refugees. Here, my life began to have meaning and purpose. Every day I take care of needy children and teach them. I feel satisfied. In the evening, I visit the camps and take care of orphans. My mother sends me money regularly, but I don't need it. I donate it to the children and the schools. That's my life and I am happy with it.'

'Mai, listen to me,' Humaid begged, not letting go of her hand. 'I have never before been this sure about anything in my life. I love you. Just think about why heaven brought us together three times in unexpected circumstances. Is the universe trying to tell us something? You're lying when you say you are happy here. Look at you. You look miserable. Mai, please. Let's not lose each other again. I'm sure you love me too.'

'Yes, I do Humaid,' Mai replied. 'I admired and liked your strong personality at college. When we met in Syria, I had feelings for you, but I didn't want to make your life miserable like mine. Now that you've treated me and saved my life, I owe my life to you and I want you to be the happiest man on earth.'

'Then marry me, Mai. If you want me to be happy, marry me. My life will be meaningless without you.'

'Are you proposing to me, Humaid?' Mai asked, her eyes brimming with tears.

'I sure am proposing to you Mai Ashraf. Will you marry me?'

'Yes, I will, Humaid. Yes, I will.'

Humaid held both Mai's hands between his palms and raised them to his lips and kissed them.

He went back to his room that night and called his parents right away. He informed them that he was in Beirut and that he had met Mai there and that he loved her and wanted to marry her, if they *so* agreed.

'I would never impose my opinions on you, Humaid,' Abdullah said. 'It's your life and your future and I will always respect your choice.'

'Are you sure you want her to be your wife, the mother of your children?' Maryam asked, a bit skeptical.

'Yes, Mama. I am sure.'

'All I want is your happiness son. You have my blessing,' Maryam told him.

Humaid started making flight arrangements for him and Mai to travel back to UAE.

The next morning, Gibran came back to the camp. He and Humaid checked old and new patients and performed a few more surgeries. Late that afternoon, Humaid said to Gibran, 'I must go see my love now.'

'Okay, Romeo,' replied Gibran. Humaid went to the emergency room where Mai was waiting for him. She was sitting on a chair, ready to leave. She smiled when she saw Humaid.

'Are you ready?' Humaid said as he offered her his arm. 'I have already made arrangements for us to fly to Dubai.'

'Yes, but I must show you something before we leave,' Mai replied.

They left the hospital on foot and walked towards an open area within the camp where a small school for refugees stood. As soon as she arrived, around one hundred children rushed out of the classes and surrounded Mai chanting, 'Mama Mai! Mama Mai!'

'You see Humaid?' Mai said. 'These are my children. I teach them. I spend my money on them. They are all orphans without a father or a mother. If I leave them, they will be lost. I must come here every few months to see them. Will you accept a wife who already has one hundred children?'

'What you have done is the most noble deed on earth, Mai,' Humaid told her, feeling genuinely astonished and proud of her. 'I will never stop you from seeing and helping them. In fact, I will support you and help educate them. We will talk to donors in the UAE and collect funds to support the children and give them the best education possible. I won't let them become beggars or terrorists. Most importantly, we will teach them to love everyone and hate no one, even their enemies. We will teach them that all humans are the same and a difference of opinion is not a reason to fight.'

Mai was extremely happy. She knew that Humaid was full of compassion and would do all he could to help the poor orphaned children.

'Now, if you want me to come with you to the farthest corner on the earth, I will,' Mai said to Humaid, squeezing his hand. And then she turned to the kids and said, 'This is baba Humaid.'

The kids jumped around them excitedly.

'Now go back to class and make me and baba Humaid proud of you,' she ordered firmly but affectionately.

After the kids went inside, Humaid held Mai's hand and said, 'Let's go, honey. Otherwise, we'll miss our flight.'

Chapter Twenty-Five
Only Love

Mai and Humaid sat next to each other in business class on the Emirates fight from Beirut to Dubai. They both felt exhilarated and over the moon. They held hands the entire flight as if they were afraid to lose each other once again.

'Are you happy that you made this decision?' Humaid asked Mai.

'I have never been happier,' Mai replied.

'Me too,' Humaid said, smiling.

Their faces were smiling with happiness. Their eyes full of love.

'I'm also very happy that you took care of those orphans, Mai. You have changed. For the best, I must admit.'

'I used to think life was about wearing fashionable dresses, modern accessories and makeup. I now understand the real meaning of life and the real happiness that comes from looking outside myself and caring for others.'

'I know you have one hundred kids to take care of, but I want to have some of my own and I want them to have beautiful blue-green eyes just like you,' Humaid said with a sly smile.

Mai blushed and replied shyly, 'I don't mind having a hundred babies with you.'

To change the subject, she asked, 'What are your plans for your post-graduate studies?'

'After we get married, we'll go to Germany. I'll finish my cardiac training there. You can learn the German language and then continue your own post-graduate studies.'

'Sounds like a plan,' Mai said. 'You know, after you left Damascus, I fell in a deep depression. My uncle took me to a psychiatrist who prescribed these tablets for me.' Mai took a bottle of pills out of her handbag. 'Actually, I'm still taking them.'

Humaid laughed so loudly that the other passengers in business class looked over at them. He too reached into his bag and brought out a similar bottle with the same prescription. Mai and Humaid looked at each other in astonishment.

'No way!' she said quite audibly.

The passengers looked at them again, but this time, purely out of interest. Mai took both bottles and pressed the button to call the flight attendant.

'What can I do for you love-birds?' the flight attendant said with a big smile as she approached their seats.

'Do you have any windows on the plane that can open?'

'Why?' the flight attendant asked, startled.

'I want to throw these lousy pills out of the plane,' Mai told her.

'Well,' the flight attendant said, smiling again. 'That can be easily arranged without having to open any windows. You can just give them to me.'

Maryam, Abdullah, Saleh and Afra were all waiting for them at Dubai airport. Humaid kissed his parents' hands and foreheads. Maryam hugged Mai tightly. She had special feelings for her because of what she had been through in Syria; but most of all, because she was going to be her son's wife. Feeling the warmth of Maryam's love, Mai's heart filled with gratitude and her eyes with happy grateful tears.

Humaid hugged Saleh and Afra. Saleh remember Mai from college.

'How are you, Cinderella?' Saleh asked.

'I'm fine. But why this name?' Mai asked, bewildered.

'Humaid might have forgotten to tell you,' Saleh replied. 'I used to call you that in college.'

'He told me about *Daloa*,' Mai said.

'And that too,' Humaid replied. Everyone laughed.

Humaid's sisters were waiting for them at their house in Sharjah with little Jamal. As Humaid entered the house, Sara and Maitha ran to the door. They hugged and kissed him as if they were seeing him for the first time in ten years and not just six months. Both girls had grown into beautiful young ladies.

Humaid picked up Jamal and showed him to Mai.

'He is so cute,' she said, kissing Jamal. 'He has your beautiful face,' she said to Afra.

Saleh pulled out the handcuffs from the pocket of his *kondora*.

'Not again!' Humaid said.

'What are these handcuffs for?' Mai asked.

'These are for you,' Saleh said as he handed the handcuffs to Mai. 'It will be your job to keep this man from throwing himself into danger from now on.'

'Mai, you're more than welcome to stay with us,' Afra offered. 'We have enough room at our place.'

'I don't know,' Mai said, confused. 'What do you think, Humaid?'

'You're only engaged,' Saleh opined. 'It's against our culture for two engaged people to stay in the same house without being officially married. Put your sandals on, Cinderella. You may leave one of the sandals here though for Humaid to find you, just like in the Cinderella story.' Everyone laughed.

Mai took her carry-on and said goodbye to everyone.

'I'll miss you,' Humaid said to her as he saw them to the car.

Over a cup of sweet tea that afternoon, Afra explained to Mai Emirati customs, wedding ceremonies and what would come next. Mai listened attentively.

'I used to live here. I've been to so many Emirati weddings,' Mai said when Afra was done. 'But now that it's my wedding, I feel like I don't know anything. I want to do everything right to make Humaid happy.'

The wedding date was set for the next week. Mai went out with Afra every day to shop for the big day. She started wearing long Emirati dresses and abayas.

Humaid and Mai decided not to spend too much money on their wedding. Instead, they wanted to donate as much as they could to the refugees. Instead of buying a wedding dress, Mai rented one. Humaid booked two separate event halls, one for the men and one for the women, in the same hotel. They invited only relatives and close friends. Two days before their wedding day, they went to Sharjah court to sign the marriage agreement.

Mai wore a *shaila* and a nice abaya like Afra. 'We must pass by Humaid's house and take someone with us,' Saleh told Mai on the way to the court. Mai was surprised because she expected them to ride in separate cars. Saleh stopped in front of Humaid's house and said, 'Come, Cinderella. Let's go inside.'

Another big surprise was waiting for Mai inside. She found her mother, her younger brother, her uncle Abu Basil and Um Basil there waiting for her.

'Mama!' Mai cried incredulously as she hugged her mother and her brother. Then she kissed her uncle and his wife. 'How? When? No one told me.'

'Humaid arranged for us to be here today,' Abu Basil said.

Humaid came out from his room and looked at Mai.

'Thank you, Humaid,' she said. 'Can I at least hug you for this nice surprise?'

'No, you can't, Cinderella,' Saleh jumped in. 'Not yet.'

Humaid and Abdullah rode in one car to the court with Abu Basil. Mai, Saleh and Afra in another to sign the marriage agreement.

It was essential for one of the bride's male relatives to witness the marriage agreement and sign it. Without it, the agreement would not be complete. That was why Humaid made sure Abu Basil was present.

Humaid and Mai signed the papers. Saleh, Abdullah and Afra signed as witnesses.

'You are now husband and wife,' the judge said.

The wedding was held after two days. All their family members and close friends were there. The men and the women were in separate halls. Humaid made sure he invited his college friends. Rajan, John and Gibran came with their wives. Mona and Farah came with their husbands.

After dinner, and when the men left, Humaid was taken to the women's side by Abdullah, Saleh and other close relatives. He was received by his mother and sisters who were wearing beautiful sequenced long dresses. They took Humaid to the stage where Mai was waiting for him. Humaid lifted Mai's veil and kissed her on the cheeks. Mai looked stunning in her white dress; her blue green eyes gleaming like emeralds. Humaid was suddenly reminded of the first time he saw Mai at the university. Mona and Farah came up to the stage and congratulated them and posed for photographs with the bride and groom.

After the guests and relatives had their photos taken with the new couple, it was time for Mai and Humaid to leave. Mai laced her arm through Humaid's as they walked outside. Since grooms didn't usually drive on their wedding night in the UAE, Saleh had decorated his car for the occasion and assumed the responsibility of driving the newlyweds to their next destination, with Afra sitting next to him. Humaid and Mai sat in the backseat. Saleh and Afra had booked a honeymoon suite for them for a week at a beach resort in Ras Al Khaimah.

Sharjah University was not far from the hotel where the wedding took place.

'Do you mind driving us through the university parking lot?' Humaid asked Saleh. Saleh knew exactly what Humaid had in mind. He turned the car into the university parking lot and stopped where Humaid indicated for him to stop.

'Come,' Humaid told Mai as he got out of the car, opened the door for her and held her hand.

'Why are we here?' Mai asked him, perplexed.

There were few streetlights in the area, but there was a full moon in the sky. Mai's face gleamed in the moonlight. She walked with Humaid to the exact spot where they had met the first time.

'Do you remember this place?' Humaid asked.

'It's the parking lot, Humaid,' Mai replied.

'This is the place where you stole my parking space on the first day of college and my heart for eternity,' Humaid said.

Mai, remembering now, replied, 'I might have stolen your parking space and your heart, but you have claimed every part of my being, Humaid. I hereby confess that I willingly give you my heart, my body and my soul.'

Humaid pulled Mai towards him and they kissed on the lips for the first time.

The End